ANGIE FELT DELICATELY ALONG THE THREADS OF HER POWER.

In the real world, she was aware of sitting inside a protective circle with Esmerelda on the hardwood floor near the sliding glass door at the back of Ezzie's house. She was aware that Sebastian was nearby, guarding them from outside the circle. But that awareness was peripheral to her main focus.

Her web of power.

If she let herself relax, really feel it, it felt like she could do anything with all that magic. Not just open portals to demon realms, but break open reality if she really wanted to.

Which she did *not* want to.

"That's why we're here," Esmerelda's voice filtered through her mind, an echo, a calming breeze that rippled across the delicate lines of Angie's web. "So you can *choose* how to use this power. When to use it."

"It feels like my anger," she murmured, not sure if she was speaking out loud so that Sebastian would hear, but knowing Esmerelda would. "Maybe that's why it reacts when I get mad?"

"Power and anger can feel…similar. But you need to differentiate. It isn't your anger. Your anger is separate. This is just power, to be used as you see fit, at your command."

"Is this witch magic or demon witch magic?"

"It's all *you* magic."

Bone Lantern Witch

Spiderweb Witch

Storm Shadow
Witch

Darkling Mist
Witch

Apocalypse Witch

STORM SHADOW WITCH

A DEMON WITCH NOVEL

KAT SIMONS

Storm
Shadow
Witch

For my love, my husband, for all you do…

CHAPTER ONE

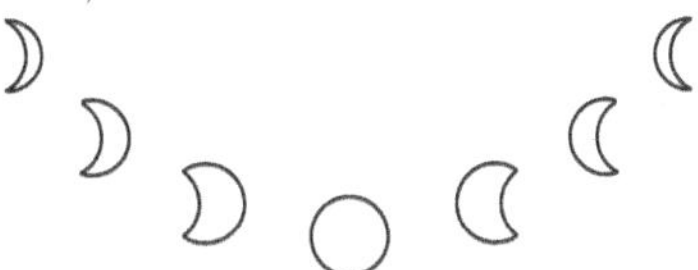

ngela Jordan held very still and tried not to let the smell of sulfur and the heat from the lava overwhelm her, but the stench still clogged her throat. The trees around her rustled in a gentle breeze, the spring sunshine touched the back of her shoulders. That warmth so sharply contrasting with the heat pouring out of the natural V in the tree trunk in front of her, it felt cold. A shiver crawled along her shoulders as another cooling breeze blew through her hair. But she didn't turn away from the V in the tree trunk.

Or the demon realm beyond.

"I hate this," she muttered to the man standing at her back. "And I'm never not going to hate it."

"I know," Sebastian said into her ear. "But you need to keep practicing."

"I need to make my flight."

Holding open a portal to a demon realm, on purpose, was not her idea of a good time. But it came naturally to her. It was part of what she was. Despite her efforts to reject the role.

Demon witch.

And now, demon hunter. A job she'd never wanted, but found herself doing. Because she was a demon witch, and the hunters just couldn't let her go.

This ability to open portals into demon realms wasn't anything she'd asked for. She'd tried to run from the ability on more than one occasion. Suppressing, ignoring, trying to forget. Getting very good at not looking directly at trees that had natural Vs in their trunks. But she couldn't get away from it. No matter what she tried, this skill, this innate ability, always came back to bite her in the ass. Now, she purposefully used the skill again, purposefully embraced her demon witch talents, because she no longer had an option to cut herself off from that part of her magic. To survive, she had to learn to master the skill once and for all.

And *wow* was she grumpy about it.

She loved her magic, she loved being a witch. But this demon stuff, it was…intertwined with her witch magic now, more so than ever before. Recently, the two magics had started to blend together, in a way she couldn't seem to stop. And that blending affected everything she did, including her ordinary spells. Even her touch psychic skills. All of it changing in ways she couldn't predict. And frankly, resented.

"You'll make your flight," Sebastian said. "You have hours."

"I don't like being late."

"You like sitting in airports for four hours to avoid worrying," he said, a slight smile in his voice.

"So."

That brought a chuckle, and his laugh helped relax her shoulders. A little. She was still staring into a demon realm so there was only so much relaxing she was capable of.

Beyond the V in the tree trunk, the hellscape beckoned. A land of black rock and belching volcanos, lit by a red sky and rolling rivers of lava. This was one of the closer realms, the more easily accessible ones. Many of the demons summoned by humans came from this realm. Which meant it was one of the places she needed to understand and be able to control her ability to access it. Sending demons back to where they came from was her *job* now. At least one of them—her other was providing psychic readings to clients at Dana's Cauldron, an all-things-pagan shop in Greenwich Village. She *liked* the job at Dana's, though. Demon hunting was not her calling.

Angie had tried to walk away from the demon hunter world more than two years ago, despite that requiring she also walk away from the man she loved. All of that effort had blown up in her face in the last year. Now she was right back in the middle of the demon world, training to be a demon hunter or else—a threat from the demon hunter council forcing her hand—and the only good thing about any of this was that it had brought Sebastian back into her life.

If she were being honest with herself, all of this was worth it to have him again. Even though she hated all the other stuff.

"We could have waited to do this until after I got back from New Mexico," she pointed out. "We didn't *need* this last session."

"I'll feel better letting you go back alone if I know you've got this under control."

She'd been putting off this trip for months, but she could no longer avoid it. She had to see her former mentor, her first teacher, the woman who'd taught her how to master both her magic and contain her demon witch skills when she'd been a child. Esmerelda didn't take on pupils anymore—even the girl Angie had sent to her last year for training had moved on to another teacher. And Esmerelda hadn't been one of Angie's primary teachers, or even an active mentor, in a long time. But she'd been the most important mentor in Angie's life. She was the one person who might be able to help Angie now.

When all Angie's magics, which had previously been separated, seemed to have mixed just enough to screw everything up.

She could do things now she'd never been able to before. Like open a realm breach into a demon world without the framing natural V in a tree trunk. Until a few months ago, she'd required the tree, had to look through that natural shape to open the portal. Now… She could do it whenever and wherever she wanted. An ability that terrified her so much, she hadn't done it since being forced to do it by another witch whose motivation in all this was suspect to say the least.

Since that night last Halloween, she'd tried to lock down

her ability again, to confine it to only opening portals using trees. She'd even started practicing that again, so she'd have better control over when she did and didn't open a breach. With Sebastian's help, she'd been forcing herself into tree-filled areas, finding the right shapes, and ripping through the barrier between demon realms and the human realm on purpose. Then closing those breaches. Again and again. Until she could do it safely, without feeling caught. Without the panic overwhelming her.

Except sometimes, the panic still overwhelmed her, and she still felt caught and unable to turn away from the portals. Months of practice weren't enough to overcome all the past terror, the experiences that still haunted her nightmares. But it had helped. Like exposure therapy. She'd been standing in the middle of the cool forest in a park in New Jersey for a solid fifteen minutes, holding open this particular portal into a demon realm, all without panicking. And without letting her fear overwhelm her.

She wasn't sure she'd ever *not* be afraid, though.

It probably helped that she hadn't heard the chittering yet. There were no passing chittering demons that might spot the breach. That's when the panic really got to her.

"We really should get to the airport now," she said.

"A few more minutes. You can do this."

"I'm distracted. Flight to catch."

"Just a few more minutes."

She growled. She hated this, even as she forced herself to do it. Forced herself to do all of the demon hunter stuff.

Beyond the realm breach, the chittering sound she hated

and dreaded with every ounce of her being started up. Oh that sound. It scratched against her soul and set her teeth on edge. It nibbled at her inner ear like a swarm of bugs. It haunted her nightmares, even when she wasn't asleep.

Her breathing sped as anxiety crawled over her skin. Carefully, slowly, she breathed in through her nose, out through her mouth, held the portal open a few moments longer. Repeating the mantra, *I am in control. I can close the portal when I want to. I am in control.*

And she was. Surprisingly. She felt more in control of this process than she ever had. At least, she didn't feel like the portal had taken over her entire being. She knew she'd be able to close it. She could look away whenever she was ready.

The demons wouldn't drag her into their realm. Not again.

With the stability of the tree shape as her anchor, she didn't even need to take hold of that part of her magic that linked to this skill. She didn't need to hold those threads of power to master her control of the breach. That had been the real lesson over the last few months of practice. When she did and didn't need to grasp the threads of power that made up the spiderweb of her magic.

She was still too afraid of all that raw power to want to use it. Yet another reason she needed to see Esmerelda.

When the chittering got closer, when she could see darker shadows on the red line of the horizon detaching from all the other blackness beyond, when she knew with heart-pounding certainty that the demons had seen her, that they were on their way…

She very slowly blinked. And turned away from the breach.

The sense of wrenching was still there, like she was ripping herself physically away from a tight grip. A grip around her soul as well as around her throat. The feeling of physically tearing away from the connection with the portal had lessened enough it no longer stole her breath. And she didn't need a physical shock from her realm to ground her enough to look away. Those startled moments, those unexpected sensations that brought her gaze away from a breach and back to this realm, those broke the connection the easiest, allowed her to turn away with a suddenness that could close the portal quickly.

But the sense of breaking the contact was always sharp. Even with those sudden calls back to this physical realm.

After the months of practice doing this without the help of some outside force, without the coincidental—or when Sebastian was around, the determined—effort of someone else to break her concentration, she could do this on her own now, much more easily. And the sense of panic just before shattering the link no longer left her overwhelmed and shaken.

The noise and stench from the demon realm cut off the minute she turned away from the breach, but a lingering sound of that chittering and the glow of the lava flows in her peripheral vision remained for a brief moment. Now that she'd looked away, though, the thinning between realms thickened again and closed the portal to possible demon escape.

Once again, she managed to *not* unleash a demon plague. Good day. Good day.

She still didn't like it. "I still don't like it," she said to Sebastian as she turned and let him wrap her up in his arms.

"But you've gotten a lot better at it." His soft English accent rolled over her, warm and deep and delicious.

She sank against him, a part of her still so *relieved* to be back in his arms. She'd tried not to love him. She'd tried to stay away from him so she could stay out of his world. None of that had worked. She'd been forced back into his world. So if she was going to be here, she was going to be with him. Fuck everything else.

Wrapping her arms around his neck, she leaned in a for a kiss. Soft and gentle as the cool breeze blowing across her neck, cooling her sweat. Sebastian's clean soap smell replaced the stench of sulfur in her nose, his taste and flavor banished all hints of the demon realm and grounded her back firmly in this reality. She sighed into his mouth and held him closer, easing away only reluctantly when the incessant *tick tick tick* of her internal clock insisted on reminding her she had a plane to catch.

Sebastian ran a hand up through her hair, loosening the already loose bun. "I wish I could go with you," he murmured.

She did, too. They hadn't been apart since they'd gotten back together. Because he was training her, he didn't have to leave her behind when he went on a demon hunt. And since, despite the outward title of "demon hunter," she still couldn't *feel* the call to a demon hunt, he'd had to stay with her to ensure *she* got to the hunts she was supposed to go on.

That was still a real sticking point, that she didn't *know* when a demon was about to escape. That she wasn't pulled to the fight. And boy oh boy was she going to use that against the council when they finally realized she wasn't meant to be a hunter. The "I told you so"s were going to be epic.

"I'll miss you, too," she said against his mouth, kissing him again. "If this was anything other than witch training, I'd bring you with me." She smiled. "My parents are relieved we're back together. They want to see you again."

Her parents knew what Sebastian was and did. Because they also knew what Angie was and did. Her family were generally mundane, except for her mother's small magic skills, but her brothers and father had never shied from Angie's magic or made her feel like a burden. In fact, her family were strangely protective of her even though she was the one with the skills to protect them. And none of that had kept her two brothers from giving her grief growing up.

The whole family had met and, after an appropriate hazing period, approved Sebastian. Angie had always suspected his job reassured her mother, who—maybe better than anyone—knew what Angie was capable of and worried more about the demon aspects of her powers. Her mother had always assumed with Sebastian around, Angie would be safe from those powers.

Her mother didn't know a lot of the issues Angie had with the demon hunters, though, and because Angie didn't want to worry her, she never told her those finer details. She'd taken the blame for the breakup and given hand-waving reasons for it. But now that she and Sebastian were back together, she'd practically *felt* her mother's relief through the phone.

"When it's not witchy work," Sebastian said, "we'll plan a family visit so I can pass the gauntlet of suspicion again."

She chuckled. "You know they love you." She sighed. "I'm…nervous about this. About being away from you. Especially since I still can't feel the call to a hunt."

"I don't want you hunting while I'm not with you anyway."

He didn't say it out loud, but they both knew she wasn't ready for that yet. Probably never would be. If she was meant to be a hunter, she'd be able to hunt alone by now. The training period and mentorship for most hunters went on for some years, but usual by the six-month mark, a hunter could fight a demon without their mentors so long as it was a relatively straightforward fight.

They both knew she couldn't do that yet. Not least because she couldn't sense the need to hunt. If a demon was about to get loose anywhere near her, she'd have no idea. Another hunter would have to show up.

At least, she hoped another hunter would be called to the fight. No one, not even the council, knew what would happen if she was in the area of a possible demon escape and yet didn't sense the call. The council member Angie could actually tolerate, Gabriella, seemed to think without

Sebastian around, Angie would better feel the need to go stop a demon escape. Angie doubted that.

Unfortunately, Gabriella had used the anomaly to talk Angie into continuing with the demon hunter efforts longer than she'd intended. She'd given Gabriella and the council three months. Six months later, she was still "trying."

She had ulterior motives for that, though, that had to do with the information the hunters had on demon witches.

Still, going to New Mexico alone was risky. But she needed to do this on her own. "I'm going to need the focus, and you know full well you shatter my focus," she said, leaning into Sebastian. The hard plane of his muscles against her softer curves made her hum under her breath.

"Which is why I'm not arguing to go with you," he said, his arms flexing around her. "But I'll miss you. A lot."

"Yeah. You too." She kissed him again before the ticking clock in her head got the better of her, and they headed back to the car he'd rented to take her to the airport.

Dread that had nothing to do with the upcoming flight crawled along her spine as they left the trees behind. Dread that they were missing something.

She'd been avoiding this trip home for months. But not all of that was because of her new job, or not wanting to be away from Sebastian, or even just assuming she could master the skills herself without help. Since Halloween, she'd had a sense of waiting-for-the-other-shoe-to-drop following her around, biting at her heels.

She hadn't seen Carmen again since that night in the empty short-term office building. Angie still didn't understand Carmen's reasons for challenging Angie to unleash her full powers, but the witch was definitely dangerous and a threat.

Angie hadn't seen the demon hunter Jacob since just before that night either. Jacob had attempted to talk her out of becoming a hunter back when Angie was still trying to avoid the job herself. Then he'd disappeared. Disappearing wasn't unusual for a hunter. They rarely stayed in the same place because they were always being called to a new hunt. The fact that Angie had had Sebastian to herself and they'd been able to stay mainly settled in New York for the last six months was highly unusual. Still, she'd expected Jacob to show up at some point. And because he hadn't, and because Angie still didn't know his motivation in all this, she'd been on edge for months waiting on…something.

Going home meant potentially bringing that something to her loved ones. To her family. To her former mentor. That something being anywhere near her colleagues and friends at Dana's was bad enough. But they were all witches and psychics and even mundane people that were just used to the weirder aspects of reality. Her family, outside of her mother's small magic, were so very ordinary. Angie didn't want to bring demon trouble into their lives.

At least, not any more than she already had.

And going home felt like she'd be bringing all these unknown dangers back with her. Doing it all without Sebastian there to help.

They were nearing Newark Airport when she started to really worry this was a huge mistake. That leaving without him, that going at all, would be too dangerous. A sort of panic gripped her middle, and even as Sebastian drove into the temporary parking lot, she opened her mouth to say she was going to cancel the trip.

She snapped her mouth shut just as quickly, when a visual image of her magic, a spiderweb of lights rose into her mind's eye. The web was almost entirely blue, but had a single red thread running from the center to the edge. And that red had bled into some of the neighboring threads last Halloween. That mix had started to spread more lately. Or maybe it was a slow seep and she'd only noticed how bad things had gotten recently.

Either way, there was more blending, more of that strangely colored purple magic edging through her web. The power, when she dared touch it, felt strong and wild. It wasn't like Fae magic, which she often saw as purple, but it wasn't ordinary witch magic either. Or even the ordinary line of her demon witch powers. The magic was becoming something else. She was becoming something else. And she needed to figure out what and how to control it.

Or she'd be more dangerous to those she loved than any outside force.

Which meant she couldn't back out of this trip. She *had* to go.

"You okay?" Sebastian asked after pulling into a parking spot and turning the car off. He faced her, his brow creased. "You've been very quiet."

"I'm not sure," she said. "I'm panicking about leaving. I want to cancel the trip. But I can't. The magic... I have to learn what to do with it, how to control it. See if I can—" She cut off the thought because she was afraid to even say it out loud.

But she wanted Esmerelda to tell her she could reverse what was happening. That she could tuck all that demon witch magic back up inside the red thread and cut herself off from the thread. That she could return to being an ordinary witch if she wanted to.

Sebastian cupped her cheek in his large hand, holding her gaze. She took those precious moments to study his beloved face, memorizing. The firm jaw and chin, now circled by a small goatee, full lips, his dark brown skin showing few signs of his age. His tightly curled dark hair peppered now with just a few flecks of silver and cut close to his head. His dark eyes luminous in the car's dim interior. That faint hint of red in their depths barely visible just then.

"I'm a phone call away if you need me," he said. "And if you've changed your mind about going alone, I'll get on that flight with you."

She smiled. "Last minute tickets cost a fortune and my flight is full."

"You think that'd stop me?" He raised a sardonic brow and looked so smug she chuckled.

The laugh eased the clawing panic. As he no doubt knew it would. "Thank you. But our original plan is the right one. I need the time with Esmerelda alone. To concentrate." To ask questions she didn't dare speak aloud to anyone else yet. "I'll be fine. Just a shaky moment."

He leaned forward and set his forehead against hers. "I will be there if you need me. Remember that."

She gripped his wrists and nodded, letting out a sigh. Then she straightened away and sucked in a fortifying breath. "Let's go. I don't want to miss my flight when I'm already this close to the airport."

"You still have three hours," he pointed out.

"Right. Like I said." Her comment made him chuckle, which had been her aim.

Saying goodbye at the security line was another tough moment, when the panic swept her again and she almost changed her mind. This sort of panic about leaving wasn't entirely normal. When they'd been together the first time, he'd had to leave regularly to hunt. And sometimes she went with him, but not always. She'd had an actual job at the time —working in a psychiatrist's office where she'd learned for sure she wasn't cut out for office work—and so couldn't just drop everything to follow him and have his back on every hunt.

She went as often as she could, whenever the hunts were close to home, and most especially if they involved freed demons, when her ability to open a portal really came in handy. Still, they'd separated often enough that being apart wasn't so very strange.

But this time felt...ominous. For a witch like Angie with psychic skills, that foreboding *meant* something beyond just her natural nerves. She knew it did. But she couldn't pinpoint what was wrong. Well, honestly, there was so much wrong in her life right now, she couldn't say which of the varied things was causing her such worry.

She knew leaving was necessary, and she needed help with her magic. Letting it go any longer was dangerous, not just for her but for everyone around her. But going felt dangerous too. Like she was missing something. Something important.

With more reassurances from Sebastian, and the deep knowledge that he could take care of himself because he had been doing so for a long time now, she made it through security and to her gate and onto the plane without incident.

Mostly without incident.

She thought she spotted Carmen in the ebb and flow of Newark's central shopping and food area. Even chased down the woman she'd thought was Carmen. Only to grab the arm of a perfect stranger and had to apologize. Her nerves were so jumpy, she'd been seeing enemies where there weren't any.

Her mood and her edginess didn't bode well for this trip. But what could she do?

She either learned what to do with her magic and this new increase in power. Or she accidentally loosed death and destruction on the world.

A result she feared, even after she got help.

CHAPTER TWO

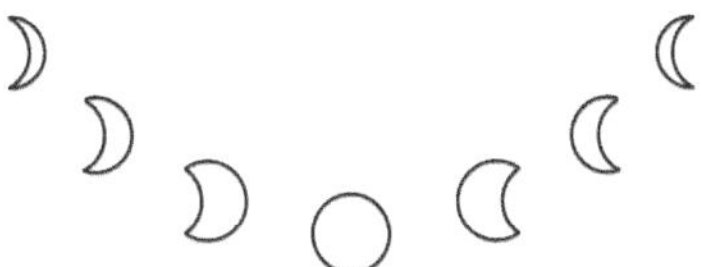

Angie went right to Esmerelda's house after picking up her rental car at the airport in Albuquerque. She texted her parents, so they would know she'd arrived safely and where she was going, but she needed to see Esmerelda before she faced her family. She realized on the flight that some of her trepidation about this trip was because she didn't trust herself at the moment. And she didn't want to bring any danger to her family. She went to a great deal of trouble to keep them out of the magic and demon mayhem that often permeated her life. Knowing about a lot of it was one thing, experiencing it for themselves was another.

The fact that she thought she saw Carmen again in the luggage pickup area hadn't helped her paranoia. While she wouldn't want to lead Carmen to Esmerelda, Esmerelda was perfectly capable of taking care of herself against a hostile witch. Angie's family was not. And she didn't want that woman with her mysterious goals anywhere near the Jordan family.

Again, though, she wasn't sure she'd actually seen Carmen or if, like in Newark, her imagination was getting the better of her. The uncertainty was almost worse than knowing the witch was around. Without knowing for sure, she wasn't sure exactly how to protect those around her—if she even needed to.

By the time she reached Esmerelda's sprawling ranch house in the desert at the edge of the city limits, her nerves were no more settled than they'd been in New York. Thanks to the three-hour time zone shift, the sun was only just setting when she reached the ranch house. The sky over the desert painted in pinks and oranges and purples. The smell of creosote and the dry warmth of the spring day settled around Angie like a childhood blanket.

Home.

And also…not quite anymore.

The nostalgia didn't dissipate as she studied Esmerelda's home. The house was a long, single-story building that bent into an L-shape at one end. The yard was wild in the front, left for the desert to landscape as it saw fit, with only a single bit of paving for a driveway at the base of a freestanding, single car garage that connected to the house by an overhang. Stucco walls painted a bright blue, white trim, red ceramic tiles covering the roof, hanging planters under the portico over the front door and along the breezeway from the garage. The front of the house was welcoming and well-kept. Showing no signs of age despite Esmerelda having lived here for at least fifty years.

The back of the house, Angie knew from memory, had an enclosed yard, the rough wooden fence encircling Esmerelda's planted garden. Though the last time Angie had seen it, the garden had been even more wild and untamed than the desert at the front of the house, filled with hanging plants, and herbs and lots of fragrant things that grew good in the desert. There were even a few cottonwood trees for shade. Wind chimes decorated wooden trellises and tree branches, filling the backyard with soft tinkling sounds that complimented the twitters of visiting birds. In between all the wild plant life, stone paths wound around planting boxes, and a couple of hidden cubbies with chairs and tables shaded from the desert sun popped up suddenly around bends in the path.

That back garden was probably Angie's favorite place in the whole world outside Dana's Cauldron. So many memories of growing up and learning who she was and what she could do, right there in that garden surrounded by the rich scents of herbs and the sound of wind chimes.

Angie had spent a lot of time at this house as a child, learning how to control her magic, learning the basics of how to *do* magic. Learning how to *not* loose a demon plague on the world.

Again.

She'd found Esmerelda through a demon hunter, Sebastian's mentor, and the first demon hunter Angie had ever met. Aidan was a legend for good reason, but she'd also saved Angie's life when, at five years old, Angie had stumbled on her demon witch powers for the first time. The demons escaping their realm into the parking lot behind her dad's church had been one of the most terrifying things Angie had ever seen. And she'd had no idea how she'd done it, why it had happened, or how to fix it.

The view of the hellscape through the tree's split trunk had been so unexpected and so fascinating, so dark and spooky, that five-year-old Angie hadn't been able to resist looking. But once she'd started looking, she couldn't seem to look away until a bunch of the demons beyond the tree had climbed out from between the branches and started charging around the parking lot.

And then…

Angie had no memory of Aidan's arrival. Suddenly the demon hunter was just there and the demons were screaming and somehow going back through the tree into their realm, and then the woman with the gentle voice was telling her to look away from the tree. Honestly, a lot of that first meeting was…fuzzy. More than twenty years had passed and she'd suppressed a lot of what had happened that warm, sunny Sunday morning. She just knew Aidan had arrived in time to save her and everyone else. No one had even realized what Angie had done. And if it had been up to her five-year-old self, no one ever would have known.

Aidan had talked to her parents though, explained the situation, and introduced them all to Esmerelda. Who'd been a lifesaver on many levels. Especially since Angie's ordinary magic was growing beyond what her mother had been able to handle.

The front door opened as Angie stood beside her rental car, letting nostalgia wrap around her, and the witch herself stepped outside, hands on hips as she looked at Angie from the threshold.

Esmerelda was a solid, sturdy woman whose age was impossible to guess beyond "older". Her once black hair was steel gray now, pulled back into a loose bun at the base of her neck. Her tan skin comfortably lived in, soft and creased with her age, her dark eyes bright and sharp as ever. She was dressed in a long white skirt decorated with huge red flowers and a black t-shirt with some Mexican rock band on it that Angie didn't know. Her feet bare. Her shoulders hunched a little forward now. Her only jewelry a necklace of brown beads with a little silver charm in the center that winked in the sunlight.

At this distance, Angie couldn't see the charm, but she knew it was a tiny, etched sugar skull.

"Hello, Esmerelda," Angie said, smiling at the older woman.

"You should have come months ago," Esmerelda, Ezzie to her students and family, said. "Come in. The kettle has just boiled." She turned and returned into the house, leaving the front door open.

Angie left her luggage in the car and, properly chastised, followed Ezzie inside.

"I missed you, too," she called after the older woman and was rewarded with a grunt.

The inside of the house was just as comfortable and rich with textures and scents as the outside of the house. Plants hunt from ceiling hooks and sat on tables throughout the open space. A living room area with a fireplace off to one side, an open wooden floored area near the back door which, when Angie had been studying with Esmerelda, served as the sacred space and teaching area. There was a permanently marked circle in the wood, though if you didn't know what you were looking for, it would be hard to see. The imbedded crystals of salt simply looked like a texture in the wood. The open kitchen took up much of the area behind the living space. And around the bend in the L of the house were Esmerelda's bedroom and the guest bedroom that she mostly used for storage.

As far as Angie knew, no one stayed with Esmerelda. Her family all still lived in the area, and students never stayed. Ezzie had told her once that she and her students needed the space after lessons, to absorb the sessions and clear out the conscious part of the training. A lot of magic was study, memorizing spells and herbs and processes. But more of it was letting those lessons sink into the subconscious and become muscle memory. At least for witches as powerful as Angie.

Ezzie had mostly taught her control over her various gifts. How to use some of the actual magic at the basic level, and how to keep her touch psychic skills and her demon witch powers from overwhelming her and making life impossible. Though, when she'd studied with Ezzie, she hadn't had a name for her ability to open portals into demon realms. In fact, she'd only learned recently that there *was* a name for people like her.

The demon hunter council still hadn't given her access to their records about demon witches. Angie hoped if she got full control of this melding and mixing magic that was creeping through her powers, she'd be able to convince the one council member she had a grudging respect for, Gabriella, to let her finally see those records. The others thought it was too dangerous. She had to convince them it was more dangerous keeping her ignorant of this history.

Ezzie stood at the kitchen counter pouring water into two large, blue ceramic tea mugs, filling the airy house with the scent of rich peppermint, which mingled pleasantly with the scents of greenery.

"Peppermint?" Angie asked as she took in the changes in the house since the last time she'd been here. Not many. A painted wall. A few different plants. The large silver fridge looked new.

"To settle your stomach after the flight." Ezzie handed her a steaming mug. "Let's sit outside. It's a nice evening."

It was indeed a lovely evening, warm still with the heat of the early spring day, but the breeze was light and cool, dry and flavored with Ezzie's herb garden. Though there were no clouds overhead, in the distance, Angie heard the rumble of thunder and a faint flicker of lightning popped up over the distant mountains.

"Be hours before the storm gets close," Ezzie said as she eased down into the plastic patio chair at a large round metal and stone topped patio table just outside her back door. The patio itself was encircled with wooden tresses covered in plants that gave shade in the middle of the day but didn't completely block the sky overhead. The sun had fully set, leaving only a faint glow of red in the west, and the stars were just beginning to bejewel the sky.

Because Ezzie's house was just outside of town, there were more of those stars than Angie had seen in ages living in New York. She settled into a plastic chair opposite Ezzie, cradling her tea mug, and leaned back to take in the pinpoints of light as they brightened, picking out the spring constellations. The night sky wasn't as dark as it used to be, when she'd come here as a kid. Too much of the city had crept too close. But there was still an impressive array of visible starlight popping to life overhead.

"I still have one of your old telescopes in the back room," Ezzie commented as she sipped her tea.

"Might borrow that while I'm here," Angie murmured without looking down.

"You'll be here long?"

She sighed. "I don't want to stay away from my job too long, but they're understanding. My bosses. I have the time I need."

"How has the aura reading been going?"

Angie smiled. One of her work colleagues and friends, Laura Fuentes, was a superb aura reader and she'd been helping Angie better that skill. "Good. I can actually see auras on command now instead of haphazardly—if at all. Progress."

"All we can ever hope for," Ezzie said. "Progress." She

fell silent for a moment. Then, "Why did you wait so long to come to me?"

"Fear," Angie admitted without hesitation. With Esmerelda, she didn't have to hide any of this. In fact, it was better if she didn't. Her mentor couldn't help her if she kept her fears to herself. "Hope that the…that whatever is happening would just resolve itself." Quieter, she admitted, "And I didn't want to leave Sebastian, even though I knew I'd have to to concentrate."

Ezzie grunted. "Love always complicates things."

Angie finally looked down. "Did it for you?"

"In my youth." She shrugged. "My love gave me children. Who've given me grandchildren. And I love them all. So I accept willingly the complications that come with that love."

Ezzie had lost her husband to cancer before Angie had ever met her. She'd always known her mentor as someone who lived her life at a distance from her family and loved ones. And it had never occurred to Angie to think of what Ezzie might have been like before she was how she was now. When she'd had a husband and children in this house.

"But you've come to work on your powers, not talk about relationships," Ezzie said after a deep breath. "The demon magic is mixing with your witch magic now."

"Not fully. But some of it has blended." She'd given her mentor a broad strokes explanation of the problem on the phone. Now she gave her all the details. What Angie could *see* in her mind's eye of her magic, the spiderweb of her power that she'd stumbled upon in a vision, the threads of blue, the single thread of red that connected to her ability to open portals.

And the way she'd grabbed those threads on the magical plane, using the red one to open a portal without needing a tree.

"Hmm," Ezzie said as Angie finished telling her everything, nodding to herself as she sipped the last of her cooling tea and set the mug aside.

"Can you help? Can you…explain what's happening?"

"Yes. And yes. But you want to reverse what's happening, don't you?"

Angie sighed. "I'd love to. I'm afraid that will be impossible."

"Another fear." Ezzie tisked. "We'll see."

CHAPTER THREE

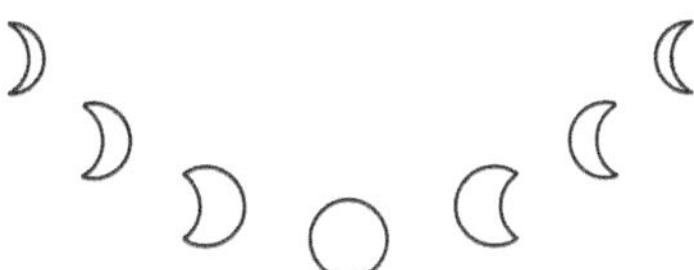

They left the sliding glass door that led to the backyard open, screen closed to keep out bugs, as they settled into the permanently etched circle inside. The space within the circle was large, taking up enough of the wooden floor to allow plenty of room to work. Space for an altar if needed. Space to move if needed. All the ways Ezzie taught magic could be accommodated inside the circle. And with the winking clear salt waxed into the wood, the circle, once activated, was strong enough to contain every working that happened inside.

Cool night air filtered through the open room, bringing the scents of Ezzie's garden and the surrounding desert into the house. As Ezzie turned off house lights and brought out candles to set at the cardinal points in the circle, Angie swept the circle clean with a ceremonial sage broom, mentally as well as physically cleansing the space.

When they'd established the things they'd need, they both settled into seated positions—Ezzie gently onto a cushion, Angie on the wooden floor—and Ezzie closed the circle. In her mind's eye, Angie watched the flare of blue magic encompass them, leaving a cone of safety and security so that they could work without worry.

At least not worry about how this would affect the outside world. Angie still worried about how this might affect her teacher.

"Show me this web," Esmerelda said, motioning with one hand in Angie's direction.

"I'm not sure how to show you. I've only seen it on the magical plane."

Ezzie shook her head. "It's been too long. You forget why I teach the young ones. Close your eyes and open to the web. I'll see it."

Angie let out a rueful huff. She had forgotten. But only because Ezzie had only "looked" at her powers when Angie had come for training the first time at five years old, then never did it again. Twenty-three years later, she'd forgotten that moment, the sense of being *seen* and not having to try and explain what she didn't understand herself.

She closed her eyes as instructed, let out a few deep breaths, took the time she needed to clear her mind. Accessing the view of the web of her magic had gotten easier in the months since the image first appeared to her—during a spell for clear thinking, which did *not* have the expected outcome!—but she still needed a few moments of concentration to call it up when she wasn't in the middle of a life-or-death situation.

In those moments, the web was just…there. Easy for her to grab. But easy access in dangerous moments was precisely what had gotten her into this mess.

After settling her mind, Angie looked for her web and the image rose, sharp and clear. Blue lines of magic arrow out from the center of her body, circular lines of power twining around the radiating threads, all spun around her as the central figure inside the web. The waiting spider. That aspect, that image of being a spider waiting for prey, never ceased to bother her. Mainly because she wasn't sure what sort of prey she was supposed to be waiting for.

In the midst of all the blue, a single red thread speared out from her chest, running the full length of her web. Before taking hold of that thread, it had been a distinct, separate line, twined with the other threads, but none of the red bled into the other parts.

Now, though, a few of the surrounding threads, some of the connecting, circular lines, showed a purplish hue where the red magic and blue magic had begun to blend. The red hadn't overtaken the blue, as Angie had once feared it might. But the blending was almost more terrifying. She didn't know how to *unblend* the magics that were mixing together.

If the red had simply been taking over the blue, scary as that was, she could visualize forcing the red back, letting the blue magic push the red into place in its single thread again. That was the sort of image she could work with to form a spell to fix the problem. At least in theory.

But this was much worse. She couldn't think how to separate the magics now that they were intermingled, couldn't figure out how to separate them into distinct powers that she could segregate. And it was really only sitting inside the safety of Esmerelda's circle that Angie realized how much she'd been hoping to do just that. To once again separate her demon magic from her ordinary witch magic and simply go back to being a witch. Maybe even find a way to cut off the demon witch magic all together.

A possibility she'd never really entertained. A web didn't work like that. Cut one line and the integrity of the whole thing was compromised. She might lose all her magic. Or she might unleash a devastating magical disaster. There was no way to be certain. But that didn't stop her from carrying the fantasy around in her heart.

Now, looking at the blue and red mixing, the purple color seeping deeper into the blue, really looking at that melding of her magics, here where she knew Esmerelda would see too, even the fantasy of separating the demon witch power from the witch magic faded. This mixing was too extensive now, too set. The hope she hadn't know she was harboring died in that moment. Leaving her close to tears.

Esmerelda's voice filtered through that sense of hopelessness. "The magic is powerful like this. You'll have to learn to control it."

Angie sighed. "I know. But I guess a part of me wanted you to say I could fix this and go back to the way I was."

"Oh. I think we could find a way to do that. If you wanted to. But then you would be right back where you started."

Angie frowned, even with her eyes closed and the image of the web still firmly in place. "What do you mean?"

"You have two paths ahead of you, mija. Two paths. But I'm not sure you're going to like either one."

Angie wasn't sure whether to feel relief or panic at the idea of a choice. "Explain, please. I thought my only choice was to accept and learn to handle this magic like this."

"And that is why you should have come earlier. The longer you wait, the more permanent these changes will be, the more the decision is made for you."

Given that the decision had already been forced on her to use the magic in that red thread directly, or at least use it enough to be in this position, the thought that she'd almost lost a chance to make another choice for herself left her a little breathless. So much of what was happening in her life lately were choices forced on her. Not things she'd do if given other options. Attempting to work as a demon hunter. Accessing the magic in that red thread of power. Hell, even her initial attempts to break up with Sebastian and move to New York had felt like a choice she wouldn't have made if she'd thought she'd had any other option.

Now Ezzie was giving her an actual choice. A choice to return to a place where she knew what to expect from her magic. A choice entirely up to her that wasn't forced on her by circumstances and other people's manipulations and agendas.

"Tell me. Please."

"With a great deal of work and concentrated effort, there is a way to move the magics apart again. A way to separate them. The window is closing. We'd have to start soon, and it will take several weeks of effort. You will be exhausted. And all your magic will be a little weaker when we are done."

All of her magic? "Even the ordinary witch magic? My psychic skills?"

"You probably won't feel the difference," Ezzie allowed. "But only because you never used your full potential anyway. Had you ever fully embraced all that you are, you would notice the difference."

"You're not the only teacher to tell me that I haven't been accessing all my magic," Angie murmured. "But… But it's always felt complete. As much as I could control."

"You've hesitated to embrace everything since you were a child, and it's so second nature to you, I'm not surprised you don't feel the lack. But there has always been a great deal more there for you to tap. The limits have always been your own doing."

Angie swallowed and slowly opened her eyes, letting the direct image of the spiderweb fade from her mind's eye. But she kept her gaze on her hands, not wanting to meet her teacher's gaze when she said, "It's the demon magic, that red thread. I've always been afraid that if I access too much of my witch magic, this other magic would get out of my control."

She stared at the white beaded bracelet on her wrist, the little dime sized pentagram hanging from the silver thread holding the beads. Rubbing her fingers over the pentagram, Angie said, "You gave me this as a touchstone, a way to step back from and control the demon portal magic. If you weren't worried about me embracing everything and…" She let out a breath. Then, "If you weren't worried about me accessing my full magical potential, why give me this?"

"That was always meant to center you and give you the balance you needed. It wasn't meant to stop you from using all the power you could. Just give you breathing room so that the power was in your control and not out of it." Ezzie reached across and touched the bracelet. "I'm afraid it's become more of a crutch than it should, though. That you rely on this like a security blanket."

Angie's chuckle didn't have a lot of humor to it. "You would be right about that."

"It may be time to let the crutch go. Time to accept all that you are without these imposed limits."

"And if I'm afraid? If I don't want to?"

"Then you can go back to a half-life of only accessing the minimum of your potential. And hope the world doesn't make you regret that decision."

Angie was more afraid the world would make her take hold of her full potential. More afraid of what she'd do with all that magic. "Have you heard the term demon witch?"

Ezzie's dark eyes widened a moment and then she gave a reluctant, sharp dip of her chin.

"Why didn't you tell me that name? Why haven't you told me more of the history of witches like me?"

"You weren't ready to hear," Ezzie said. "Just like you're not ready to embrace all your magic. The demon hunters finally told you?"

"Some of it. Not everything. But some. They won't let

me see their records on the other demon witches yet, but one…" She couldn't mention the council. Most people outside demon hunters didn't know there was any kind of governing body for the hunters. She hadn't even known when she was working with Sebastian the first time. She'd known about the history keepers. But not that there was a council who set down rules for the hunters.

Since thanks to a hunter trick of some kind, she physically couldn't mention them, she said, "One of the hunters who has seen the records told me a little. That all the demon witches they had information on went on to lose control of their power and unleash demon plagues that the hunters had to stop. That all the witches ended up dead. Either by the demons they unleashed or they were killed by others. Usually hunters. Once their own coven."

Ezzie sighed and nodded. "That one. She is infamous among the few who know of her."

"You've heard about her?" Why Angie was surprised Esmerelda knew more than she'd ever told Angie, she wasn't sure. "Never mind. I get it why you didn't tell me any of this before. But I'm ready now. For everything you know. I can only make this choice if I have all the information. *All* of it this time."

Ezzie's frown was contemplative as he studied Angie's expression. "Yes," she said after a moment. "Yes. I do think you're finally ready. To hear the full truth at least. Then you must decide. To embrace all that you are. Or cut off this one part of yourself permanently."

"Wait... I'd be cutting off the demon magic permanently?"

She wasn't sure how to feel about that. For most of her life, she'd wished that skill away. She wanted nothing to do with demons and demon portals. The only thing in the demon world she wanted was Sebastian. Everything else was just trouble and nightmares and felt antithetical to her witchy calling.

But knowing she could cut that part of her skills out, could consciously break that thread and never have to worry about unleashing a demon plague again?

The thought was both exhilarating and terrifying.

And she wasn't entirely sure why she was scared.

"Essentially the break would be permanent," Ezzie said. "And this is not a decision for you to take lightly. Or to make tonight." She waved a hand in the air, then abruptly cut the circle. The suddenness startled Angie. "Go to your parents and spend the night thinking about all this. Come tomorrow and we'll discuss more. You will have three days to consider. Then you must choose."

"Why three days?"

"I like the balance. And I like the number three."

That comment surprised a genuine laugh from Angie. She rose and helped Ezzie back to her feet, though the older witch hardly needed the help. Then silently they cleaned up their work area.

Angie left with a promise to think and to return early, but not too early, the next day—Esmerelda wasn't a morning person.

On the drive to her parents' house, though, Angie couldn't stop wondering what it would mean to give up her ability to open portals into the demon realm? Would her life be better without that skill? Safer? More her own to control? The demon hunters would no longer have any use for her. She'd be freed from that, and she'd no longer be a threat the hunters had to worry about. Almost all the things in her life she *didn't* want right now were tied to that particular skill, to that magic. Cutting it would eliminate all those problems and struggles.

But if she did give it up, what would that mean for her and Sebastian?

CHAPTER FOUR

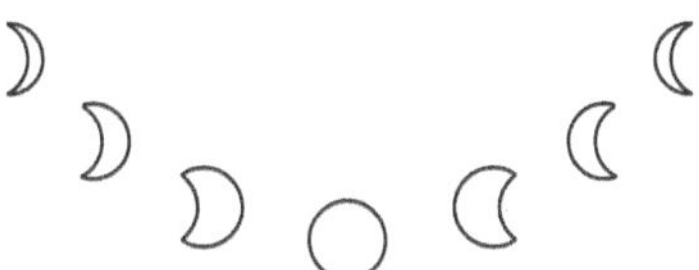

When she returned to Esmerelda's the next day, Angie still didn't know what she wanted. She'd spent the night visiting with her parents, her brother and his wife, meeting her brand new baby niece in person for the first time.

She'd sent Sebastian a text to let him know things were fine but didn't go into detail. What could she tell him when she had so much still to understand herself? And honestly, she was afraid to tell him what Esmerelda had said. Afraid to even consider that she could separate her magics and break off her ability to open realm breaches. Afraid of what that would mean for her and Sebastian.

She'd talk all this through with him when she understood it better. She just didn't want to rush things and confuse the situation.

Which was the excuse she kept telling herself all night.

The excuse she still repeated when she rang Esmerelda's front doorbell that morning. The chime let out a little tinkling bell sound, a bit like the wind chimes in the back garden. Angie smiled. That sound brought back a lot of memories.

Instead of Esmerelda opening the door, however, a woman Angie hadn't met before answered. A young Black woman dressed in light blue scrubs, her dark curly hair pulled up into a puffy bun.

She smiled politely. "You must be Angie. Ezzie said she was expecting you. I'm Tara, the visiting nurse. We'll be finished soon." She stepped aside so Angie could enter.

From the backyard, Ezzie called, "Come and sit in the sun with me, mija."

Angie gave nurse Tara a hesitant smile then went directly to Ezzie's side. She was sitting at the same table they'd sat at last night, mostly in the shade but with her legs stretched out to catch the sun. She was dressed in a loose skirt again, the material pulled up so her calves and ankles were exposed to the bright spring light.

Tara collected some equipment off the table, a pressure cuff, a pulse oximeter, a small box. "I'll be right back with your pills," she murmured to Ezzie, then left them alone.

"What's going on?" Angie asked, her full attention on her mentor and teacher. Ezzie looked more tired in the daylight, the skin around her eyes more delicate, the circles under her eyes a little darker. And there were creases of discomfort around her mouth that Angie hadn't noticed last night. Even when they were sitting on the floor.

"I'm getting old," Esmerelda said sardonically. "That is

what's going on. My children insist I have help with some things. And a nurse to ensure I take my medications and the laundry gets done. A stipulation I agreed to so I wouldn't have to hear the constant worry and nagging that I move closer to them. Ha! They're the ones who moved far from me. I have always been here."

Angie rolled her lips into her mouth so she wouldn't comment on that last. But the insight into Ezzie's relationship with her children was fascinating. Especially since Esmerelda didn't talk about her kids except in vague but loving terms when she did mention them.

"Are you sick, or…?" Angie clenched her fists in her lap. The temptation was strong to reach out and touch Ezzie so she could read exactly what was wrong. But it would also be an invasion of her teacher's privacy, which Angie wouldn't do. A lesson Esmerelda had taught her.

Ezzie saw the hand clenching, though, and smiled. "No, you do not have permission to read me. This is my business, and I am fine. Just old. And dying. But not very soon. So you don't need to worry."

Angie swallowed. For reasons she'd be embarrassed by if she mentioned them aloud, she'd never considered Esmerelda getting old enough to die. She'd thought, child-like, that her mentor would just always be there. Being confronted with the reality of time passing, of life moving on and Esmerelda nearing the end of hers, was a blow. A deep one.

She looked out across the garden, blinking back the sudden tears gathering in her eyes. Ezzie would hate to have her sit there crying over the inevitabilities of life.

Esmerelda reached across and patted Angie's thigh. Then folded her hands on her stomach again and tilted her face toward the sky, looking up through the covering vegetation shading her.

"Life," she said quietly. "It's worth it, this finite time."

Angie nodded but emotions were too thick, clogging her throat and making talking impossible.

"Anyway," Ezzie said briskly now. "We have things to discuss. Once Tara is finished, we'll get on with it."

"Are you sure? Are you up to it? I can come back…"

"Stop! Don't you treat me like an invalid. I am not. I'm perfectly fine. I get enough of that nonsense from my children."

Angie chuckled despite herself and nodded. "Fine. When you're ready."

They sat outside for a while longer, letting the day's warmth sink into their skin. And Angie realized it was the first time in months she'd felt this at peace. This… quiet. Lately, her life felt like she rested on a knife's edge of other people's goals and ambitions. Nothing to do with her own wants. Except for Sebastian, and her job at Dana's Cauldron, so much of her life felt like a chaotic mess. The peaceful moment in Esmerelda's backyard was a moment out of time. A moment to just breathe.

The front doorbell chimed while Tara was still puttering around inside. She called, "I'll get it."

Angie frowned. "You excepting someone else today?"

"Probably a religious person selling their god. I'll let Tara handle them. They always leave shell-shocked when I answer the door."

Angie chuckled and turned her face up to the shaded green overhang again. But a sense of unease moved through her gut as she tried to find that sense of peace from just moments ago. Something raised her hackles, set her on edge. When Tara walked back outside, Angie's foot was bouncing against the stone tiles beneath the metal table.

"There's a woman at the door," Tara said. "She says she's here to speak with Angela." Tara's gaze darted to Angie, her frown deep. "She specifically asked for Angela Jordan."

Angie sat up, that sense of unease sharpening into something close to fear. "Did she give a name? What does she look like?" Memories rose of those brief moments where she thought she'd seen Carmen at the airport in Newark, then again at the airport here.

"Dark hair. Pale skin. Tall but not as tall as you. Speaks with a heavy Spanish accent."

The description overall could fit Carmen. But the description could also describe half of Albuquerque and a fair number of people in the U.S. Carmen did put on a Spanish accent when it suited her, though she dropped it with Angie. Actually, Carmen was a chameleon, blending into her surroundings in whatever guise suited her purpose, so Angie wasn't entirely sure if the accent was an affect or if dropping the accent was the affect. Given Carmen's accent waivered, though, Angie assumed it was adopted rather than natural.

"She didn't give me a name," Tara finished. "Just said you'd know who it was."

Angie flexed her fists against her thighs and stood. This could be nothing. But it could also be a threat. And she couldn't take the chance that it was nothing.

"Stay here, please," she said to Tara. Glanced at Ezzie. "You too."

Ezzie was already murmuring under her breath. Angie caught a few words and realized she was setting a protective circle around herself and Tara. Angie nodded, got out of the circle before it closed, and stalked to the front door. She trusted her teacher to look after Tara. Even sick and old, Esmerelda was a force to be reckoned with.

And Ezzie knew the world Angie was part of now. She would understand the potential threat.

Angie approached the front door already starting a spell, setting it up in her mind, murmuring the words, forming the appropriate finger gestures, getting the spell to the stage of almost ready to cast, then holding it there so that all it would take was a single word to trigger it.

The big problem with Angie's type of magic was that it took time. Time to build a spell. Time to cast. No instant wizard bolts or streams of flames from her palms. Witch magic was spells and potions and things that took time. But over the years, she'd learned how to prepare a spell ahead of time and keep it ready to trigger. She could hold up to two different spells if necessary. That skill had been serving her well these last few months.

She approached the door cautiously, which Tara had left closed—smart woman—but Angie couldn't see a silhouette through the smoked glass at the top of the door. She listened, but there was no noise from outside either.

Anxiety tightened her gut. She flung open the door, suddenly…

Only to find no one there.

She stepped just outside, blocking the door to protect those inside in case this was a trap, and scanned the surroundings. The wild front yard appeared empty. There was no strange car in the driveway or along the street besides her own and Tara's. No one walking away from the house.

Swearing under her breath, she searched the front porch. About a foot away from the door, a little envelope with her name written in neat, curving lines. Angie swore again as she approached the envelope.

She opened her senses to it, to *see* any magical spells on the paper. There was no tell-tale blue light shimmering around it. Nothing even when she turned her head and looked at it just so from the corner of her eye.

Before touching the envelope, she went back to the door and touched the knob, opening her psychic sense. She didn't do that with doorknobs often because the damned things were almost always too chaotic to read, having been touched by so many people. But she tried this time anyway.

A flash of Tara coming in earlier. Esmerelda. Angie herself. She picked up one of Ezzie's children. But nothing from the woman who'd just been there.

Angie tried the door next, where someone might knock. Remembered the bell chime and tried the doorbell. Nothing but herself, Tara, Ezzie, and some of Ezzie's children. There was one impression from a young man on the door who wasn't familiar, but after studying that impression a moment, she realized he was a grocery delivery man—one who apparently adored Ezzie because she tipped well and she'd helped him with some romantic trouble.

Angie smiled briefly at that impression, the flash of his emotions and situation a nice break in her worry, but she moved away from that and back to the issue at hand swiftly. Another scan of the surroundings, then she warily approached the envelope again.

Squatting down next to it, she hovered her hand over the blank, white square. A small envelope, not the ordinary letter-sized. No writing on the outside except for her own name. And still no hint or feel of magic.

She took in a deep breath, braced herself. And picked up the note. When nothing happened, she let out the breath in a whoosh and stood. The back of the envelope wasn't even sealed. It was easy to open and pull out the single sheet of notebook paper inside. The kind of paper torn out of a spiral notebook with the spiral at the top, leaving the ragged edges behind.

She opened her senses to the page and the envelope, trying to read them. She was better with people but still capable of reading objects when the need arose. Yet she got nothing from the note. No sense of the person who'd held it. No impressions of…anything. No psychic impression at all. Damn it.

But then what had she expected. Carmen knew enough

about her to know she was a touch psychic. She'd have found a way to ensure the envelope was clean.

"Everything okay?" Ezzie called, her voice strong and a little deep from the magic she'd just worked.

"Fine. No one here. Just a note."

"What's it say?"

"About to find out." She flipped open the folded paper.

The note said: *Time's come. You've survived too long. Too well. They'll try to kill you now. Directly. Gonna have to kill them first. ~C*

Angie scowled at the note, another curse bubbling up in her throat. Not something she could discuss with Tara around. But the minute the nurse left, she had to talk about this with Ezzie.

And then she needed to call Sebastian.

She folded the note and slipped it back into the envelope, stuffing the whole thing into her jeans back pocket. Another slow scan of the area. But there was no sign of Carmen. Or anyone else for that matter. Still, the minute Tara left, she was drawing a circle around Ezzie's entire house while they talked.

If Carmen was right, and not just trying to stir the pot—which was a real possibility with the revenge-minded vigilante—the people among the demon hunter council who wanted the demon witch, *Angie*, dead weren't going to wait for a demon to do it anymore.

Angie knew for a fact that some of the council members wanted her dead. She even had an idea which ones. Though there was at least one she hadn't met yet and that one definitely wanted her dead. Then there were the hunters Jacob claimed to represent who wanted her as far from demons and demon hunting as Angie wanted to be. She'd suspected for a while now that the ones who wanted her dead were just waiting for her to fail as a hunter.

Demon hunters didn't do badly at their job and get fired. Demon hunters didn't retire. They didn't just quit. A demon hunter only stopped being a demon hunter when their will wasn't as strong as a demon's and they were killed in a fight.

And what better way to kill a reluctant demon witch than to force her into being a hunter, knowing she didn't have the will for the job, and then just letting the demons get her.

But six months later, and she was still alive. A lot of that was down to Sebastian. With him on her every hunt, and with her witch magic and ability to open portals to demon realms, she'd managed to survive even without the hunter's will or instincts.

Apparently, her enemies on the council were tired of waiting.

Or Carmen was lying in the hopes Angie would destroy the council. A very distinct possibility.

What Carmen had to do with the hunter council, Angie wasn't sure. There was a connection there. Carmen had killed a demon hunter years ago and yet she still walked free. She knew things that most people—even Angie until recently!—didn't know about the hunters.

Carmen had been deep in the demon world for years, convincing people she thought deserved it to summon demons and then watching as the demons killed the people when the invariable loophole in the demon contract came due. Carmen *arranged* for demons to kill and possibly escape their summoners. She'd worked closely with a horrid demon called a Molder demon for years as its servant.

And yet the demon hunters had never stopped her. She'd escaped justice over and over again.

Carmen had a link to the council. Some connection that allowed her to maintain her freedom. Yet she was trying to goad Angie into attacking the council, kill the ones who wanted to kill Angie. There was something deeper there, some revenge plot Carmen was engaged in—she was patient and often worked for years in a revenge scheme—but Angie had no idea what her ultimate goal was.

And Angie didn't kill people. Not unless attacked and left with no choice. She wasn't a murderer. She believed in the witches' creed that what she put out would come back to her. There was even a spell for that. She would defend herself however she needed to. But she didn't attack and murder people.

Which was what Carmen, apparently, wanted her to do.

But what happened when Angie refused?

ANGIE WENT BACK INTO THE HOUSE AND PRETENDED everything was fine for Tara's sake. Waiting until the nurse had finished giving Esmerelda some medicine and then left. Angie watched the pills, frowning, worry for her teacher and worry about Carmen's note doing complicated things in her chest as she waited to explain everything to Ezzie.

Even after the nurse left, Angie hesitated to show the note. She didn't want to worry her teacher when she had other things to worry about, like her health.

It took all of two minutes of silence before Ezzie snapped, "What's going on?"

Angie reluctantly pulled the note from her pocket. She held it up without opening it. "So, I told you about the witch who…forced me to open the demon witch powers?"

Ezzie nodded, a crease forming on her brow.

"The note is a warning. Of sorts." She stared down at the envelope. Since she couldn't mention the council directly, she said, "There are people in the demon hunter world who would like to see me dead, because of what I am and what I can do. Others want me to succeed. Still others just want me to stay away from all things demon. It seems the ones who want me dead are tired of waiting for a demon to do it."

"They're coming after you here?" Ezzie said, her tone hard.

"I don't know. Maybe. At least, it sounds like they're coming for me soon." She picked at one corner of the envelope. "The witch thinks I should go after them first, kill first. Which, obviously, I'm not going to do. But it's possible she's followed me here and left the warning note because my enemies have come here, too. Which means my family is in danger. And so are you."

Ezzie waved that last away. "I'm in no danger inside my own home, on my land, from anything but old age and the fussiness of my grown children. No demons, no hunters, no witches can get at me here if I don't let them in." She closed her eyes a moment, took in a deep deep breath, and let it out slowly.

Angie could practically feel the magic rolling off Ezzie. Her particular brand of magic didn't work exactly like Angie's. No two witches were completely alike. And Ezzie's Brujería discipline was different to Angie's more Celtic-based approach. But there were basics, fundamentals that were similar across disciplines.

Early in her study, Angie had learned about the permanent protection circle encompassing Ezzie's home and a significant portion of the surrounding land. The circle was set and ready to be activated or dismissed as needed. Angie had learned how to set such a circle, and had tried to place one around her apartment in New York. But apartments were tricky. Too many other people in and out of the building as a whole. Land and houses made the setup of a full protective circle easier. Angie'd had to settle for mostly warding her door and windows, a sort of witchy alarm to warn her of intruders.

The circle was stronger. A better way of keeping danger out.

As she waited the moments it took Ezzie to activate the spell, she decided she'd better place something like this around her parents' house. Her mother had resisted the idea of a permanent circle for years. Insisting they didn't need it when she and her coven could just throw one up if a specific situation arose. Angie thought the resistance to a permanent circle might have been her mother's way of trying to reassure Angie that they trusted her to wield her magic wisely. But this had nothing to do with Angie's magic—even if it was currently unpredictable—so maybe her mother would finally relent.

Ezzie opened her eyes and looked directly into Angie's. "We're both safe and no one will overhear us." Her eyes fluttered closed again, though there was still movement behind the thin barrier of her lids. "Eagle and fox are patrolling. They'll let me know if anyone is near."

Ezzie had a unique skill that Angie had often envied as a kid. She could ride inside the minds of animals, after asking permission of course, and see and hear and smell and taste all that they could. She'd maintained links with certain animals who lived and hunted on her property the entire time Angie had known her. Not the same animals, as they passed away. But from what Ezzie said, the different animals over the years were from the same lineages. This fox and this eagle were related to the fox and eagle Ezzie would have first bonded with years ago when she moved to this house.

"Now," she said, snapping her eyes open, all business. "Tell me what you're trying not to tell me. I can't help you if you keep secrets."

Her teacher's voice was hard to resist. But Angie said, "There are things I can't tell you. Even if no one is listening. It's better you don't have certain information. Just in case. But I can tell you that there are certain hunters whose efforts to turn me into one of theirs were primarily motivated by the hope that I'd fail. And die in a demon fight."

"You've foiled that plot quite neatly so far."

Angie almost smiled. Wanted to preen a little, too. But she refrained. Barely. "I've had help surviving."

"Sebastian."

She nodded. "But this skill, the way my magics have blended. That's made the fights… I don't want to say easier. Because they never are. I can't face a demon the way a hunter can. I don't have that sort of will and keep defaulting to magic. *But* the magic is working in these fights. Better than it should. Like…like it was made to be wielded in just this way. I suspect if I stopped trying to fight like a normal demon hunter, and fully embraced the magic as it's changing, I could fight without needing the will a hunter uses."

"But you fear making the blending of the magics worse if you do that."

"I'm afraid I'll…destroy the magic I've always had, the magic that makes me the witch I am. That it'll be subsumed under whatever this blended magic is and I'll never be able to access the original again."

Ezzie nodded. "A valid fear. A possible outcome. And one of the points you must weigh in your decision to keep things as they are or permanently cut off the demon magic."

"If it was possible to cut that magic off," Angie asked, "why didn't you do that for me when I was a child? Why not nip the danger in the bud before I accidentally loosed a demon plague again?"

"First, that would take away your choice. The path of your life, the way you wield your powers, which powers you choose to wield, those are all decisions you must make for yourself. I would never force a student down a certain path, even if I thought the path was safer for them. That is always and forever something you need to choose."

Her tone was sharp and brook no refusals. Angie had learned a long time ago not to argue with that tone.

"Second," Ezzie continued, "I cannot see the future. And even though you can, you know as well as I do that the future is always changing. That any reading of it is subject to shifting currents and decisions and whims of fate. Had I taken your choice and separated you from a part of your magic, I may have made things much worse. Though I'd like my children to think differently, I am not omnipotent. Any choice I made when you were still just a child could have had consequences we couldn't foresee. I had to allow the future to play out as it would."

Angie nodded, understanding. As often as not, attempting to change the future only brought about the future you were hoping to avoid. There were entire Greek tragedies written about just that point. Everyone, even non-magical people, knew that attempting to control the future was a fool's errand. Even if those everyone's didn't listen to that instinct.

"Third," Ezzie said, "you were always going to be safer learning to control the demon witch powers. Learning about your magic and how to control it, even the parts of it you would prefer not to use, is ultimately safer than trying to eliminate what you don't want. I chose the safest route available to us." She shrugged. "I think I chose wisely."

Angie relaxed back into the plastic chair and gave in to

Esmerelda's logic. "You're right. Of course you are. That's why you're the teacher."

"Yes. It is."

They both chuckled, but Angie's worry overtook the moment of humor. "I won't go after my enemies the way Carmen is trying to push me to do. I will defend myself. And those I love. But I won't attack anyone. Still…"

She lifted the envelope from the table, tapping the end of it against the metal edge. The *tink tink tink* sound blended with the wind chimes around the garden as a warm breeze fluttered through her hair. "Still, knowing they're coming sooner rather than later means I need to understand the way my magic has changed. I'm not sure I'll get the three days you've given me to make the decision whether to cut the demon witch power out or not."

"If that's the case, we'll deal with that when it happens. Until then, you're safe here and we have work to do. We should get to it now."

"Are you sure you're…?" She swallowed the rest of the question at Ezzie's annoyed look. "Fine. Let me call Sebastian quickly, to let him know about this so he's forewarned. Then we'll get started."

Ezzie grunted and turned her face toward the sun, closing her eyes. She looked both vulnerable and indomitable in that pose. Definitely a force to be reckoned with.

And the thought of losing her, even if that loss came years from now, stabbed sharply into Angie's heart.

What would she do in a world without Esmerelda in it?

CHAPTER FIVE

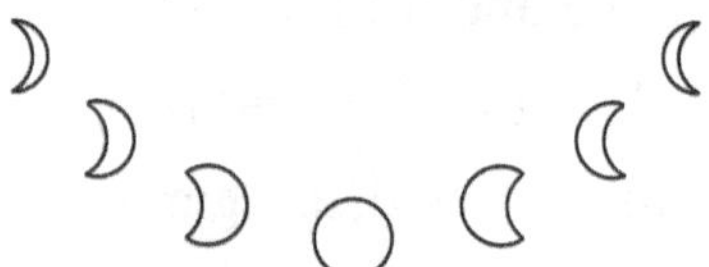

Sebastian answered on the first ring. "Is everything okay? What's happened?"

"You're more suspicious than I am," Angie said, smiling at just hearing his voice, deep and strong, that lovely English accent rolling the words.

"This is a phone call instead of a text, and it's not at the time we arranged," he said, though she heard the hint of humor in his voice. "Can't blame a man for worrying."

"I can't. And I hate to confirm you're suspicions but something is wrong. Carmen is here."

"What's happened?"

She told him about thinking she'd seen the witch at the airports but writing that off as anxiety. "And then a woman came to Esmerelda's door looking for me. She didn't wait around. But she left a note."

"Signed?"

"Only with a C. But that was enough." She told him what the note said. "Obviously, I'm not going to attack and kill anyone. But the fact that she showed up again after all these months and is trying to manipulate me into… Well, I think into going after the hunter who wants me dead, but I'm not sure."

She checked over her shoulder. Esmerelda was still in the garden, her face turned up to the sun, her eyes closed, giving Angie privacy as Angie paced in the airy kitchen. But Angie had left the sliding glass doors open, and sound carried, so she had to be careful what she said aloud.

"I never know with Carmen," she finished, turning back to the magnet-covered, silver fridge and the silly donkey shaped magnet from the Grand Canyon she'd been staring at without really seeing. "Whatever she wants, though, I'd rather not give it to her, and I have no intention of launching an assault on anyone."

"It is possible certain people have gotten impatient. I'm not sure they thought you'd survive this long."

"Have been a few close calls," she said with a twist of her mouth. "I thought they'd realize the error of their ways at this point, though, and give up trying to make me a hunter."

"They'll never give that up," he said, his tone harsh. "Even if it would be better for everyone that they did."

Which was how she'd ended up in the middle of this mess. They couldn't just let her be a witch and ignore the portal magic. They were terrified she'd open a realm breach and unleash a demon plague. And she had no way to assure them she wouldn't, other than stating repeatedly that she had no intention of doing that. She didn't *want* to loose a demon plague on this world. Ever. It was her world, too.

But how did she make the sort of people who regularly dealt with humans who summoned demons understand that? That *she* wasn't someone they needed to fear.

If she were being completely honest, she'd have to admit she even understood their point of view. Knowing what she did now about all the other demon witches, about them all either losing control or unleashing the demons on purpose. Hard to blame the hunters for worrying about her. She did get why they couldn't just take her word that she was different from the others.

That rationale didn't make her any happier about all this, though. And it certainly didn't make her a demon hunter.

"Have you heard from Gabriella?" She leaned against the kitchen counter and idly twisted the tea kettle Tara had left sitting on the stove top. The speckled blue metal was still warm but the kettle felt mostly empty. Restless and anxious, Angie took it to the sink to refill. The sound of the running water glugging into the metal pot did nothing to settled her nerves. But maybe a cup of chamomile would help.

"I haven't heard from any of them." Sebastian paused. Then, "But Jacob put himself in my path."

"That's…unexpected." She straightened away from the sink. "He always approached me when there was no possibility of you being around." And then only twice. He hadn't tried to talk to her since last October. Vanished the same as Carmen. "What did he say?"

"That our time has run out."

Angie snapped off the water but left the kettle sitting in the bottom of the sink. "Same as Carmen. What the hell is going on?"

"You haven't died. And you haven't managed to become a proper hunter. Neither camp is getting what they want."

"Which is exactly what we told them would happen," she huffed. "At least the part about me not being a proper hunter.

Actually, though, she wasn't sure what Jacob wanted in all this, if he wanted her dead or not. He hadn't wanted her to be a hunter. Had tried to talk her into turning down the job— as if she'd had a choice. And he'd claimed he didn't want her dead. But that didn't mean much in this world. He could have changed his mind in the intervening months.

Except why warn Sebastian that their time had run out if he wanted her dead?

Yeah, Jacob's motivations were as cloudy as Carmen's. But having them both show up again, now, when her powers were growing and her control was shaky, felt…like an omen.

A warning as much as the warning that her enemy on the council had finally stopped waiting for her to die by demon.

"Esmerelda says I can reverse the blended magics," she blurted to Sebastian, then winced. This wasn't exactly the way she'd wanted to tell him. But now that it was out there… "She says I can even cut myself off from the red thread. But it would probably be permanent."

Sebastian was silent for a long moment. Long enough for

her to get the kettle back on the stove and turn on the heating coil beneath it. Long enough for the water to begin boiling.

"Is that what you want?" he asked finally. "To cut yourself off completely from the demon witch thread?"

"I'm not sure. Esmerelda's given me three days to figure it out. And in the meantime, we'll work on how I can control what's happening if I decide to continue letting the magics mix."

"You've never liked that skill. You'd prove yourself no threat to the hunters, too, if you cut yourself off from it. They'd have to leave you alone."

"Maybe. Or maybe they'd still want to kill me."

"Without the ability to open the portals, you're not a threat. Killing you then would just be murder. They won't be able to get away with that."

Didn't mean they wouldn't try. But she kept that part to herself. They both knew, even if Sebastian didn't want to admit to it out loud.

"Esmerelda said if I cut off the demon thread, though, it could have a knock-on effect for my other magic. Make me weaker than I am now. I'll probably still have all my skills, but... But there may be consequences that we can't anticipate. I'd likely be giving up more than just the ability to open portals to demon realms."

That particular skill she'd dump in a minute. It was all the other consequences that made her hesitate. That worried her.

Especially if the hunter council still came after her, still tried to kill her even after she was no longer a threat.

"I know you didn't want me to join you there so you

could focus," Sebastian said quietly. "But I'm having trouble staying away. Especially with Carmen and Jacob back in the picture."

"Are you asking to come to Albuquerque?" She smiled into the phone as the kettle whistled and she removed it from the heat.

"I'm worried about what they'll try while we're not together. I'm worried they'll use this moment to attack you, when I'm not there to have your back."

"I'm worried they'll come after you because you do always have my back," she admitted. It was a constant fear in the back of her mind, one she'd never admitted out loud to him. One she'd only barely admitted to herself. She was terrified the hunter who wanted her dead would use Sebastian, or have him killed, to get at Angie.

The same way Carmen had used Sebastian to force Angie to break open her powers.

"I'm able to handle them," he said but quietly, his reassuring tone doing a lot to calm her nerves. "Remember I've been dealing with them for a lot longer than you've had to. But it's nice to know you worry about me."

"Come to Albuquerque," she said in a rush. Even as the words left her mouth, her shoulders relaxed and a tension in her gut eased.

"I'll be on the next flight I can get. This will affect the work you do with Esmerelda, though."

"The minute Carmen knocked at her door, our work was affected. I'll figure it out. Given the circumstances. Having you here will be less distracting than the worry."

Silence for a moment. Then, "I hope this doesn't piss you off, but I was coming one way or another. To guard your back. I wouldn't have distracted you by letting you know I was there, but I would have been there no matter what."

The soft smile he couldn't see would have given her away, even if her next words didn't. "I probably should be pissed at that, but… I'm not. I'd do the same for you."

"I love you, Ang. I'll always be there for you."

Her heart thumped harder and her smile widened. "Text your flight details when you have them. I'll pick you up at the airport."

A brief hesitation, then, "I arrive tonight. Nine."

"You already had the flight booked?"

"I already had the flight booked."

She chuckled. "You're lucky I'm understanding."

"I am. See you soon."

When she rejoined Esmerelda on the patio, her teacher said, "When does he arrive?"

Angie rolled her eyes and huffed out a breath. "How did you know?"

"You two have loved each other for a long time and weathered some…unique storms. He wouldn't stay away when you needed him."

Angie had no idea why that made her want to tear up, so she pushed the rush of emotion aside. "Nine. So we have time to work today. So long as you're up for it."

"Ask again and I'll hit you with that spark spell I taught you to fend off your brothers."

Angie laughed. "That spell's come in handy over the

years. And not *just* with my brothers." She'd even used it once to survive being trapped in a demon realm.

But since that memory still closed her throat and stalked her nightmares, she pushed it aside, too. One day, she might tell Esmerelda about that moment. That breaking point. Maybe. For now, they had other things to do.

Before the second shoe—whatever it might be—dropped.

CHAPTER SIX

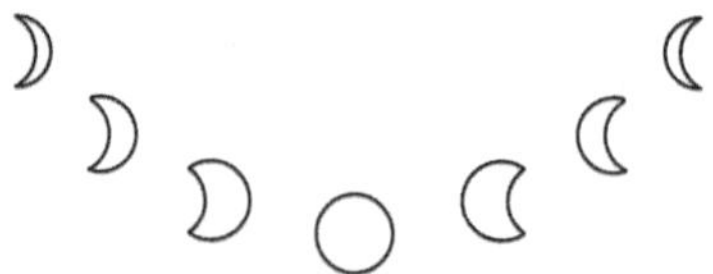

The training went okay. But sitting in a secure circle in the middle of the airy space in Ezzie's living room, with the desert wind blowing in through the open, sliding glass doors and the scent of creosote and Ezzie's garden filling the air, was a very different experience to trying to use that magic under stressful circumstances. Angie had learned the hard way that she couldn't rely on her mind in moments of terror, couldn't rely on her memory of spells and finger movements. If it wasn't baked into her muscle memory, into her bones, all the training and learning went out of her head the moment panic set in.

Which meant learning how to use this new, more powerful magic either had to be trained into muscle memory. Or she had to cut it off now so she didn't hurt someone with it.

"Take another deep breath," Ezzie said quietly, her voice filtering through Angie's mind.

With her eyes closed, that voice was Angie's only link to the physical realm. Most of her existed in the metaphysical spaces, the realm of her magic. She sat in the center of her spiderweb of power, the center of those threads of mostly blue magic. Every time she mentally touched one of those filaments, the familiarity filled her, settled her. Here was the power she was used to wielding. The home of all those spells she'd learned and practiced and trained over the years. That magic felt like *her* in a way that was hard to explain with words. The sense of it was like recognizing her face in a mirror.

Then there was the single red thread. The link to her demon witch magic, the power to thin the barrier between this realm and the demon realms. There weren't any active spells or training built into that thread. No years' worth of effort. Opening a realm breach wasn't something that took physical effort on her part. Not like casting a spell. All she needed was to look into the right shape in a tree and the barrier thinned, a portal opened, and demons could move through.

So could she, but she tried not to think about that moment, being trapped in a demon realm, the portal she'd opened closing and no trees for her to open another and escape. There were no trees in a demon realm.

The lack of effort needed for her to open that portal, compared to her actual magic, was a puzzle she'd never been able to solve. But it was similar to her touch psychic skills.

She didn't require effort to do that either. For both, all the physical effort went into *not* opening barriers, *not* reading every object or person she touched. Those skills were a sort of mirrored image of the effort required for her actual spellcasting.

And that connection, which she couldn't explain yet, was one of the reasons she hesitated to cut herself off from her demon witch thread. If the two things were linked in some way, in the complex weave of her magic, she risked cutting off her psychic skills. The very skills she used to make a living, to make a difference for people. To help. She'd lose one of her core abilities.

She didn't want to lose that skill, even if it meant never having to fear opening a portal again.

Thanks to her last encounter with Carmen, though, Angie also knew now if she touched that red thread in her web, if she grabbed it, she could use that magic in a more active way than she'd ever used it before. No longer needing a tree, no longer a passive sort of power that just happened. She could literally open a portal anytime she wanted. Anywhere.

But she hadn't tried to open a portal again that way because she was afraid of the power. The feel of it was… heady. She'd never been the type of witch tempted by great power, never necessarily wanted to have *more* magic. But the metaphysical act of grabbing that red thread filled her with *more*, more strength than she'd ever experienced before.

Even more terrifying, that *more* also felt like her. Felt like something she was always supposed to feel. Always supposed to be.

Except that she didn't want to *be* this.

"Your resisting," Ezzie said, her tone firm but calm. Washing over Angie as surely as the breeze through the open patio door.

"I don't want this much power," she admitted as she hovered a mental hand over the red thread. The mixed purple magic spread out into the neighboring strands. But for the moment, Ezzie had decided Angie shouldn't touch that magic. Not yet. They needed clear boundaries. And if she decided to separate from this new, more powerful mix, she was better off not getting too familiar with it.

"You never have," Ezzie said, with a sound Angie thought might be a rueful chuckle. "That doesn't mean you haven't had it this whole time. This has always been you, mija. You've always held back. But the magic will consume you if you don't learn to use it all."

She'd been hearing that same admonishment her whole life. She was only just now starting to understand what Ezzie and her other teachers had been talking about.

Reluctantly, she settled a mental hand on the red thread, without touching any of the blue magic. She usually anchored in the blue witch magic first, before risking touching the red thread. But Ezzie wanted her to practice accessing the demon witch power on its own. To learn to control it on its own.

The power surged through her, a flash of white light behind her closed eyes. A shock of energy through her limbs. Always before, this led her to open a portal, like it or not, conscious or not, touching this power opened demon portals.

Her lesson now was to access the magic and *not* breach a demon realm.

Which was easier said than done.

The moment she came into contact with that thread she felt the barrier between realms like a physical thing. Like an actual wall that she could touch, except it was all around her and didn't fit neatly into a three-dimensional boundary. The "wall" was everywhere, like air.

With her hand on the power in that red thread, she could topple that wall. Break down every last barrier between demon realms and this one.

But she could also…not.

That's what she focused on. Holding the thread and mentally feeling that barrier and *not* letting it thin. Not letting it break open. It felt like she was physically holding the barrier up, though. Like her shoulder to the wall was the only thing keeping it from falling over. The effort it took caused sweat to break out along her spine, drip down her temple.

"You're trying too hard," Ezzie murmured. "You're forcing the barrier up instead of allowing it to remain in place."

"Feels like if I don't, it'll crumble," she muttered, hearing the strain in her voice. "If I relax, it'll fall. Demons will escape."

"They won't. You have control of this. This is your will. Yours to command."

Angie shook her head as the demon witch power continued to surge through her, warm now, like heat dancing over her skin, along her nerves. A part of her still faintly aware of her physical body felt her muscles tense and tight, felt the sweat dripping down her spine. Her labored breathing.

The part of her not in the physical realm, the part of her existing in the magical realm *knew* if she dropped her guard, the power would consume her, washing over her like a literal dam breaking and drown her. She'd unleash the demons.

She shook as she tried to loosen her grip on that mental image, to relax as Ezzie instructed and *control* the power, in the same way she controlled her other magic. But this was too…too easy. Her other magic took effort to work. This was effort to force it not to work. It wasn't the same. It was so hard to keep the barrier up. Would be so much easier to let it drop. If she stopped, everything would crumble. But that would be so so easy.

"Angela." Esmerelda's voice in her mind. Strong. Powerful. Vibrating the web of Angie's magic to get her attention. "Angela. Release the thread. Take a deep breath. Move back into your body."

"Can't," she muttered. Though whether out loud or in that metaphysical plane she wasn't sure. "Too much. Too strong. So hard to control."

"Let go, Angela. Pull away from that power now."

Everything in Angie tightened, her body vibrating now too as she willed her mental hand to open, to release the thread. If she looked, she thought she saw the red power encompassing her hand, holding her grip on the thread more firmly. She lifted one mental finger and it was like pulling two strong magnets apart.

More sweat dripped down her face, but she lifted another finger. The connection weakened. The hold no longer so strong. She lifted a third finger, and now her hold on the thread was more tentative.

The power surging through her eased back to something manageable, and only then did she notice how hot her skin felt. The cooling breeze from outside brushed her cheek. Another anchor to the real world.

With a settling breath, she refocused on her center, on the middle point in her that held her balanced with the world around her. Balance was everything to a witch like her. This was where she needed to be, this delicate central point.

The very center of her web.

She eased down into that point and released her hold on the red thread. Watched as it vibrated and settled. Felt the web around her as the final vibrations moved over it like a brush of a breeze echoing the air swirling around her in the real world.

She took in another deep, long breath, releasing it slowly.

And opened her eyes.

"Well," she said with a deadpan that belied the panic that had gripped her. "That was interesting."

Ezzie snorted. "You have so much power and you have refused to tap it. It will take time and effort to learn to control it. The good news is, you didn't open a portal. Directly accessing that magic and not breaching the realm barrier is progress.

Angie didn't feel like she'd made progress. She felt drained, exhausted, and like she'd just discovered how little control she actually had over her magic. "This will take longer than we have. Longer than three days. And I'm not even sure I have that much time."

"You don't need full control right away. Just knowing, in your mind, you can touch that magic and not open a portal is enough for now. Feeling the energy there is important, too. The more you are acquainted with it, the better you'll be able to judge if you can cut yourself off from it or not."

Angie nodded, the decision before her still weighing heavily on her.

"Enough for today," Esmerelda said, clapping her hands. "Come back tomorrow. And bring Sebastian. I haven't seen him in years. It's nice having such a handsome man in my home. I'll make him pollo con arroz."

"Do not go out of your way to cook for us," Angie said, thinking again of Tara the nurse and all that medicine Ezzie was taking. Of the years that were catching up to her mentor.

Ezzie waved a hand. "Don't fuss. I love cooking. It's good for me to do the things I love. And if you don't stop treating me like an invalid, Angela Jordan, I will force you to do the dishes after I've spent all day cooking. I can go through many pots and pans."

Angie chuckled and shook her head. "I can't help worrying about you. But I'll try to stop fussing. Just know it comes from love."

"I know." Ezzie waved her hands in a shooing motion. "Now go away so I can take a nap in the sunshine."

Angie hesitated at the door, thinking of the fact that Carmen had come to this house, knew where Esmerelda lived. "Set your wards after I leave. Please. And the larger circle." She held up a hand when Esmerelda opened her mouth. "This isn't me fussing. This is… Carmen is dangerous. I can't predict what she'll do. And the other people after me, they might use you to get to me. So, please, just…be extra careful and protect yourself."

"I will," Ezzie said gently. "I will."

Angie still left reluctantly. But she trusted Esmerelda's magical skills. More than her own at the moment. Her teacher was one of the strongest witches she knew. If Esmerelda didn't want Carmen or any of the demon hunters to get through to her house, none of them would.

Now Angie had to figure out how to protect the other people she loved.

And not get killed herself.

The text popped up on Angie's phone while she was at a stoplight. Thinking it was Sebastian, she flicked a glance at her screen. But the number was one she didn't recognize and wasn't in her contact list.

Frowning, leery after receiving Carmen's note that morning, she drove into the parking lot of a coffee shop. She wasn't holding out much hope that Carmen didn't know where her parents lived, but if there was even a chance that the witch didn't know, Angie would do what she had to to avoid leading her to them.

Once parked, she looked at the text. The number still wasn't familiar, but the first three numbers were a 917 New York cellphone area code. Still thinking about Carmen, she scanned the message.

The council is done waiting for you to die. They'll come for you now. He'll come for you now. Watch your back.

There was no signature, not even the "C" written on the note. Nothing to say who this message was from, except that it was from a New York cellphone.

But it was essentially the same message she'd gotten from Carmen. Almost exactly the same message. The same message passed to Sebastian from Jacob. Either a lot of people were privy to the thinking of her enemy on the council, or this was some kind of a trap.

Given the machinations that went on in the background of the demon hunter world, she was leaning toward trap.

Angie dialed Sebastian's number, hoping to catch him before he got on his flight, but the call went to voicemail. She considered the text message again. Glanced around the parking lot. No one seemed to be paying her any attention. No cars had followed her into the lot. Still, the sense of being maneuvered into a trap didn't ease. She snatched up her huge, brown leather purse, dropped the strap over her head, and went into the coffee shop, watching her surroundings, the people she passed.

The moment she stepped inside, the scent of roasting coffee beans hit her, along with the quiet drone of a busy café. There were people waiting for their orders at the high black counter, one person at the register, three efficient workers behind the counter making coffee at speed, and a handful of people sitting at the available tables. A couple at one, busy leaning in close and talking intently, paying no attention to their surroundings. A woman with a laptop tapping away, taking occasional sips from the paper to-go cup beside her but her full attention on her screen. A man and a boy playing a game of chess on a foldout board as the man showed the boy how to move the pieces. And another man near the back reading a book.

No one glanced in her direction. No one looked familiar.

Not that that meant anything. Not when dealing with demon hunters.

If a demon hunter didn't want her to see them, they could be sitting at one of the supposedly empty tables and she wouldn't spot them. A demon hunter could will her gaze to dance right over them. She'd seen Sebastian's mentor Aidan do just such a thing on more than one occasion. She'd seen Sebastian do it, too. So she didn't take the disinterest of the other people in the coffee shop for granted. Or take for granted that she was seeing everyone in the room that was there.

But from appearances, no one in the place took any notice of Angie.

Two people walked into the café behind her. A man in a business suit, checking his Blackberry and frowning fiercely at whatever he was reading. Another was a harried looking woman with a baby in a stroller. Her toddler was trying to lift himself out of the stroller's harness and half crying, half screeching at his inability to break free. The mother gave Angie an apologetic look and tried calming the toddler with a squeaky toy, to little effect.

Angie smiled at the mother, trying to reassure her the noise was okay. She might only be meeting her brother's daughter for the first time, but she'd been talking to him since the baby was born two months ago, and things were a lot more difficult and exhausting than he'd expected. He loved his daughter to distraction, which was fun to see, but he and his wife weren't getting a lot of sleep. Angie had a great deal of sympathy for the harried looking mother.

She got herself an excessively sweet coffee drink with lots of milk and sugar and whipped cream on top—she'd burned up a lot of energy during her training session with Esmerelda—and then paid for the mother's coffee and juice box for the toddler. The woman attempted to brush away the offer, but Angie insisted because the woman was having a rough moment and looked like she could do with a bit of kindness. The mother teared up a little but sniffled back the tears and thanked Angie profusely. The man in the business suit behind the mother gave them both a funny look, but then his Blackberry dinged again and he returned to whatever was happening on the screen.

Angie took her dessert coffee to a free table that faced the front door and sat. The other patrons in the café continued to paid no attention to her. The mother waved her thanks again before leaving, taking the now contently-drinking-his-juice-box toddler out into the sunny spring afternoon. Angie watched the business man snatch his coffee off the counter without acknowledging the barista who'd made it, his face still in his phone. He paused as he started toward the door, turned back to the barista and thanked her, then marched outside.

The rhythms and flow of the café. All perfectly normal and ordinary.

She sipped her sweet, caramel-laced coffee and watched

the door, watched the other patrons in the coffee shop without appearing to watch them. The whir and noise of the baristas behind the counter, the strong scent of coffee, the murmur of the other people inside the busy café. A few more people walked in and out with their coffees. Only one other person took a seat—a teenager with a skateboard tucked up under her arm.

When Angie was halfway through her coffee, she decided she was safe enough and pulled out her phone again. She re-read the text message, glanced around the coffee shop one last time, and rang the unknown number.

Three rings before the person on the other end answered.

"You got my message," a woman's voice said.

"Gabriella?" It was the trifecta of possible people who might warn her about her enemy on the council. Jacob going to Sebastian. Carmen leaving her a note. And now Gabriella leaving her a text.

Quietly, so the patrons at nearby tables didn't overhear, Angie said, "What the hell is going on? Why is everyone warning me and Sebastian all at the exact same moment? What's happened?"

"Who's everyone?" Gabriella's tone was sharp.

"Another hunter has been in touch with Sebastian." She didn't mention his name because she'd never told Gabriella about Jacob. She still didn't know what the man wanted, why he *didn't* want Angie to be a hunter. And until she knew if he was one of the good guys or bad, she refused to reveal his name to anyone. Especially since she didn't entirely trust

Gabriella. Respect her more than the other council members. But she certainly didn't trust her.

Gabriella let out a sound somewhere between a snarl and sigh. "Is that all?"

She'd never told Gabriella about Carmen still lurking around either. But that was mostly because Angie believed Carmen had a connection on the council and didn't know who that connection was. And while Angie didn't believe that someone was Gabriella, she didn't know for sure. Especially after Carmen had escaped after the bone lantern incident.

So Angie said, "A mysterious benefactor warned me in a note." She glanced around, being careful of her wording. But no one in the café even glanced in her direction.

"I'd like a name," Gabriella said. "There's a lot of coincidence going on."

"I don't like coincidence either. Means there's a trap. Are you part of that trap?"

"I'm on your side. I'm here to help you."

"You're on your own side and you want me to be something I'm not. If you haven't figured out in the last six months that I'm not made for this job, that's your problem."

"You're still alive. And you've stayed that way far longer than he thought you would."

"But not because I'm fit for the work. The only reason there hasn't been a disaster is because Sebastian is with me all the time. We *all* know that."

"You've banished more than one demon in the last six months. That's enough."

Angie let out a sigh through her nose, a sound that carried all her frustration with Gabriella's stubbornness. "Just… Tell me what's changed that everyone is suddenly sending me warnings. Today. All at once."

"You're not in New York."

"You knew that already." She hadn't told anyone besides Sebastian where she was going. That didn't mean the hunters didn't know. She had a feeling they'd been monitoring her this entire time, though she had yet to figure out how. Sneaky bastards.

"You're…less safe outside of New York. Especially without Sebastian around. The timing works in your enemy's favor."

"Is that all? Everyone noticed I was gone, so he's decided now's a good opportunity?" If so, he'd picked a bad time and a worse location. This was her home ground. And with her family here, she'd do a lot to keep them safe from any threat. She was more dangerous here than she was in New York. And she was dangerous enough in New York.

"Just watch your back. He knows where you are. And he's grown impatient."

"So have I," she snapped under her breath.

She scanned the café. The woman working on her laptop was staring into the middle distance now. The couple stood to leave, still intent on only each other. The man reading his book was still reading his book, and the skateboard-carrying teenager was flicking through a magazine.

Still with her voice low, Angie asked, "Would he use the people I love to get to me?"

A long silence on the other end of the line. Then, "If it was expedient, I'm afraid he would."

"How is he still allowed to be on the council when his *expedience* involves roping innocent people into his plots?"

"I've told you before, hunters are pragmatic. Some to the point of…difficulty. Ends justifying means."

"They are supposed to save people. Save them even from themselves. Not kill them to make things easier." This last sentence she muttered so quietly she wasn't even sure Gabriella would hear her. The café was noisy enough, but not so noisy the people at the nearest tables couldn't hear her. Talking about this sort of thing on the phone in a public place was complicated.

"I know that," Gabriella said, her tone irritatingly even. "And so do some of the others. But not all of the others. Some see a few innocents lost to save many more innocents as worth the price."

"It's not," Angie growled. "Especially if those innocents are my family." The build of her magic under her skin was so swift and subtle she barely noticed until she glanced down and noticed the coffee inside her paper to-go cup was boiling. She released the cup, flexing her hand in her lap as she pulled in a breath and let it out slowly, trying to calm both her temper and her rising magic.

This was something she needed to discuss with Esmerelda. Her control over her magic when she was angry was…not as good as it used to be. Ever since her first vision of her spiderweb of magic, ever since tapping directly into that red thread for the first time, her anger made her magic rise.

She glanced around to make sure no one had seen the slip. No one seemed to have. Thankfully. She didn't have that hunter trick of willing people to not see her. She turned her gaze to the table and focused on her breathing, on controlling the rise of magic so she didn't light something on fire or whip up a windstorm outside.

Her teeth clenched, her temper barely in check, she said, "You need to tell *him* that bringing my family into this, any of this, will not go well for him. And no, I'm not talking about his specific fear." The fear that she'd loose a demon plague on the world. Even at her angriest, she didn't intend on doing that. No. This would just be good old fashioned witch retribution.

She glanced down at her cup. The coffee was no longer boiling, but she kept her hand in her lap. Just in case.

"Sebastian arrives there this evening," Gabriella said, not responding to Angie's threat, even with the tone of her voice.

"He does."

"Watch your back until he gets there." Quieter, her voice strained, "You might want to…send your family on a holiday. A cruise. Something that gets them out of town."

"That better not be necessary," Angie said. "You tell him what I said. If he gets anywhere near any of my family, this ends badly for him. And anyone working with him."

She disconnected before Gabriella could say more. Her temper was too frayed and she needed to calm down. It was one thing to threaten her life. It was another thing all together to threaten her family.

All of this was because they didn't trust her not to lose control of her demon witch powers. Yet they kept pushing her, pushing her temper, her anger, in just the ways that would tempt her to do that.

She blinked suddenly as that thought sank in. It was like her nemesis was *trying* to get her to lose control. Like he *wanted* her to unleash a plague. But…why the hell would he want that?

She groaned and dropped back against her chair, running both hands up through her hair, pushing the curls away from her face. If she did lose control, that would pit *all* of the demon hunters against her. All of them would come for her to stop her, not just him and whoever was sympathetic to his cause. She'd become the thing he feared, but it would give him the grounds to send everything the hunters had after her.

That sort of logic baffled her because it was so fucking dangerous. What if she was the one demon witch they couldn't stop? He had no idea. He couldn't know what would happen. All of this, *all of it*, could be avoided if they would just leave her alone!

Outside of giving him leave to throw all hunter resources after her, she couldn't imagine why he'd be willing to take this kind of risk? What did *he* personally have to gain?

She didn't even know *his* name. She'd never seen him. He avoided her the few times she'd been called before the council. She only knew four of the council members on sight. She wasn't even sure how many members there actually were. And no one would tell her his name because hunters were weird about their names.

The whole thing was so unnecessary. She'd been quietly reading people's futures, ignoring all things to do with demons. She'd even given up the man she loved to get out of the demon world. If they'd just left her alone, none of this would be necessary.

With her rising anger and frustration, she felt the tingling of her magic under her skin again and bit back a curse. Another few moments spent regaining control. Then she stared at the café without seeing it.

What now? What did she do to protect her family?

Because no matter what, that was her top priority. No one would hurt her family.

CHAPTER EIGHT

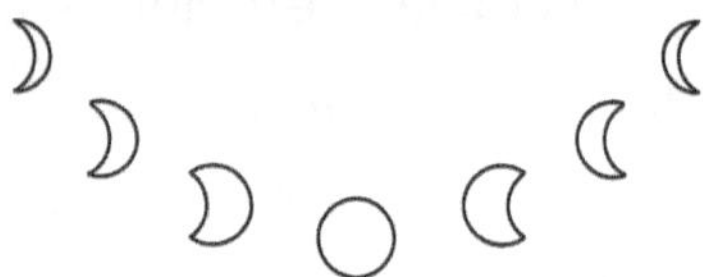

Instead of heading straight home, Angie returned to her rental car and called her mother.

Patricia Jordan wasn't the kind of witch and psychic her daughter was, but she knew her way around small magics and kitchen spells and was no stranger to stronger magic from the people she knew. She belonged to a small coven of similarly skilled witches, and her favorite thing to do with her small magic was to create healing foods.

When her mother answered, she was predictably in the kitchen. "I just put some bread dough aside to rise. Are you going to be home soon? How's Esmerelda doing?"

"She's fine," Angie started, then paused. "Actually, she's got a visiting nurse coming in regularly and is taking a lot of medicine."

Patty was quiet for a moment, then, "I see. Are you… okay?"

"With Esmerelda dying? No. But it's the cycle, isn't it?"

"Doesn't make it easier. Is that why you called?"

"No. I…I have something I need to…"

She couldn't tell her mother—or anyone for that matter—about the demon hunter council or most of the machinations going on in the background. She physically couldn't tell people about the council. Some hunter trick that made it impossible. And without that piece of information, the rest didn't make sense. She had told her mother she was back together with Sebastian but hadn't told her about being forced to work as a demon hunter. She didn't want to worry her parents by telling them everything that went on in her life, but they were some of the few people she could talk to about most things. The balance she struck between what she revealed and what she kept to herself was a delicate one.

"Should I be setting a circle around the house?" her mother asked before Angie could figure out exactly what to say.

Angie dropped her head, her shoulders sagging, and she chuckled. "Yes. Please. If you can get the others in your coven to help strengthen it, that'd be great, too."

"Demon stuff or witch stuff?"

"Demon stuff. But not, I hope, actual demons. Just things related to demons."

Silence, then. "Is Sebastian coming now?"

"He arrives tonight."

"I knew I liked that man. He'll come for dinner tomorrow night."

"Not tonight?"

"You two will need time alone tonight I think."

"Mother!" It didn't matter that she was now a twenty-eight-year-old woman, having her mother telling her she needed a night to have sex with her boyfriend was just too much.

"To talk," Patty said with a chuckle. "Of course that's what I meant. And the other thing too. But with this demon thing bringing him all the way across the country, I assume there needs to be some talking as well."

Her cheeks warm, she shook her head. "Do you talk to Paul and Christopher this way?"

"Yes. And it delights Nicole when Paul blushes."

Angie grinned. Good to know her brother's wife had a sense of humor about their mother's teasing bluntness. And that Angie wasn't the only one taking the brunt of that teasing.

"Now," Patty said, back to business, "I need to set a circle here. Your brothers? Their homes?"

"It would help. What's happening… They'll try to get to me through my family. I won't let them. But it would help if I knew you were safe while I…take care of things."

"Will you be okay? Do you need help beyond Sebastian?"

"No. I'm good." She didn't want her mother involved in any way more than she already was.

"Fair enough. I assume we won't see you until tomorrow. Call before you arrive so I can let you in."

"I will." She was quiet for a moment. Then, "I'm sorry I

brought this to you. I don't like you being roped into these things."

"We're your parents. We love you. And we've got your back. Besides, you're not the one roping us in. It's the bad guys, right? They're the ones to blame."

"Thanks," she murmured, as warmth seeped through her limbs. "Careful what you tell Dad. I don't want him trying to help."

Her father and brothers were all extremely *not* magical in any way. They were the definition of mundane humans. And while they were very accepting of her mother and her magic, taking it as just part of normal life, they didn't have any skills to help in the non-mundane world.

"He knows better," Patty said softly. "At least when it comes to this kind of thing. If your sink is broken, or your cabinets need the doors re-hung? Well, that's a different story."

"But Dad is a disaster at the handyman stuff." Her parents' house had one or two very specific quirks that were directly related to her father's skills—or lack thereof—with a screwdriver.

"He is. But he means well."

"I'll call if anything comes up that you need to know about. Otherwise, I'll be back tomorrow with Sebastian."

"Don't you need a change of clothes?"

"Better I don't come back today. Just in case." She was worried someone was following her, even though she hadn't been able to spot anyone yet. But if someone was following her, she didn't want to risk leading them back to her parents. Bad enough Carmen had followed her to Esmerelda's house. "I'll be fine until tomorrow."

"Sounds bad, whatever is happening."

The worry in her mother's voice made Angie wince. She hated worrying her parents. But she couldn't let them just walk around unprepared when there was a potential threat either.

"I'll take care of it."

"I have no doubt," her mother said. "I believe in you. I just wish you didn't have to 'take care' of things that were dangerous."

"'Fraid that stopped being an option when I was five."

Her mother sighed. "Whichever ancestor is responsible for the demon stuff deserves a good talking to."

Angie chuckled. "Couldn't agree more. Text after the circles are set around your house and Paul and Christopher's places."

"I will. Tell Sebastian hello from us. Don't forget dinner tomorrow night. And stay safe. Keep me updated as much as you're able."

Angie stared for a long time at the steering wheel after disconnecting with her mother. She truly hated that they were even peripherally involved in this demon shit. But she was also glad she was nearby in case they needed her. If her enemies had decided to go after her family while she was still in New York, that would have driven her crazy. The fact that they might go after her family only because she was here with them, though, settled a lump of guilt in her throat no amount of caramel-laced coffee would ever dislodge.

She finally glanced at the clock. Sebastian's flight wasn't due for a few hours. She had time to kill and a potential threat following her. Time to lead them away from her loved ones.

And she knew just the place.

CHAPTER NINE

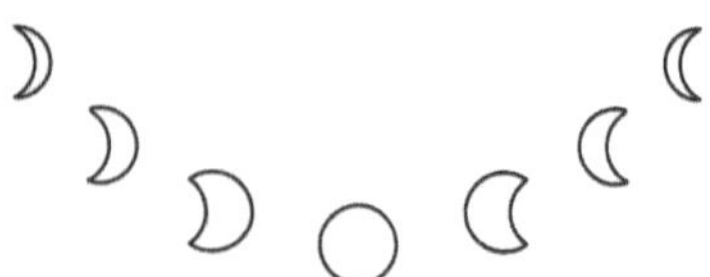

ngie parked at the base of the short, easy hiking trail at Rinconada Canyon and climbed out of her rental car. The lot was mostly empty. This late in the afternoon, there were a few people here, but being the middle of a work week and a school day, the easy hiking trail was less active. This particular area had always been one of her favorites as a kid, because of the petroglyphs, but also because it was mostly shrubs and low ground cover, some cacti…

And no trees.

The sky was a bright blue, not even a few stray clouds fluttering overhead. The horizon cut a sharp line against the expanse of pink rocky sand and tan and green desert scrub. The smell of creosote always reminded Angie of home and it was stronger here as the desert blew a dry, gentle breeze across her cheeks.

Without trees, she'd never had to worry about accidentally opening a portal here, so she'd always felt a little more comfortable. Freer to just relax and enjoy the walk. There were other hiking trails here, other places that did pass through patches of trees, but this trail wasn't one. Here, she didn't need to think about where her gaze fell.

She was probably cutting things close coming all the way out here when she still had to get all the way back across town to the airport by nine tonight to meet Sebastian. But this was a place far enough from anyone she loved to feel safe. On the two-hour drive, she'd pulled off once to get food at a drive thru and watched for anyone following her. She hadn't spotted anyone, but that didn't mean anything.

If a demon hunter was following her, she'd never know. And it seemed she couldn't tell when Carmen was following her either, which was more than a little irritating.

Locking the car door, she dropped her long purse strap over her head, adjusting it across her chest, then started down the flat, ambling dirt path. She wasn't prepared for a long hike. She had a water bottle in the depths of her huge purse, but she was wearing tennis shoes better suited to city streets and jeans that didn't breathe enough or a hard hike. It wasn't as hot as it would get in another month, but it was still too warm for a long walk in what she was wearing, with only a single bottle of water.

Fortunately, this path didn't require a lot of exertion or preparation. This was the place families brought young kids without having to worry.

The afternoon warmth seeped into her skin. The exertions

of her training session with Esmerelda that morning had left her sleepy. Not as exhausted as she'd gotten a few months ago when accessing that red thread. The first time, she'd dropped into a sleep that had lasted hours and inadvertently scared the crap out of Sebastian. Over the months, with the mixing of her regular magic and the magic from that red thread, the exhaustion didn't wipe her out anymore. But with warm sunshine sinking into her, the lovely, light breeze brushing through her hair, and her stomach full of greasy fast food burger and fries, she could take a nap.

Probably not the best time to put herself in a position to confront whoever was after her. But better this than anywhere near her parents' house.

She was passing a small lava rock with a bird-like petroglyph drawn in lighter pink on it when someone behind her cleared their throat. She swore. She hadn't noticed them. Hadn't seen or even felt them there.

Fucking demon hunters.

She turned slowly, already building a shield spell in her mind, her fingers moving in the required gestures to set the spell.

"Probably should have built the shield spell ahead of time."

The speaker was a stranger to Angie. Not that that was a surprise. He'd been avoiding her up to this point. Now that she saw him, though, she vaguely recognized the business man with the Blackberry in the café.

"Thought that might have been you," she murmured. If she'd looked closer at the café, she might have even seen the telltale hint of red in the depths of his brown eyes. A tell that gave all the hunters away—if you knew what to look for. When you didn't, that flash of red just looked like a trick of the light.

Other than that, though, the man before her did look a bit different to the business man in the café. The charcoal suit was the same, though the tailoring looked better now. The dark brown hair and pale skin, same. But his chin was a bit longer. His eyes were shaped differently. Cheekbones higher. Jaw line narrower. Same but different. And no sign of the Blackberry.

"Good disguise. Nice suit."

He snapped down the lapels on his jacket and flashed her a faint smile. "Thank you. This meeting has been a long time in coming."

"Agree."

He glanced around. "You led me to a place with no trees. Interesting choice."

"Tough call, actually. Considered surrounding myself with the right kinds of trees. Decided I didn't need them to threaten you."

He grinned at that. "You are a powerful witch, Angela Jordan."

"One that won't let you hurt her family or the people she loves." She flicked her fingers and her shield popped up in front of her, an invisible barrier against any magic the hunter had brought with him.

"Is that why you think I'm here?" He tilted his head to one side, studying her.

"Why are you here? We could have had this conversation back in New York. In fact, I thought we might have. Once you realized your plan to kill me wasn't going to work."

"Only because of Sebastian."

"If you hurt him, I will kill you." The threat was out before she could consider it. Even when she did, she knew it was true.

"By unleashing a demon plague?"

"I don't need one to kill you."

But that right there… That revealed his fear. And his problem. He feared her anger and her reactions. Didn't trust her not to use the demon witch powers in revenge. And he wanted her eliminated to get rid of that threat. But it was more than just wanting her dead. He would have just arranged a way for her to be killed before this. The threats, the pushing her to unleash demons he might not be able to put back…

"Why all this? I was living quietly outside the hunter world. Would have stayed there. Your people brought me back."

"Your feelings for Sebastian would have brought you back eventually. There was no chance the two of you stayed apart indefinitely. Love." He chuckled at the word, spread his hands and shrugged. "Such a pain in the ass, that emotion."

Since she sort of agreed with him, she kept her mouth shut. She didn't want to give him any more information about her than he already had. Though why she tried, she wasn't sure. He obviously knew more about her than she did.

"Do you intend on killing me now?" he asked, his head tilted. Curious but not scared.

He was very good, she thought. Because he was afraid of her and what she could do. But there wasn't a hint of it in his tone or body language. A very very good bluff. "I don't kill people randomly and just because. I will defend myself if attacked. But I'm not a murderer."

"You just threatened to kill me if I hurt Sebastian."

"For him and my family, I'll take the consequences of revenge." But she wasn't Carmen. She wasn't interested in revenge for the sake of revenge. She believed the witchy creed that what she put out came back on her. She knew if she went after him for hurting her loved ones there would be consequences. It's just that, in this case, she was prepared to take those consequences if he pushed her. "Better for all if you leave them out of it."

"It was almost always the death of a loved one, loved ones, that drove the others you know?"

"What are you talking about?"

"That's why your downfall is inevitable. The demon witches who broke? They did because people they loved were hurt. Killed. They lost control, or rather, they chose to unleash their power, because of heartbreak."

She pressed her lips together so she wouldn't snap out a knee-jerk comment. But his words hit their mark. And she didn't like it.

Gabriella had told her about some of the other demon witches, the ones who the hunters had actual records of. She'd told Angie how they'd died. Even the motivation of one in particular. But she hadn't told Angie that all of them had been motivated by revenge for the death of a loved one.

And Angie couldn't decide if Gabriella had kept that from her on purpose, or if the man in front of her now was lying. Picking up lies from demon hunters who could will you to believe they were not standing right in front of you was almost impossible. Still. There was a truth somewhere in what he was telling her, because the rightness of it hit her in her instincts. And yet… Yet she suspected he was telling her a selective truth.

Dealing with these people was a pain in the ass. The machinations made her head spin and just pissed her off. Not knowing if she could trust what she'd been told, who to trust. She respected Gabriella but didn't trust her. She trusted Sebastian but he was obviously also her weakness. And this stranger who wanted her dead because of who she was was pushing her into a corner that would force her to react. Instead of letting her just be a witch, he was trying to force her to become the very thing he feared.

And all of that just enraged her.

Overhead, clouds gathered across the blue sky, dropping the surrounding temperature as a strong breeze swiped her hair over her shoulders. The scent of creosote mixed with the crackle of electricity in the air.

Angie fisted her hands at her side, but her anger still snapped in her blood. "I just want to be left alone. To be a witch. Live quietly. Read palms. I'm not the one pushing buttons and limits and forcing confrontations."

The man glanced at the sky, back down at her. "You can't

help what you are. And what you are will get the best of you. Eventually. It's inevitable. It's what demon witches do."

"This isn't the demon witch talking," she said, her voice deepening as her power rose. "This is just the witch. And the witch is pissed off."

His gaze flicked up to the sky again as the first few drops of rain pebbled the dry orange dirt on the trail. "I noticed. But you really think you'll be able to stop with witch magic when you have access to so much more?"

"What the hell is your name?" she asked suddenly, and had the pleasure of watching him blink. She relaxed her fists, took in a deep breath. The breeze settled and the clouds overhead splintered into soft white whisps flowing over blue. "What do I call you?"

"You think I'll give you, a witch, my real name?"

"Of course not. I'm not looking for that. What would Sebastian and Aidan call you?" The reminder that Angie had friends among the hunters was no accident on her part.

He subtly shifted feet at the mention of the legendary hunter. Nothing obvious, just a rearranging of his body. But demon hunters had such control over their bodies, the movement was telling.

"You can call me Morty."

She snorted. "Morty? Seriously? That's the name you chose?"

"What were you expecting?"

"Something more dramatic, less... New Jersey cab driver."

"That's precisely why I like Morty."

"Okay." The build of her magic sparked by her anger had fully calmed, back in her control. But she needed to work with Esmerelda on the way her anger now tested her control. "Morty it is. So Morty, what's the end game? What's the point? You forced a meeting with me here, where my family is. You've grown tired of waiting for me to be killed in the normal hunter way. What's going to happen now?"

He tilted his head again as he considered her. "You're training with your mentor now. To what end?"

"Same reason any witch trains. Improving my skill set."

A half-truth, but they both knew she wasn't going to tell him the full truth. Morty was already afraid of her. He didn't need to know he might be right about her control teetering.

"You'll break, Angela," he said, quietly. Almost regretfully. "All demon witches do. Sooner or later, you'll break. I can't allow that."

"You can't be sure about that either. But instead of working with me so I don't, you're pushing me hoping I will. Seems to contradict that tone you're using, like this isn't something you want to do. You *want* to push me. You want to kill me." Her turn to consider him. "Why wait? Why not just kill me now?" She glanced around. "No witnesses. No trees."

"You think I'm a murder? A man who's dedicated his life to saving people from themselves, from the demons *they* call?"

Yes, actually. She did think he'd murder her outright. Pragmatic. That's what Gabriella had said. He was very very pragmatic. Ends justified the means. Even if the means were murder. And eliminating the demon witch *before* she lost control was the pragmatic solution.

"Either you want to be able to justify the murder," she murmured, watching him closely—that was a very real possibility, that he needed to be able to justify his actions to his people and so he needed to push her into attacking him so he could claim he'd killed her out of self-defense. Or… "Or you can't kill me. You aren't strong enough. Don't have what it would take to actually kill me. Not on your own." And that struck a chord of truth, too.

He didn't reveal anything to her in his expression, in a shift of body language. He didn't even blink. His reactions were perfectly controlled, his expression mild. But he didn't have to show her a reaction for her to know she'd hit on something. The truth of her words hung in the air between them.

Both her statements were true. He needed justification to arrange for her to be killed, but he couldn't kill her himself.

That was why he'd hoped she'd fail as a hunter and be killed by a demon. Neat and tidy. No blood on his hands. But also no need to figure out another way to get to her when he wasn't strong enough to take her out on his own.

She knew, from Sebastian, that Morty wanted power, wanted the council to be more than they were among the demon hunters. Wanted the council to actually have control over the hunters, a governing body more than figure heads who helped keep the history of the hunters.

Until Morty's tenure on the council, they hadn't tried to exert any control over individuals. Demon hunters were solitary and independent and not good at accepting other people's authority. They had to be that way to do what they did. But Morty wanted authority. And he'd been moving the council in a direction that would give him power and influence.

But he couldn't control Angie, and he didn't have any influence over her, and he would never be able to exercise any authority over her. She was dangerous. On many levels.

And he couldn't do anything about that danger on his own.

Well. That made some things clearer. And he didn't even have to confirm her suspicions. Watching him carefully *not* react to her statements was more than enough confirmation.

"I think we're done for now," he said. "If we talk much longer, you'll never make it back across to the airport in time to collect Sebastian."

"Why are we talking now, Morty?"

"Perhaps because I wanted to take your measure."

She snorted.

He glanced up at the sky, now clear and blue with only a few whisps of clouds flowing past. The breeze was a light cooling kiss. The scent of the desert sand dry and sharp and pleasant.

When he looked back at her, he said quietly, "I have plans, Angela Jordan. A demon witch is…not in those plans."

"She'd remain out of anything to do with demon hunters if you'd just leave her alone." She felt like she should get that sentence tattooed to her forehead, she had to repeat it so often. If they just left her *alone*, none of this would be happening. And it didn't seem to matter how often she said just that phrase, they still dragged her in.

"If only it was that easy," Morty said. "There are things you don't know."

She huffed a sarcastic laugh.

"And things I hope you'll never know."

"Stop pushing me into a corner, then. You want me out of the way, let me *get* out of the way."

"It's not that easy. I'm afraid my hands are tied. You're dangerous. This…confrontation is inevitable."

"Nothing's inevitable," she said. "We got here because of decisions made. We can change course. Those decisions are ours."

"You can't change who you are. And that, in the end, is what matters." He turned and walked away from her without giving her a chance to say more. But over his shoulder, he called, "Tell Sebastian hello."

She watched him walk away as her anger swept through her again. Thunder clapped in the distance, echoing across the low foothills. None of this made sense to her and she hated when things didn't make sense. But she hated the subtle—and not so subtle—threats to the people she loved even more.

And Angie had no doubt, after finally meeting the man, that Morty's last sentence was a threat.

CHAPTER TEN

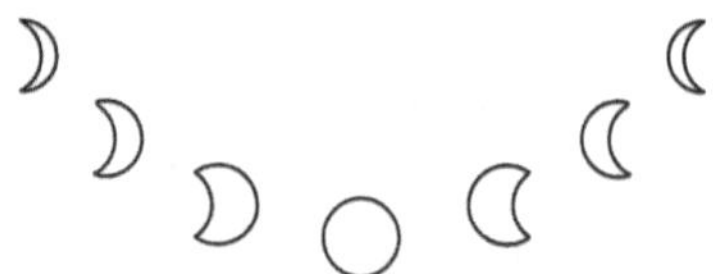

The drive back to the airport took hours and gave Angie too much time to think. She swung into a drive thru for more food because that spark of barely controlled anger, the storm she'd accidentally called and had to release, left her body hollow and in need of calories.

Morty needed her dead for obvious and not-obvious reasons. He couldn't kill her outright. He didn't have the skills or strength. He needed some sort of justification for having her killed, too, now that the plan to have a demon do it wasn't working. To do that, he needed her to break. Needed her to unleash the demon witch powers.

If she broke, he'd have proven himself right about her, and not only would have justification and support for killing her, he'd have earned himself the sort of clout and power that comes with being right about a dangerous situation. The other council members would have to acknowledge he'd been correct about her. And if he was right about her...

Then maybe he was right about other things.

Whatever the hell those other things were. Though she suspected they had to do with the power he wanted.

The best way to push her beyond her control was to endanger the people she loved. Apparently, that had been the tipping point for all previous demon witches. Though, to be fair, that had been a tipping point for people throughout history—demon witch or not. She had no doubt she could be pushed into losing control despite all her work and effort. Despite her belief in the law of return for witches. Especially now, when access to this greater power had already pushed her control to the teetering edge.

But if she cut herself off from the demon witch power, if she severed that thread...her threat as a dangerous demon witch went away. She'd be an ordinary witch. Maybe even a weaker one than she'd been. If she eliminated the threat of her unleashing a demon plague, would that get Morty and the others off her back? Would they finally leave her and the people she loved alone?

Would it be enough?

Her gut tightened as she pulled into the short-term parking garage at the airport. The thought of cutting off a part of her power was terrifying, when she didn't know what the outcome might be. But the thought that it wouldn't be enough... That she'd go to all that trouble, risk the very magic she used to make a living, the magic she loved, and Morty and his ilk would still come after her...

Or worse, come after the people she loved when she was no longer capable of protecting them.

That thought was the part that scared her the most.

She glanced at the clock on the dashboard before turning off the engine. She was a few minutes late. Sebastian's flight had probably landed by now. But when she checked her phone, no text from him yet, so maybe she wasn't too late.

Locking the rental car, she went inside to check the boards. Anxiety crawled through her, so strong now she wasn't even sure if the source was her confrontation with Morty, worry for her family, worry for Sebastian, or the uncertainty of whether to cut herself off from the demon witch magic or not. Probably all of the above, she thought as she entered the noisy Arrivals hall and hunted for one of the electronic Arrivals and Departures boards.

Once she'd confirmed Sebastian's flight had actually landed, she dodged around people and their suitcases to reach his luggage carousel. Not that he usually had much luggage. A backpack at most that he'd have carried onto the plane. But it gave her somewhere to look for him in all the chaos.

People with too-large bags pushed around her, juggling stuff and kids and other people to find their way out of the airport. The sound of luggage dropping onto a nearby carousel competed with the noise of a toddler having a meltdown and a couple of older men to her left, one of whom was wearing too much aftershave, debating where to go for a taxi. Under normal circumstances, Angie liked Arrivals halls. She liked the people-watching opportunities. But at the moment, all she saw were the crowds of vulnerable humans that she'd have to protect if Morty chose now to attack.

She reminded herself that he could have attacked earlier that afternoon, in the middle of nowhere, with no innocent bystanders in the way. If he could have killed her then, he probably would have tried. He was waiting for something. She had to hope that *something* didn't involve a situation where there were a lot of innocent people in the way.

Though she was watching for him, Sebastian found her before she found him. Or rather, he let her see him when he found her. One moment her gaze scanned over a group of people near the luggage drop, the next, Sebastian was walking out of that crowd, almost like he'd materialized there.

Demon hunter will really could look like magic.

She walked right into his open arms. His familiar scent, the warmth of his skin sunk into her, and she took a deep breath. The first relaxed breath she'd taken since getting Carmen's note.

"Glad you made it," she murmured.

"Glad to be here," he said against her hair.

"Why were you hiding yourself from everyone?"

"Habit when I'm traveling." He pulled back, holding her shoulders, and looked into her face, studying her.

She studied him back. He'd shaved that morning, but his cheeks were still stubbled with scruff around his goatee. There were dark patches under his eyes, but otherwise, he looked good. Worried, though. The crease between his brows didn't ease as he studied her.

"What's happened?" he asked.

"We'll talk in the car." She looked around him for a bag. Just the backpack over his shoulder. "No suitcase?" She grinned.

"Got all I need right here."

He pulled her close for a kiss and Angie's heart beat a little harder. She wrapped her arms around his neck and sank into him, letting the zing that always came with kissing Sebastian run through her blood. She'd been in love with this man since she was twenty-one years old and he still managed to take her breathe away.

Conscious of all the people around them—even though kissing was pretty mundane in the Arrivals hall at an airport —she eased back, but she rested her hand on his cheek as she looked into his gorgeous dark eyes, with that hint of red in the depths that could almost be a trick of the light.

"Thanks for coming," she murmured.

"I'll always be here for you, Ang," he said.

He'd pulled her out of a demon realm once. When she'd been dragged in, terrified, surrounded by demons, the portal she'd opened closing and her without a tree in the hellscape to open another one. He'd reached through a breach between worlds that he couldn't even see and pulled her out, back to the safety of his arms.

She might hate the demon hunter world. But she loved this particular hunter with her whole heart.

"We have a lot to talk about," she said. "But we can't go to my parents' house."

"Carmen?"

"And Morty."

His eyebrows jumped at the name, and his mouth tightened. "What's happened?"

"In the car. I got us a hotel room not far from here. We'll have more privacy to talk."

Though as she twined her fingers with his as they made their way out of the crowded terminal toward the parking garage, she realized she'd rather not talk when they got to the hotel room. She'd rather lose herself in Sebastian and forget all the things she had to worry about. It would be very easy.

But her current worries involved her family. She had to make sure they were safe above all else.

—

THE HOTEL ROOM WAS A DECENT IF BLAND PLACE WITH A king-sized bed, clean sheets, and plenty of towels in the bathroom. The décor leaned toward browns with a few hints of pink in the carpet. There was a mini-fridge and a large TV and a decent sized desk with a pretty good office chair in front of it. Nothing fancy. But not the worst hotel she'd stayed in.

"Remember the motel in San Diego?" Sebastian said, chuckling as he dropped his backpack onto the office chair.

She groaned. They'd been on a hunt…well, he'd been on a hunt. She'd been able to join him to guard his back because she'd been between classes. They hadn't been together for very long at that point. A few months, maybe. And she was only just starting to join him for as many of his hunts as she could swing around working on her Master's degree and her part-time job at a psychologist's office.

"Definitely the worst room ever," she said, thinking of the twin beds that had nearly collapsed under Sebastian's weight and the mold in the bathroom. The off-brand motel had seen much better days. By the time they'd checked in, the place was one more citation away from being shut down as a health hazard.

Sebastian smiled. "We've had some adventures, haven't we?"

"We have." She dropped onto the bed. "I'm afraid we've a few in our future, too. But not the ones I might have planned for us."

"Would have preferred a Caribbean island and piña coladas, too," he said. "You met Morty finally."

He settled next to her on the mattress, taking one of her hands in his as she told him about the confrontation with the hunter that afternoon.

"You took him out to a desert location instead of surrounding yourself by trees?" Sebastian asked.

"He noticed that, too."

"Because you were worried your control would slip?"

"My control did slip. On my magic. But…I didn't want the first encounter to be quite so blatant a threat. From me anyway. He made no bones about threatening me." Her hand flexed in Sebastian. He rubbed his thumb over her wrist in a soothing circle that calmed her anger. "He doesn't know I don't need trees anymore."

At least, she didn't think he did. She and Sebastian had

been careful to keep that to themselves. But Carmen knew. And Carmen was in contact with someone inside the demon hunters, someone with power, so Angie couldn't be absolutely certain if Morty knew about her evolving powers or not.

"If we can keep that from him, it would be good," Sebastian said.

"I still can't get over the fact that he calls himself Morty. It feels…like a name that shouldn't belong to a mysterious and deadly enemy. It's the guy who works at the local bodega and knows which soda I like best."

"He has a strange sense of humor?" Sebastian suggested. "Don't underestimate him. I suspect the moniker is designed to make people think he's a harmless everyman. But he's ambitious and ruthless."

"I told him I'd kill him if he went after my family."

Sebastian nodded. He knew what that meant to her, that she'd actively kill someone. "Has your mom gotten the circles set up around everyone's houses?"

"When I texted her from the airport parking lot, she said they were all set, but she hadn't seen any signs of anyone. I called Esmerelda earlier and no one has been back to her place either. So far, everyone is fine."

"Ruthless as he is, I think he'll come after you more directly, rather than through your family. That would be too…obvious a move. Too obvious he was pushing you to break."

"Maybe. Unless he makes it look like someone else came after them."

"Who?"

She shrugged. "No idea. Carmen?"

"Except I doubt Carmen is working with Morty. One of the other members of the council…" He shrugged and his jaw tightened. He did not like that some hunter, any hunter, might be helping the woman who'd murdered a demon hunter. The fact that Carmen had put him into a position that nearly got *him* killed seemed less troubling to him than a hunter actively protecting the vigilante.

Angie's turn to sooth with sweeps of her thumb over his hand.

Some of the tension relaxed in his jaw as he said, "Carmen warned you he was coming. I don't think she's working with him."

"Jacob warned you. We still don't know what his part in all this is."

"Except that he seems to be working against whatever it is Morty's doing. I'm not sure they'd pair up to push you into unleashing your demon witch powers."

"Who else is there? Another member of the council?" More than just Morty wanted her dead, she was sure. But the four she'd met in person—before today—were very careful about hiding that fact. The only one she was pretty sure didn't want her dead was Gabriella, but that was because Gabriella still believed Angie could be a hunter. Despite all evidence to the contrary.

"Given how practical Morty is," Sebastian said, "I wouldn't dismiss him hiring outside criminals. Someone who can't be traced to him. Someone who can easily be eliminated later."

"A scapegoat."

"He'd picked a horrible person, and feel righteous for taking them out afterward, but that wouldn't prevent him from using them to his own advantage first. As he would see it, a win-win."

"I hate that. On many levels. Including that he thinks in *win-win* terms like a corporate shill."

"The problem with him picking a criminal or horrible person who he could justify eliminating later is that we won't see them coming. We can't know who, or when, or how someone like that might strike."

"Fuck." Her muscles tightened again instantly. "That makes it even more dangerous for my family. It could just be some asshole with a gun and not magic at all."

The thought sent a rush of adrenaline through her. She hadn't even thought… Had just assumed a magical threat in this magical world of hers.

But hunters weren't witches or wizards. They didn't use magic. Their will, yes. But not magic. They wouldn't necessarily discount mundane things the way Angie sometimes did. And that hadn't even *occurred* to her.

Damn damn damn.

Magic circles had to be specially designed to work against mundane weapons. They took power and time to set up and even Angie would have trouble setting one large enough to circle a whole house. Her mother wouldn't have thought of using one of those circles, and working that kind of circle was well past her power level anyway. Even the powers of anyone in her coven. They were mostly kitchen witches, some without any magic at all because they were just pagan in their religious beliefs.

Angie rushed to her oversized purse for her cellphone before she'd even thought through what she wanted to tell her parents. What she thought they could *do* to prevent a mundane attack.

Sebastian's hands were on her shoulders before she got her phone out. "Take a breath, Ang. You'll panic your parents if you call them like this."

"I have to warn them."

"We'll do better. Let them know we're coming tonight. You won't rest if you aren't there to make sure they're safe."

She turned into him and wrapped her arms around his neck. So tight she came up off her toes. They were nearly the same height—he only had about an inch or two on her—and that made wrapping him up in a fierce hug easier.

That he understood. That he knew her this well…

Sometimes she forgot. And then he'd go and read her mind, make things easier for her, and she'd be swept up in just how much she loved him all over again.

"Thank you," she said into his neck, breathing in the familiar scent of him, that subtle clean soap smell that was *him*.

"We'll keep them safe, Ang." He rubbed his hand down her back. "I promise."

CHAPTER ELEVEN

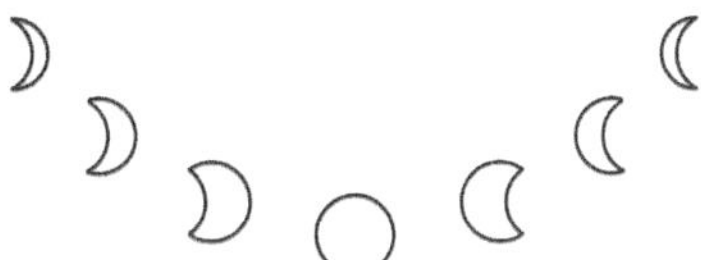

She texted her mother on the way over, letting Sebastian drive because she wanted to start working on spells she might use to protect her family's homes. When her mother's "all's well" text came back, Angie nearly doubled over as the relief left her nauseas.

"Good thing you're driving," she muttered as she bent forward and focused on breathing the adrenaline rush away.

"They're okay?"

"So far." She glanced at her phone. "I'm getting a question mark for why we're coming over." She texted: *Tell you when there. All OK. No one hurt.*

Given how worried Angie was, she could only imagine how worried her mother was after these texts. Especially after the call earlier. Patty Jordan was a smart woman. She wouldn't be fooled if Angie tried to minimize the danger. But she also needed to know Angie wasn't in current danger.

This was one of the many reasons Angie never wanted kids of her own. She loved kids. But she couldn't take the anxiety and fear that came with worrying about them all the time. Hard enough to worry about herself and Sebastian. To worry about her family, her brothers, her brand new baby niece. Worrying about her *own* kids… No. She was happy being the eccentric aunt to her brothers' kids, and then doing her best to keep her strange life away from them. That would be her contribution to the future of her family.

That and keeping them safe from Morty's not-so-subtle threats.

"If he's going to use something mundane…" She started, then swallowed hard. Mundane was a lot harder for her to protect against. Mundane didn't have to be some asshole with a gun. It could be a car accident when her mother was on the way to the grocery store, or a gas leak that blew up the house, or a fire sparked by cut wires. Mundane was…well, mundane. The sorts of things that just *happened*. And there were a lot of ways to cause harm that looked like an accident.

"How do I stop an accident?" she murmured. "How do I keep Morty from *causing* what looks like an accident but any mundane human will see as just unfortunate bad luck?"

Sebastian didn't answer, which wasn't reassuring. But at least he wasn't feeding her platitudes they both knew wouldn't help.

She ran through all the spells she knew, everything she'd studied since the age of five, all the knowledge Esmerelda, as well as her other teachers, had tried to pass down.

There were wards she could put on the doors to keep

strangers from entering the house. That might protect from someone coming in and setting up a supposed accident that led to fire or something. Not that her mother would let a stranger in right now, but the ward would keep them from approaching the house.

There were some luck charms that Angie could put into her parents' cars. That might help deter accidents. Luck charms were…finicky and didn't always do what a witch wanted them to do, but Angie could at least try. That was something her mother might be able to do, as well. Or someone in her mother's coven.

Angie could strength the circle around her parents' house, use some solid grounding materials like salt—her mother was going to hate that, though, because it would kill some of her plants in the backyard—and maybe add an illusion spell to the circle that made the house look different enough anyone looking for it would miss it.

While Sebastian was in the house, he could will people not to notice it. Anyone in the neighborhood, walking by, would just miss the house. But that would impose a huge strain on him. Might or might not work against another demon hunter. And would leave him vulnerable if demon trouble arose. His will was impressive and strong but not infinite. He could wear himself out.

So, yeah, the illusion spell would be safer. Since Angie had no idea what Morty would do, if he'd use something mundane or magical, they couldn't afford to have Sebastian weakened by over-exerting himself in a place where a spell might do.

What else…?

She wasn't great with charms and potions. They weren't her forte—she was better with power spells, and illusions, elemental spells, and occasionally just brute force magic. She knew people in New York who were excellent at potions and charms. But they were too far away to help her now.

Sebastian pulled up to her parents' house as Angie was still racking her brain for protective options and ways she could ensure her family was safe from all possible dangers. The big problem was, she couldn't *know* what "all possible dangers" were in this case.

"Should have tried to shake Morty's hand," she muttered as she stepped out of the car.

"He wouldn't have," Sebastian said without missing a beat.

Of course Morty wouldn't. The hunters knew she was a psychic. Still, she hadn't even thought about it at the time, and she should have tried at least. A mistake that could get her family killed.

Her mother was waiting in the doorway as they walked up the path through a well-tended front yard filled with patches of desert plants and succulents on hills above decorative rocks. The water her mother used for the gardens went into her extensive herb garden in the backyard. So the front yard was designed to take advantage of the desert environment and require less watering.

There were no trees around their house at all. Her father had cut those down years ago.

Like her daughter, Patty Jordan was tall, and slim, though

thicker and curvier as she aged. Her dark brown hair was straight as a pin and her eyes were a deep brown fringed by darker lashes—Angie had inherited her green eyes and curly light brown hair from her father. With the light at her mother's back from inside the house, Angie couldn't see her expression clearly, but she didn't have to. The worry was obvious in her mother's posture, in the hands she had planted on her hips and the way she stood braced in the doorway.

"We're fine," Angie said as soon as they were close enough for her mother to hear her without having to shout. "I promise. No one is hurt."

Her mother nodded, looked past her to Sebastian and smiled, lifting her arms to him. He went in for the hug like he was greeting his own mother. Angie wanted to roll her eyes. Her mother had not taken to Sebastian initially. Mainly because he was sixteen years older than Angie. But he'd won Patty over. Not least because he was a demon hunter and Patty thought he'd be able to keep Angie safe from her own ability to open portals.

Her mother had…worried when they broke up. She didn't question Angie's decision—for which Angie was grateful— but she'd made the occasional *concerned* comment.

Patty patted Sebastian's cheek, like he was one of her own kids, and invited them both into the house with a sweep of her arm. She gave Angie a hug as soon as she was over the threshold.

"I'm glad you're okay. And frankly, I'm glad you're here where I can keep an eye on you for the night," Patty said.

Angie shook her heard. "I'm here to keep you safe." She

leaned back to study her mom's expression. "What's in place?"

"Circle around the whole property." She raised a hand when Angie opened her mouth. "Reset right after you came in. This isn't my first rodeo."

Angie didn't argue, but she sort of wanted to. Her mother hadn't had to face anything like this before.

"Nita came over and helped with that, set the circle with salt." Patty sighed, but Angie let out a relieved breath.

"I'll need to add a few things to it. Thanks for letting Nita use salt." Especially because Angie didn't have to argue for that anymore. "What else?"

"Becky brought over some warding pouches and I've got them tucked at the doors and windows. I made a little protective hex that I set into the steps by the back door. And there's another one on the mailbox."

"Won't that zap the mail carrier?" Her parents had had the same woman delivering their mail for the last fifteen years, and Angie didn't want Consuela hurt.

Her mother dropped her chin and gave her a look. "Sometimes you act like I don't know what I'm doing. I'm older than you, you know."

Angie huffed out a half-laugh half-groan. "You know our magics aren't the same thing."

"But I've been working with mine for more than fifty years. I know how it works. Better than you."

"Fine." Angie sighed. "Anything else, or does that cover it?"

"That was what I thought I needed. Do we need more?"

They stood just inside the door, talking with lowered voices, but Sebastian had moved ahead to greet Angie's father. From the living room, Angie heard the back-patting hugs and introductory sports comments that reacquainted her father with Sebastian. Her dad followed English soccer so he and Sebastian had always had something to talk about. Behind the quiet conversation, Angie heard the sounds of a gameshow on TV.

The house itself smelled like *home* to her in a way she probably wouldn't have been able to describe accurately to anyone. It smelled like her mom and dad. Like the lemon polish her dad used on furniture, and the herbs her mother grew in the kitchen windowsill, and the carpets in the living room and den that had seen them through many a Christmas and birthday party and still managed to survive looking decently—though her mother kept swearing she was going to pull them out and replace them with hardwood floors.

The cool white walls, with marks from Angie and her brothers growing up. The paintings her father had done over the years hanging on the walls alongside a few beloved pieces of kid-art. The kitchen table piled with books and paperwork since no one ate there. The well-worn fridge and dark blue kitchen counters. The bright sunshine that poured into the back of the house during the day, drawing the family in the cooler winter months, and the cool, shaded rooms at the front that drew them all in when the summer heat baked the roof.

The feel of this house was just home in a way that not many other places were. And yet, it wasn't quite *her* home anymore. Which also felt familiar. She was more comfortable here than most other places in the world. Like Esmerelda's home, she felt…safe in this space. But she was also aware of not living here anymore.

Sometimes that left her feeling a little adrift. But she didn't quite know how to put that feeling into words, so never discussed it with anyone. Especially because her mother would argue with her about it.

"I only realized tonight," Angie said, leaning in closer so her father wouldn't overhear, "that the people I'm worried about…they aren't witches. I've been thinking about defending against magic, but that was a bad assumption. These people don't use magic, so they might not come after you with magic."

"Demons can't get through the wards I've put up. Becky and Nita made sure of it." Patty's two best friends in her coven didn't have much more magic than Patty, but combined, they could work stronger things to fend off stronger entities. If they needed to.

"I'm worried about more mundane things," Angie whispered. "Accidents. Fires. Electrical issues. Things that could look like an accident."

Her mother pulled in a deep breath and nodded, her gaze turning inward. "Only so much we can do against that, but… Daniel can help. His magic bends toward the mundane in a way the rest of ours doesn't. I bet he even has a house ward or something for preventing mundane accidents."

That was news to Angie, but a relief. She leaned against

the wall. "That'll help a lot. But it won't prevent car accidents. It won't keep you safe at the grocery store."

"I can't live inside the safety of the house forever," Patty said, raising her hand again when Angie would have spoken. "But… We don't have anywhere we need to go for the next week. I have work in the garden to do. Your father is working on a new painting. That'll keep him occupied." She frowned. "Your brothers might be tricky. But Paul is heading to Flagstaff to visit Nicole's parents for a week so they can spend time with baby Hannah. And Christopher… Not sure what to do about him."

"If he'll let us ward his apartment against mundane things, that'll help."

"*If* he'll let us. That's the problem."

Angie's younger brother didn't like their mother's magic, small though it was, invading his space. He claimed it threw off his creative vibes—he worked for an advertising firm, mostly writing copy—but Angie suspected he just didn't want a life with magic in it. He preferred the mundane world and didn't always like the reminders that his family wasn't *entirely* mundane.

In fact, Angie was pretty sure he often *forgot* she was a witch even though she'd spent their childhood hitting him with low-level spark spells whenever he picked on her too much. He told people she was a psychologist who liked astronomy—true as far as it went because her bachelors and master's degrees were in psychology, and she did love astronomy—and left out the part about how she worked as a psychic in a New York pagan store.

But he had let their mother put a protective magical circle around his apartment today. So…

Family was complicated.

"Okay." Angie let out a sigh. "If he won't take more warding on his apartment, maybe you can talk him into taking a spontaneous holiday and not tell anyone but us where he's going."

"That he might go for. Apparently, work's been tough the last few weeks."

Under normal circumstances, she'd love the diversion of hearing all about her brothers' lives. They were ordinary, so normal compared to hers, she liked the balance of those stories. But she was too jittery and nervous to relax and enjoy gossiping with her mother.

Patty seemed to sense that, too. She gave Angie a shoulder hug and tugged her toward the kitchen at the back of the house. A huge open space where they'd spent nearly as much time growing up as in their own rooms.

"We'll leave your father to entertain Sebastian. They seem to be talking about some soccer league thing or other. That'll make them both happy. Let's have a cup of tea and you can tell me…as much as you're willing to."

Angie swallowed. She really did want to tell her mother everything. One of the few people in the world who knew most things about her and who she knew she could be open with. But… She was still Angie's mother. The person who worried about her maybe more than any other human on the planet. Telling her *everything* might only make the situation worse.

"Tea sounds nice," Angie said, deciding she could tell some of what was happening. Not about the council, obviously. But she could talk about where she was at with her own magic and the training with Esmerelda. How her anger was making her lose control. She could explain how there was a hunter who wanted her dead because of what she could do—that would probably spark her mother's protective instincts so that would take some easing into—and she could explain what she was afraid he was trying to do.

How she worried he'd hurt them to push her over the edge of her control.

Ensuring her parents understood what was at stake meant they'd hopefully be extra cautious. For her sake as much as for theirs. And while they were safely holed up inside their very comfortable home with their very engrossing hobbies, she would do her damnedest to find a way to stop Morty.

That was the real problem. She just didn't know how to stop him.

How did you convince someone not to try killing you because of something you would absolutely not do so long as they *stopped* trying to kill you?

CHAPTER TWELVE

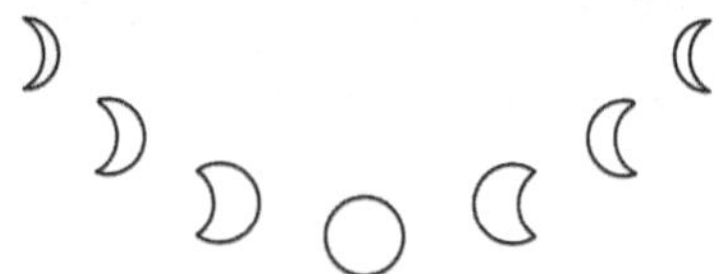

Because her mother was a witch by religion and creed as well as having magic, and didn't have any puritanical hangups, Patty didn't even blink at putting Sebastian and Angie into the same room—Angie's old childhood bedroom. Her father mentally glossed over the fact that his adult daughter and her long-term boyfriend had lived together and just ignored the fact that they were sleeping in the same room because her father was more old-fashioned about those kinds of things.

Being in her late twenties hadn't seemed to change an awful lot in her relationship with her parents. And for some reason, Angie found that extremely comforting in the circumstances.

Her old bedroom had been changed and rearranged over the years. It wasn't the same as when she'd lived here ten years ago. No shrines to her youth waiting for her whenever she came home. Her parents had packed away all her old things she didn't want to throw out, school report cards and projects, yearbooks and some old collectibles. But most of the posters and clothes and teenage paraphernalia had been donated or thrown away. The room had had a makeover about three years ago, too, so it was a grownup guest room now, with a comfortable king bed, fresh coat of soft terracotta-colored paint on the walls, new dresser and night stands in light wood, and a mostly empty closet. Even the smell of the room was a little different now. No lingering teenage attempts at perfume and makeup. Not even the faded scent of her candles and incense. Just a simple, clean air freshener smell, something with a hint of lavender in it, from the plugin at one side of the room.

So while the room was still in the same place near the back of the house, three doors away from her parents' bedroom, it didn't feel like her childhood bedroom anymore.

For which she was grateful.

She'd had a lovely childhood outside of a few demon incidents. And one or two magical lapses. The teenage years had been…well, teenage years, so a little fraught. But there was no reason for her to hate this room. She'd had many good memories here. She'd also confronted a lot of her deepest fears in this room, late at night, and those kid fears haunted the place less now because it didn't *look* like her childhood room anymore.

She wondered if her mother hadn't done that on purpose, knowing a preserved room would make Angie more uncomfortable and bring back too many fears? If her mother had known that and changed the room on purpose, then her mother was a genius. Something she'd always suspected anyway.

In the quiet, after everyone had gone to bed, Angie rolled against Sebastian, breathed him in, and sighed. "I'm not sure I'll be able to sleep," she murmured. They'd already been laying there in the dark for a half hour. Her brain was on overdrive, swirling through all the bad things that could happen.

"You won't help them worn out," Sebastian whispered into her hair. "You've done what you can tonight."

"And tomorrow?"

"Tomorrow, we'll call Morty out. Somewhere of our choosing."

She sat up in bed, leaning on his chest, and stared him in the face. "First, will that work? And second, to what end?"

"Will it work? Yes. He's here in person. He's confronted you once. He'll follow where you go. We'll force his hand."

"How?"

"You could always open a portal."

She closed her eyes and shook her head. "No. Why? No. I don't want him to know I can do that without a tree."

"We'll go where there's trees then."

"What will that do for us? What will that get us?"

"It'll get him to come out of hiding. Maybe force him to try and kill you right then and there. And we can…take care of him."

"I told him I wasn't a murderer. You're setting me up to be a murderer."

"No. I'm setting him up to have the opportunity to back down and leave your family alone. It'll be his choice, his decision to escalate. No one can blame you for defending yourself and your family."

"No one will care if I accidentally unleash a demon?"

He sighed. "I don't know what else to do, Ang. We either force his hand, or spend another six months waiting for the other shoe to drop. He's grown impatient. I don't think we'll need to do much to force the confrontation. It's coming anyway. It'd just be better if we picked the location, far away from your parents."

"Which he'll know is a set up."

"Won't stop him from coming for you."

"What if I just…kept doing my training with Esmerelda? What if I just went about my life, just with more protections on my family?"

"You think you can keep that up for another six months? Even another month? Not knowing when or if he'll strike? Not knowing how?"

"I hate this to the depths of my soul."

His arm tightened around her. "I know. But we've been waiting on them for months now. Doing the work. Surviving. Morty isn't the only one whose growing impatient." He tilted her chin up so she was looking him in the eyes. In the darkness, his very dark eyes were little more than luminous points of light. That red flash at the depths more visible and obvious. "I'm tired of waiting for them to attack you. I'm tired of worrying they will when I can't help you. And I hate that your family is in danger right now. It has to stop."

Her heart hammered, love that had never gone away, even when she'd wanted it to, swelled in her chest. She lifted up enough to kiss him, to tell him what she was having trouble finding words to express. Gratitude. Love. Fear. Worry. All of it. But mostly love. All poured into her kiss.

When she eased away, she cupped his cheek in her palm. "It does have to stop. Soon. But I need one more day to meet with Esmerelda. I…" She swallowed. "If I make my choice, do what I have to to separate my magics and then cut the red thread… I wouldn't be a threat anymore. They'll have to leave me alone. Morty would have to leave me and my family alone."

"But?"

She chuckled without much humor. He knew her so well. "But I'm still afraid of what it will do to my other magic. And if I have access to less, and Morty decides not to leave me alone, I'd be leaving us all vulnerable."

"You'd have a very good argument with the rest of the council that you were no longer a threat, though. That would…limit what he could do."

She nodded, nibbling at her bottom lip.

"You're still not sure."

"I'm afraid it'll somehow end my psychic abilities. And it'll almost certainly leave me with less magical power than I could have now."

"Could have?"

"I've never accessed my full potential. According to my various teachers."

He raised his brows, leaning back to look her in the eye

better. "You've always been pretty powerful even without doing that."

"Sort of." She titled her head to the side, a shrug. "I… have only trained so far. I've resisted being much more than I am. A lot of that is to do with the demon witch powers, but a lot is also down to fear." She looked away, not meeting his gaze when she whispered, "You see what happens when I *do* access all that power. The portals in the middle of nowhere… What other dangerous things could I do if I tapped it all?"

"Losing power you're afraid to use won't be much of a loss. Especially since you've never tapped it fully." He brushed a hand over her cheek. "Why are you still hesitating?"

"Because losing my psychic skill would be a huge loss." She sighed. "That one started out a bit of a bane, too, until I learned to control it. Knowing about other people and things when I touch them without *meaning* to was horrible. But… but once I got full control, was able to use it and not be used by it all the time… It's how I make my living in a way that really helps people. I like that."

"You could always go into regular counseling. You've got the degrees."

"With an ordinary office and ordinary office hours." She had to work not to shudder. She really hadn't enjoyed the time she'd worked in an office setting. "I guess I could. I probably would if I had to. But… I'd rather do what I'm doing."

"You want to spend the rest of your life reading palms?"

She snarled. "Why does no one believe that's fulfilling work? I don't just 'read palms'."

"Ang." He tugged her closer, into a tighter hug. "I know you find the work satisfying. It's good work." He sighed. "I didn't understand that…before."

An oblique reference to their breakup. She heard the regret in his tone and wanted to wipe it away. He didn't have anything to regret. She hadn't been clear enough with her feelings. Until terror and fear had pushed her over an edge.

She'd prefer her terror and fear didn't do that to her again, though. She wanted to make this decision, about her powers, her own magic, from a place of logic and open eyes. She didn't want to run away from her powers because she was scared of them.

Which was, she acknowledged, exactly what she'd been doing her whole life.

"I trained the psychic skill," she murmured. "To the point that I would hate to lose them now, even though at first I didn't like that power." She met his gaze. "I don't want to *use* my ability to open portals to demon realms, but… But do you think I could train that magic, all my magic, in a way that I no longer hate it or am afraid of it? The psychic skill is…is like the demon witch magic in that it doesn't take effort to *do*. It takes effort to prevent doing it. Both of them take a specific type of training. Except I've never trained the demon witch magic. Not fully. Not really. I know we've been practicing my control over tree portals, but… Well, I haven't embraced that practice."

He snorted at her understatement and that made her huff out a chuckle, rolling her eyes at herself.

"I know, I know," she said. "But what if, instead of cutting myself off from all that power, instead of making myself weaker because I'm afraid…" She hadn't even dared voice this possibility to herself before.

In fact, she hadn't considered this as an option until just this moment. But it was that link between her psychic skill and her demon witch magic, the way they both came easily and without effort. How the effort with both involved *not* doing them. And yet, she'd mastered that with her psychic skills. Gotten control so that she only occasionally read without trying. She could live without fear of those moments because they were rare and fast, and she could pull back from them when they did happen. She knew what to do with her psychic skills because she'd worked at controlling and *using* them.

What if, instead of limiting herself…what if…

"What if I train the demon witch magic the way I trained my psychic power? What if I learned to not just control it, but use it. In my control. When I wanted. And *only* when I want to use it."

"What would you use it for?" His voice was quiet, his brow creased, but thoughtful. Not shutting down the idea. "You use the psychic powers for making a living reading people and helping them with their problems. The demon witch magic won't help with that."

She shrugged. "I'm not sure… That's part of the problem. What good is it to anyone?"

"It's always helped in my work," he reminded her. "Being able to send the demons back to their realms when they've escaped, doing it so easily… Without a battle of wills to untether them from this realm?" He let out a long breath. "I'm not sure either Aidan or I have ever really explained…" His arms tightened, almost reflexively around her. "No. I know we haven't. And we haven't on purpose. But I think I should now."

"Explain? What exactly?"

"Escaped demons are… They're a lot more complicated for the hunters to deal with than we let on."

"I figured." She frowned a little, though, when she realized she'd never actually seen him deal with a freed demon on his own. If she'd been around to witness him fighting a freed demon, it meant she'd been there to open a portal to send the demon back.

"Once they've escaped, the only way to return them is a challenge. And once they've broken free, their will is stronger even if their powers are weaker. If a hunter is going to be killed, it happens…more often once a demon is free."

She nodded but held her tongue. She knew this part already, at least in general terms. But he seemed to be leading up to more.

"We don't allow demons to break free if we can help it. And so, freed demons are…rare. They usually only happen after a hunter has been killed, or move fast before a hunter can find them. Once they're out, hunters only have a few options. The challenge, as I said. Or…if the demon is powerful enough, there have been situations when we've negotiated a truce with the demon. Sanctuary here in exchange for them not burning down the world."

She tightened her jaw to keep from commenting on that. Sanctuary for the weak demons who broke free and just wanted to live normal lives pretending to be human... She understood that. Sanctuary for the very powerful ones... Well, if they're so powerful they just keep killing hunters, she supposed she understood that, too. Even if she didn't much like the idea.

"But all in all," Sebastian continued, "there are not a lot of freed demons in the world. We don't allow them out of the circle. Because getting them back to their realms is extremely difficult at that point."

And demons can't be killed. Not by humans. Other demons can kill demons, but humans—even demon hunters —can't kill demons. The only option is to banish them back to their realms.

She'd assumed, all these years, that hunters just did that when she wasn't around. They fought a challenge—a sort of game of wills—with a demon, and if the demon lost, it was banished. It had to return to its realm. If the hunter lost, they were killed and another hunter took up the fight.

None of that sounded good, of course. Definitely harder than sending them back from inside a containment circle, while they were still tethered to their own realm. Or, in her case, just opening a portal. But she'd always assumed sending freed demons back was just part of the hunter's life. They knew *how* to get demons back to their realms after they were free. They just preferred for things not to get that far.

Except, it sounded like Sebastian was saying… "Are you telling me that once a demon breaks free of a containment circle, you *can't* get them back to their realms?"

"No. I'm saying a lot of hunters always die as we try."

She absorbed that reality. A reality she had been blissfully unaware of until just that moment.

She met Sebastian's gaze. "I've fought alongside you against…a lot of freed demons over the years."

Not all of the demons they'd stopped were freed. In fact, most weren't, she realized. They were always on the verge of breaking free. That's when the demon hunters sensed the hunt. That's when they went in to stop the demon. But, still, over the years of working with Sebastian, especially before she'd moved to New York, many of the demons they went after were freed ones.

In fact, her first demon hunt with Aidan and Sebastian, the first time she'd met Sebastian… That hunt had involved a *lot* of freed demons. She'd assumed they brought her in to help because of the number and her portal would make getting rid of so many of the bastards easier. But…

But maybe she wasn't just there to help.

Maybe they'd *needed* her so they wouldn't die.

She blinked hard and leaned away from Sebastian. Not much, but he still reflexively tightened his hold on her, as if she'd bolt and he didn't want to let her run away. Then his grip relaxed. Which she didn't like. Because suddenly she realized just how many times he could have died.

How many times he *should* have died.

She wrapped herself around him again as the fear of what could have been, what might have been, clogged her throat.

Swallowing that fear, trying to calm the sudden adrenaline rush, she said, "You're telling me... On that first hunt. When we first met... You and Aidan would have been killed if I hadn't been there."

"Not necessarily. Aidan is very good." He kissed Angie's head. "So am I. But... The odds were not in our favor on that hunt, and we both knew it. But we were the only hunters close enough. No one else could have come to help. So we knew it was us or no one."

A small cult had decided to unleash a demon plague on this world, thinking they'd be handed over power or... something. One of the humans had even gone so far as to link himself with a demon, which had been very bad for him when that demon got tossed back into its own realm. The whole situation had been terrible, and she'd known that at the time. But Aidan and Sebastian had never let on that they'd essentially been on a suicide mission.

Without her.

Because she'd opened a portal for them and they'd thrown all the demons back through that portal, everyone had survived. Not, technically, easy. But no hunters had been killed. None of the humans had even died. Everyone came out of that situation alive...when maybe they shouldn't have.

"When we..." She swallowed to wet her suddenly dry throat. "When we started working together..."

"I found myself called to the freed demon hunts more," he said.

"The…the council didn't send you after the freed ones?"

"They don't do that. It's not how hunters work. We're called to hunts and we go. No one *tells* us where to go. But, with you, I was called to more with freed demons."

"What about the times I couldn't go with you?" She gripped him tighter as more panic and adrenaline shot through her. "Did you have to face freed demons without me?"

"No, no. Shhh…"

He ran a hand down her hair and she realized she was trembling. She buried herself tighter against him. All the things that might have happened, and she hadn't had a clue. No fucking idea.

"Freed demons really are rare," he said. "And when I was called to go after one, you were always there, always available for those hunts." He continued to run his hand over her hair as he shrugged. "The universe or demon hunter instincts or…I don't know. My good luck, maybe. But you were always able to come with me when I went after a freed demon. And I went after more freed demons in the years we were together than when we were apart."

She leaned back enough to look him in the face again. "Being with me put you in more danger?"

He shook his head, frowning. "No. That's not what I meant. Being with you helped me, helped me save other hunters." He glanced away. "But because it put you in danger…I resented those calls. I was glad other hunters weren't forced into those situations, but I hated…*hated* that you were in danger." He looked at her again. "That time…

I've never been so terrified in my life as I was when that demon dragged you into its realm. I know you still have those nightmares. I do, too."

She sucked in a breath. That had been the straw, the last straw, the thing that finally drove her to try leaving the demon world behind. And with it, Sebastian. The nightmares, the fears of what could have happened if he hadn't pulled her out… And goddess she'd never loved him more than in those moments when he'd reached through a portal he couldn't even see and dragged her out of her nightmare.

But she couldn't face that life and world afterward. And she knew if she stayed with him, she'd keep joining the fights. For him.

She hadn't thought about the nightmares he probably had after that night. Guilt washed through her. All she'd known was her own terror, her own inability to cope. She'd run because she couldn't handle any of those emotions anymore. But…but he'd been going through the same thing in his way. He'd had to *watch* her go through that portal.

"I'm sorry," she murmured, closing her eyes.

"No. Don't." He squeezed her tight. "I didn't say that to make you feel guilty, Ang. You had to do what you did. I hated it, but I didn't blame you. I still don't. In some ways, I was relieved when you went. You were… You were supposed to be safer that way."

Except that his council kept sending him back to her, to drag her back into the fight.

All of that took on another meaning now, though, didn't

it. Suddenly the inability of the hunters to just leave her alone made a different kind of sense.

"Is that why Gabriella is really pushing to have me be a hunter?" she murmured. "Not just because she thinks I was born to it, but because…because I can save lives by opening portals when a demon breaks free?"

He nodded. "The will to be a hunter isn't common. And there are fewer of us as the years go on. Harder to find the humans with the will to overcome a demon's. Losing any hunter is a blow. Always has been. But it's worse now. Because there aren't many to replace them. We've had to be more…compromising with freed demons than some of us would like. And it's not good. Gabriella is hoping you'll change that balance."

Angie shook her head, but she wasn't sure what she was trying to deny. That she could change anything for the hunters? That she believed Gabriella was right? That she was afraid Gabriella might be right? That any of this could be true?

She squeezed her eyes tight, and buried against Sebastian again because she felt so unmoored, so confused. Everything had to be passed through this new filter now, everything she'd assumed, thought she knew…

All of it had to be viewed differently now.

And she had no idea what to do about any of it.

CHAPTER THIRTEEN

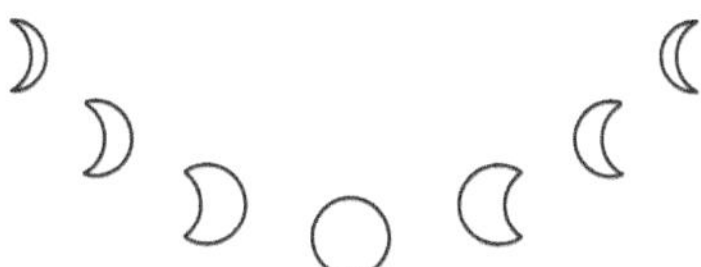

In the end, Angie drifted off to sleep, but it was a restless sleep. She turned into Sebastian every time she woke, and every time, he pulled her close, cradling her until she drifted back to sleep again.

When the morning light crowded in past her curtains, she finally gave up. Coffee and some quiet time in her mother's garden. That's what she needed. Her mind swirled with the repercussions of her work with the hunters, of what she could do to help them, and what had happened in the years before her birth, the years when there was no demon witch around to help send freed demons back to their realms.

How many hunters had died? How many other people had died?

Sebastian started to climb out of bed to follow her, but she waved him back to sleep. He'd spent the night comforting her chaotic thoughts. He needed sleep and she needed some alone time to think.

Between the threat to her family, and the revelations Sebastian had given her, she felt like she was floating away from the dock that had anchored her to reality. Like she had no idea what was right anymore.

Dark, rich coffee with a drop of milk in hand, she wandered out the back door into her mother's favorite place in the world. It was probably one of Angie's favorites too. On the same level as Esmerelda's garden.

Patty had taken the smallish space behind the house and set out a series of raised stone-rimmed boxes and terraced steps near the rear of the garden. The raised beds were filled with mostly herbs, all of them hearty and overflowing their beds. The more delicate plants were shaded with low wooden trellises covered in silver lace vines that took the heat happily. Less delicate plants were left to the full range of sunshine that hit the garden. In the terraces at the back, her mother grew vegetables and vine fruit. Anything that didn't grow on a tree, her mother found a way to grow, using the natural shaded and bright patches near the back fence to arrange her plants.

The flat stone path that wound around boxes and raised beds was also covered in giant terracotta pots filled with bougainvillea, evergreens, and flowering cacti. The garden was a working place, a kitchen witch's garden, with sections specifically for the types of plants and herbs she used in her potions and recipes, as well as plants that encouraged pollinators to visit her garden. All of it carefully tended by the hand of a woman who talked to the plants like they could answer back.

Near the back porch, her parents used to have a huge patio table with giant umbrella and enough plastic chairs for the entire family. With the kids grown, they'd downsized to a smaller table, still covered with a huge umbrella, and the quality of padding on the chairs had improved significantly, soft cushions covered in weatherproof material.

Angie took one of the four seats, setting her coffee mug gently on the table as she breathed in the heady, herby scents of her mother's garden. This place smelled like her mother to her. Backed by the sagebrush and creosote from the desert, the dry air and crackling rocks, this oasis of greenery, all without a single tree, *was* her mother in so many ways.

And sitting in the midst of that peaceful space helped calm the chaos raging through her, giving her just a little space to think.

Not that any answers came to her. She was just more clear about the lack of answers now.

Letting her eyes drift half closed, she checked on the circle surrounding her parents' house. The faint blue glow of it rose in her mind's eye, just beyond the back fence, surrounding the edge of the fence and circling around to the front of the house. Angie chuckled that her mother had ensured the circle was *outside* her garden completely. Since her friend had help her set it with salt, Angie should have assumed she'd ensure that salt was beyond the lines of her carefully tended garden so it wouldn't throw off the soil balance.

She studied the line of the circle, the magic that had gone into it, more than her mother would have been capable of alone. The blended magic of her and her two friends. A good circle. One that would keep out demons and make the skin of anyone not welcome here crawl. No one was going to be comfortable getting close to this house until her mother dropped the circle. It wouldn't keep out stray bullets and determined mundane threats, but it would definitely hinder mundane humans from getting too close.

After feeling her way through the other magics, Angie added two spells she hoped would help against those mundane threats. An illusion spell to confuse anyone coming to the house into thinking this wasn't the right place, and one that heightened the discomfort already built into the circle, making it almost impossible to get close to the house without high levels of anxiety and fear. Later, she'd try to build in something even sturdier, but for now, the combined magics would be enough to keep her parents safe.

Angie settled back in her seat with her mug then and released a slow breath, blowing across her coffee to cool it. They couldn't live like this indefinitely. She had to figure something out, because eventually her parents would have to leave the safety of this little haven.

How the hell did she end Morty's threat? Talking to him hadn't helped. Sebastian wanted to confront him, but to what end? She couldn't just kill Morty. Outside of her own, non-homicidal tendencies, that *would* fulfill his fear that she was one of the monsters, one of the demons just waiting to break free. But if she couldn't talk him out of his conviction she'd break, what recourse did she have?

"You could always curse him," her mother said quietly, as she sat in one of the free seats around the patio table, her own milky, sweet coffee in her favorite Navajo patterned coffee mug cradled in her hands.

Angie rolled her eyes. "First, I don't do curses. You taught me that."

Patty smiled. A little smugly, Angie thought.

"Second, how did you know what I was thinking about? You aren't the psychic here."

Another smug smile. "Just a guess. I actually don't know which 'he' you're thinking about. But it's a good conversation starter, don't you think?"

Angie snorted and shook her head. "Sometimes you're weird, mom."

"I try." She sipped her coffee serenely. "You should have seen the way Sade's head snapped up when I said that to her at the last coven meeting." She sighed. "I think Sade is on her way to divorce."

Talking about coven gossip was infinitely easier than trying to solve an impossible problem, so Angie was very tempted to indulge. But she couldn't run away from her current problem. She just didn't know how to solve it.

When she said as much to her mother, Patty said, "You've been running from the full force of your magic your entire life. And I promised I wouldn't interfere in that. I don't have the level of power to deal with. I can do my little spells to help the garden along, or mix a potion to help Sade's love life, or provide a poultice for Alice's cat's hinky hip joint. But I've never had to deal with the sort of power that… consumes lives. And as your mother, I just want you to be happy. If you're happy, then whatever you choose to do with your magic is up to you. Want to ignore half of it, fine."

She looked across the table, meeting Angie's gaze, the early morning light painting her lightly tanned cheeks pink. "But I think ignoring that power isn't going to help you anymore. And you are definitely not happy right now."

Angie wanted to laugh at that understatement. "It's not just trying to do work that isn't me," she said. "It's you all being in danger because of me. I hate that to the depth of my soul."

"I know. And we know you aren't to blame for that. Don't you dare feel any guilt for where we are now."

That nearly brought tears to Angie's eyes. Because she did feel guilty having put her family at risk. She knew she wasn't at *fault*, and yet she still felt responsible for all that was happening.

Her mother let out a long breath, giving Angie time to pull herself together. Then said, "You will be safer—and that's *my* priority—you will be safer, if you figure out the full depths of your magic, and how to control it."

"Esmerelda says there's a way to cut myself off from the…from the portal part of my magic." She couldn't bring herself to call that magic "demon" witch magic at that moment. She wasn't even entirely sure why. Her family knew that aspect of her magic involved demons—firsthand!

"Is that what you want?" her mother asked quietly.

"I...don't know. Esmerelda has given me three days... well, two now, to consider it. Much longer and the changes in my magic will be more difficult to reverse. It could affect my other magic, the psychic skills... I have to consider that. But not having to worry about the stuff that's not witchy stuff would be very nice. You'd be safer, I think." She hoped. "I'd be safer," she said before her mother could ask. "I think. And, honestly, until last night, I was leaning heavily toward just ending my ability to open portals. Just...snapping that power right off. Consequences to my other powers be damned."

"What did Sebastian say to change your mind?"

Angie let out a huff. Of course her mother guessed that was the change. Sometimes she forgot how easy these conversations with her mom could be because she didn't have to explain every detail. Her mother just got there.

"Turns out," Angie said slowly, then paused, her throat thick. Finally, she got out, "It turns out that my ability to open portals directly, do the thing I do... It's been saving hunter lives. I had no idea. I didn't realize... But when one of the demons gets free and the hunters go after it, it's so much harder to deal with than I knew."

She told her mother what Sebastian had told her, about the deaths, the compromises to save lives, the near impossible task of sending a freed demon back to its realm. "I understood doing that was difficult. And that's why the hunters tried so hard to ensure the demons didn't break free. But I didn't realize how...rare a freed demon was because I've seen a lot of them. Turns out, that was on purpose.

Sebastian was being called to the freed demons because *I* was with him, *I* could help him." Angie blinked down at her cooling coffee, then met her mother's gaze. "If I cut off my ability to open portals, I could well be condemning some of the hunters to death. Maybe even Sebastian. Because I won't be able to help."

Her mother absorbed that information with a quiet nod, letting her gaze travel out over the garden. "That does complicate things," she murmured.

"Understatement," Angie said.

"It's a decision only you can make. It has to be what's best for you, though. Not what's best for other people. Because that path will only lead to resentment and pain and misery. And people will still die."

Angie frowned at her mother.

Patty shrugged. "Everyone dies eventually. But you doing work you hate, because you feel obligated… Eventually, you'll resent the work. Resent the people you're trying to protect. Eventually, you'll get sloppy. And people will die."

Angie took that like a blow to the gut, literally letting out a sharp breath, rubbing a hand over her stomach. Truths hurt sometimes, but this one hit hard.

"You'll either need to learn to love the work of saving their lives, or you'll need to find another way," her mother finished quietly. "I don't envy you that decision, my love. I really don't. But we'll be here for you, and support you. No matter what you decide." She stood and gave Angie a shoulder hug, a hug Angie leaned in to. Patty kissed the top of her head and said quietly, "I'll leave you to think. But if you need to talk, I'm here."

Angie was still staring at the garden, cradling her mostly empty mug, when Sebastian came out and handed her her cellphone.

"You have a call," he said, his voice deep.

She barely had time to register how handsome he looked in the morning light before the implications of what he'd said sank in. He wouldn't be out here with her cellphone if the call wasn't important. She glanced at the screen. But she didn't recognize the number.

Frowning, she said, "Hello."

"Hey, witch," Carmen said with a smirk in her voice that was impossible to miss. "We need to talk."

CHAPTER FOURTEEN

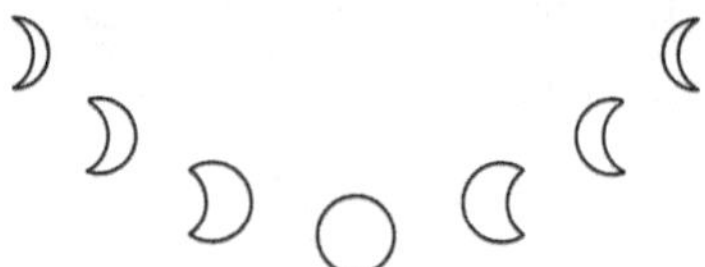

Carmen was already waiting at the open, treeless parking lot of a drugstore at the edge of Old Town when Angie and Sebastian pulled into the lot.

She leaned against a two-door, sporty little red car that didn't look like a rental. Dressed in jeans, t-shirt, hiking boots, and a thigh length sweater in deference to the cool spring morning. By afternoon, it would be too warm for that sweater, but the high desert had some cooler mornings this time of year. Carmen's dark hair was pulled back into a low bun, her makeup flawless, her dark eyes narrowed as Angie and Sebastian climbed out of Angie's rental car.

Angie expected a smirk. Carmen always seemed to have a secret that amused her and that secret was at Angie's expense. But she wasn't smirking. Or smiling. And she didn't look like she was gloating about anything.

Unusual enough to have Angie's hackles rising. She was

already leery of Carmen—she'd brought up a shield spell even before climbing out of the car and set it in front of her and Sebastian the minute they were standing beside each other. But Carmen's expression, the seriousness in her dark eyes, set off warning klaxons in Angie's head.

"We have a problem," Carmen said without preamble.

"Which one?" Angie asked. She had lots of problems at the moment.

Carmen flicked a glance at Sebastian and some of her serious expression cleared, just long enough for her to wink at him and say, "Hello, handsome."

Sebastian didn't respond. Even with a grunt. The last time he'd seen Carmen, she'd had him pinned inside a circle trying to fend off a demon in a second circle that was trying to rip the throat out of a man who was, in all likelihood, a Russian mobster. All as part of a test Carmen had set up for Angie. Carmen was not one of Sebastian's favorite people.

She wasn't one of Angie's either.

Carmen did smirk a little at Sebastian's silence, but her expression turned serious again when she faced Angie. A breeze blew through the parking lot, catching a strand of hair pulled free from her bun and fluttering the hair across her brow. She swiped her strand out of her face with an irritated gesture as she stared at Angie.

"You met Morty," Carmen said.

"And I still can't get over the fact that he's named himself Morty. Yes. We met."

Carmen snorted, though no humor showed in her expression. "I know with the name, right? But he's dangerous. And that name is designed to make people think otherwise."

"Figured. I thought you might be working with him."

Carmen actually snarled at that. "That white man? No. He wants you dead."

"And you don't?"

"I want something else. It doesn't involve you dead."

"Is that why you're here?"

"I'm here because the asshole is finally coming after me, and my…friends aren't going to protect me anymore."

"Why not?"

"You."

That was…interesting. And begged a lot of questions. Except she didn't trust any answers Carmen might give her.

"How is this my problem?" she asked instead of giving in to her curiosity.

Though *not* asking who Carmen's friends were inside the demon hunters was very difficult. She had to have someone powerful protecting her. She knew things about the hunters no one who wasn't one knew. And she'd managed to evade any sort of justice over the years even though she'd *killed* a hunter. Whoever was keeping her safe from that justice had to have a reason that outweighed that murder. The fact that the thing that shifted that balance out of Carmen's favor was *Angie* and not the *murder* was of intense interest to Angie.

"Morty is after you, too," Carmen said. "Finally coming at you directly. So we have a mutual enemy. That makes us friends."

Angie's turn to snort. "No."

"Shame." Carmen didn't sound sorry even a little bit that they weren't going to be friends. "But we do have a mutual goal of staying alive."

Angie couldn't deny she wanted to stay alive, but her feelings on Carmen's future were more decidedly mixed, so she didn't comment.

"Morty will lose control of the council if you keep living," Carmen said. "The faction that wants you alive and helping hunters is gaining strength. Especially because you aren't dead yet."

Angie thought, *I'm also not a hunter yet since I still don't know when I'm needed.* But she kept that to herself.

"Morty's run out of time. He has to prove you're a threat, and that threat outweighs any benefit to having you around."

"He's threatened my family. He's trying to push me to lose control." Angie said that as matter-of-factly as she could, without letting her inner rage show, to see if Carmen knew that was his plan or not.

Unfortunately, Carmen was a consummate con artist and she didn't let her reaction to Angie's statement show. "He doesn't know what you can do yet," Carmen said. "He still thinks you need the trees. Everyone does."

Good. Angie and Sebastian had tried to keep that to themselves. The last thing they needed was an already jumpy group of powerful demon hunters realizing she was even more dangerous than they thought. But Angie had worried Carmen might have given the truth away to the hunter protecting her.

"So they'll try to catch you out in an area without trees," Carmen continued.

"Do you know how they intend to kill me?" Angie was genuinely curious about this. Going for her family, trying to drive her into unleashing demons…what was the end game to that? If she did unleash demons, they'd have to find a way to get them all back. And how would they kill her in the meantime? Did Carmen know the plan?

"Any way they can," Carmen said without emotion. "Will you into a void if they can."

"No convenient voids in Albuquerque."

Carmen huffed a sound that might have been a laugh and looked away, swiping at the hair blowing across her forehead again. "Morty's got delusions of grandeur, but he's not the only threat to you."

"You?"

"I'm here to help you," Carmen said.

"You're here to help yourself."

"That too. I'm talking about that other hunter. Jacob."

The hunter who'd warned Sebastian that Morty wasn't going to wait for her to die a "natural hunter" death anymore. The reason Sebastian had raced all the way across the country yesterday to reach her.

"What's Jacob got to do with all this?" Angie asked, carefully.

"He has…ideas. You disrupt those ideas." Carmen scowled as she pushed some hair behind her ears again. "I hate desert wind," she muttered.

"What ideas?" Angie ignored the wind comment. Especially because it wasn't particularly windy.

"That you'll make the hunters weak. That you can't be involved with the hunters without leaving them vulnerable. Their wills not strong enough. He's..." Carmen waved a hand in the air. "If there was such a thing, he'd be a hunter... purist? An ascetic is maybe a good word."

"Demon hunting isn't a religion. How can he be an ascetic?"

"He views it as close to a religion as the hunters ever get." Carmen shrugged. "You know the types. Believe only in the fundamentals, the 'purity' of the practice. Or something." She rolled her eyes and glanced around the parking lot.

The lot was busy at one side, but their little section was quiet. No cars parked near them. No people walked by. Not even the tourists wandering out of Old Town on accident. Angie had a feeling Sebastian was providing that privacy. Willing people to be in other parts of the lot and to avoid this area.

Demon hunter wills really were amazing. She supposed she could see how someone so inclined might eventually come to center that will in an almost religious belief. But, given the work, she wasn't sure that was a good thing.

"How do you know all this?" she asked Carmen.

This time Carmen did grin. "I know so so much more than they want me to. Any of them. And that's not the point. The point is what this all has to do with you. Morty wants you dead. And will try to find a way to justify that death. Jacob wants you as far from the hunters as possible because he believes you weaken their wills. By making the job too easy. You provide a…a crutch."

When Angie continued to frown at her without reaction, Carmen lowered her chin and said, slowly, "You open portals to banish demons. That doesn't take will. And they can't do that with their wills. So all those demons that would require extreme will to send back, the freed ones, the really really strong ones, the ones requiring demon hunters to train and be at the top of their game…? You can take care of them with an appropriately placed stare. The hunters won't have to hone and train their wills to take care of those demons with you around. You're called to those hunts. But when you die—" emphasis on the *when* with a little smirk, "—you'll leave a generation of hunters without the will to fight off freed demons. So Jacob and his ilk think. He thinks that's already happening. And the longer you're part of their world, the worse it gets."

"Why isn't he on Morty's side, then, trying to kill me?" Angie asked, hiding her reaction to the news. "Or is he?"

Inside, she was churning, spinning, her mind a whirlwind whistling through her in angry blasts. Last night, she'd learned she saved hunters' lives by being called to the freed demons—or being around to go with Sebastian when he was called. She'd learned that because of her, whatever instinct drew hunters to a fight was drawing Sebastian to the most dangerous fights because she'd be there to help.

Now she was learning some hunters thought that very twist of fate and instinct would weaken the others. Would leave all the hunters worse off.

She was saving their lives on the one hand and possibly destroying them on the other? All because she was who she was. Something she didn't ask for and couldn't help. And because of that, she was damned if she did by one group, damned if she didn't by another, and a third just wanted her dead because they assumed she was a bomb waiting to go off.

The anger rose, at how impossible the situation was, at how fate and the universe had seen fit to give her *no way out* of this that wouldn't potentially cost lives. Including her own. As her anger rose, the wind around them kicked up harder, wiping Carmen's hair away from her face now, tangling Angie's hair around her head. She ignored it. She ignored the glance Sebastian sent her way.

Clouds rolled across the sky. Dark shadows fell over the parking lot.

Carmen glanced up. She stopped messing with her hair. "Jacob knows Morty's plan now is to drive you to unleash a plague. And Jacob knows that'll backfire, because, at least to him, the hunters don't have the will to fix the problem now. He thinks they've already grown too weak." She flicked a gaze up to the roiling storm clouds again. "He wants you out of the hunters' world, but he doesn't want to risk you unleashing a plague. Not while the hunters don't have the ability to stop it. That's his thinking anyway."

"And you know this because he's told you?"

"Because I am a very very good listener," she said, but her gaze was jumping back to the sky again, even as the first few drops of rain plopped onto the warm tarmac.

Across the lot, Angie heard the raised voices, the surprise. She was peripherally aware that people were rushing toward the pharmacy's automatic door. She was peripherally aware that the clouds overhead were about to open up and drench them.

And that her magic was rushing through her, tingling along her skin. She could almost see the faint purple-blue color of it at the edges of her vision, like she was standing the middle of a halo of her own power.

"Ang," Sebastian whispered.

"Yup," she said. She was very aware that her anger was causing this. That her confusion and her frustration had raised her magic. That in that moment, her control was... shaky.

It was just that she didn't care.

Let it rain. Let it storm. The hunters, hell the universe, had placed her at the center of a situation with no good answer. All she had in that moment was the storm.

"You about to unleash that demon plague?" Carmen asked quietly. Hard to tell by her tone if she was worried or just curious.

"No demons," Angie said.

This wasn't her demon witch power getting the best of her. This was her witch magic. The bulk of the power that made up her web of magical energies. But the lack of control over it... She knew that was because of the blending of magics. In that moment, she didn't really care about that either.

In fact, she could practically feel the blending of those

magics expanding, the red bleeding into more of the blue. And with that blending, she felt the surge of energy under her skin. The sheer *power* of it all.

In that moment, she felt like she could do almost anything. Take control of the elements and throw them around as she liked. Lift the sidewalks. Flatten her enemies. Strike the ground with enough lightning to release all her anger and frustration.

The force of the power surged through her, lighting her up from the inside. And it felt *good*.

"You hit me with a lightning bolt," Carmen said, glancing up, "who will tell you what no one else will?" She raised her brows. "Think Morty doesn't know what he's gotten himself into?"

"He does not," Angie said, and her voice was very deep.

"Ang," Sebastian whispered again, leaning close, but not too close. Not touching her. "You're glowing." Then even quieter, "There are kids in the parking lot."

She blinked. Damn him, he knew where to hit. He'd be preventing anyone from seeing her glow. If he could. But a lightning storm in this small space would endanger more than just Carmen.

She sucked in a slow breath, let it out slowly, focused on breathing. In. Out. Until she felt the edges of her magic again. She wrapped her mind around all that surging power and soothed it, smoothed it all, back into place.

Just like Esmerelda had taught her to do as a child.

Not to fight it. Not to struggle *against it*. To hold it gently and let it relax, melting away like ice on hot skin, sinking into her, where it—and she—was safe.

The wind calmed back to a light breeze. The plops of giant raindrops stopped. No deluge. The clouds overhead splintered and drifted away, leaving a bright blue sky and sunshine warming Angie's skin again.

She closed her eyes briefly, trusting Sebastian to watch Carmen for her, and let the last of her magic drop back into the web of power. Let those vibrating strands still, come to a stop.

When she blinked her eyes open again, Carmen was watching her closely, and Sebastian was standing near enough, she could feel his warmth beside her.

"You learn to control all that," Carmen whispered, "they won't be able to stop you doing anything you want."

"What I want," Angie said, her voice still deep, but more scratchy now than deep from her power rising, "what I have always wanted, is to be left alone."

"Too late for that," Carmen said.

Angie let out another long breath.

She hated that Carmen was right.

CHAPTER FIFTEEN

After another silent minute, while Angie got her pulse rate back to normal, as the spring sun warmed the parking lot and the breeze settled into normal gusts, Carmen finally said, "Listen, I'm here because it's to both our benefits to stop Morty. And because Jacob will… complicate things. You want Morty out of the picture. Meet me tonight. There's a trail not far from that Sandia Peak tram. Already found you a couple of believable trees. Morty will be there. He'll think you're about to unleash your plague. You can kill him and be done with it."

"No," Angie said. "I'm not killing anyone. And that wouldn't end anything. If I kill him, the others will come for me. That's not the answer." Even if she was willing to turn herself into a cold-blooded murderer. Which she wasn't prepared to do.

"Then you can try negotiating with him again." Carmen

shrugged. "You see where that's got you. This man will kill you at his earliest convenience. You strike tonight, or he'll go for your family. Up to you. I know what I'd do."

"You and I are not alike."

"More alike that you want to admit," Carmen said, but didn't smirk.

"Is that why you called me here? To try and talk me into killing Morty?"

"Morty is…a problem. But the real issue is Jacob. And what he and his ilk will do. They're the ones you have to watch. Morty is dangerous, but mostly, he's in the way."

"Morty is the one threatening my family and trying to kill me."

"Like I said. He's in the way. An obstacle. One you can take care of, if you had the…" Now she did smirk. "Will."

Angie didn't rise to the bait. Instead, she switched topics, hoping to catch Carmen off guard. "Why did you push me to take hold of powers I'd been happy to ignore? You've got a powerful enemy now, in that Russian mobster, Sokolov, and the demon he works with. All to force me to open powers that would have been better left dormant. Why?"

Carmen had given her an excuse in the moment, that it was a sort of selfish self-preservation. That if Angie didn't have control of that ability, she'd unleash a demon hoard on accident and destroy the world. Some of that was undoubtedly true since Carmen was selfish and wouldn't want the world to end, but Angie knew that wasn't the full reason. Maybe not even the main reason. Carmen had wanted her to access the ability to open a portal without a tree. And Angie wanted to know why.

"Why do you think those powers would be better left dormant?" Carmen asked. "What makes you think they'd have stayed dormant? If you can't control all your power—" she glanced up at the sky, "—you risk losing control of it. All of it. You lose control of that…unique ability of yours, you won't need trees to unleash a plague. This way, you train. You only unleash a demon plague if you want to." She smiled a little.

"That explanation seems too altruistic for you."

"You assume everything I do, I do for myself. But you'd be wrong."

"So far, I haven't seen evidence of your giving nature."

"You haven't been looking."

"You could have left me alone. Walked away."

"So could the hunters. No one was willing to risk that choice."

Risk. No one was willing to *risk* walking away from her and leaving her alone. She wasn't sure how to make people believe she was less of a threat before. Before they'd pushed her, before they'd threatened her family. She was less dangerous before they'd started forcing her hand.

She glanced up at the sky, too. Didn't wince, but her jaw tightened briefly. Maybe she hadn't been less threatening. Maybe all this power she'd been refusing for so long really would have caused a problem eventually. She'd nearly unleashed a storm on Old Town just now, because she was frustrated and angry.

But all of that loss of control… That started *after* they'd all forced her hand, forced her to this place with her powers.

What did they want from her? When would it be enough?

She folded her hand up to grab at the dangling pentagram on her bracelet, absently rubbing the small dime-sized silver charm. "And when I learn how to control all this power?" she asked quietly. "What makes any of you think that'll make me safer?"

"I never said I thought you'd be safer. Just less likely to destroy the world on accident."

"I don't trust you. Or that this is your real motive."

"I know. And I don't blame you. But none of this is the point now."

"The point is that Morty is after you and wants you dead now, too."

She smiled. "He won't stop until someone you love is hurt or dead. And you won't be able to stop him. Meet me tonight, take care of your Morty problem now. Before it's too late." She scanned the lot, and their still empty section. "Always nice talking with a demon hunter around. Guaranteed privacy, even in public." She winked at Sebastian, then turned back to her car. "I'll see you tonight, love birds. Don't be late."

They watched in silence as Carmen drove away, waiting until she'd left the parking lot and they could no longer see her sporty little red car in the city traffic. The gentled breeze whipped at Angie's hair as she stared at the spot where Carmen's car had disappeared.

"I don't like any of this," she said. "I don't trust Carmen."

"Best not to."

"This feels like a trap."

"Of course it is."

"But I'm not sure if it's a trap for me, or for Morty."

"With Carmen, could be both."

"I hate being confused."

Sebastian wrapped an arm around her shoulders, pulling her against his side. "I think you need to visit with Esmerelda today."

She nodded. "Yeah. I'm afraid…" She swallowed.

"Afraid?"

"Of what she'll tell me. I'm afraid it's too late, and I can't turn back. But I don't really know how to go forward like this. And… I'm afraid Morty will push me into killing him even though I don't want to. Or somehow Carmen will trick me into it. Or I won't have enough control over my power to stop it." She said this last very quietly. Because that was her real fear, and saying it out loud felt dangerous.

Sebastian tightened his arm on her shoulders, wrapping his other arm around her now. "I've got your back. We can do this together."

She hugged his arms, still staring at the spot where Carmen's car had vanished. She didn't miss that he wasn't dismissing any of her fears.

But he had her back. And that meant everything.

THEY REACHED ESMERELDA'S HOUSE AS THE EARLY afternoon sun gave way to some rolling clouds. Nothing unnatural this time, just the normal flow of spring in the desert. The chances of flash flooding went up if it rained, but the cacti bloomed and that was one of Angie's favorite sights.

Esmerelda was standing at the door by the time Angie and Sebastian had climbed out of the car, her grin spreading as she spotted Sebastian.

He went right to her outstretched arms, bending low for his kiss on each cheek.

"Ah! So handsome," Esmerelda said, leaning back to pat his face. "I like the goatee. I've missed you. I'm glad she took you back."

Sebastian chuckled. "I'm glad, too. How've you been, Ezzie?"

"Good, good." She released his face to wave a hand in the air. "But I think a happy reunion isn't what brought you both here today. Come in. I'll make tea."

They followed her to the back of the house and when she waved them out the back door, they went to the porch and sat at the large circular patio table under the shaded trellis while Esmerelda put the kettle on to boil.

Through the open sliding glass doors, she said, "I have good tea, Sebastian. Don't worry."

Angie rolled her lips into her mouth, but it wasn't enough to stop her grin. Sebastian simply raised his voice to say, "Thank you, Ezzie. You're a star."

"I know."

Angie gave in to her chuckle then. And oh how she

wished this was just a friendly reunion visit. Esmerelda had always liked Sebastian, though Angie half suspected it was his accent as much as anything else.

Esmerelda emerged from the house with two cups of tea and placed them in front of Angie and Sebastian before taking a seat. Angie watched her lower herself gently, and her concern from yesterday crept back in. She wasn't sure if burdening her teacher with her current troubles was a good idea. But she also knew if she said that out loud, she'd get an earful from Esmerelda. Probably half in Spanish. So she kept her concerns to herself. For now.

"What's happened since yesterday that I need to know?" Ezzie asked, leaning back in her seat and folding her hands over her stomach.

Angie quickly told her about the meeting with Morty, the fear for her family, and their encounter with Carmen that morning. "I'm being pushed into a corner. A smaller and smaller corner. And I'm not sure what to do. My magic isn't as controlled anymore. I nearly brought a storm down onto the drugstore parking lot. And that was just standing around getting angry. That wasn't anyone actually attacking me or my family." She looked down into the tea cup cradled between her hands. "I'm really worried what I'll do if someone does hurt my family."

"A fair worry," Esmerelda said, without pulling punches or trying to make Angie feel better with platitudes. That was Esmerelda's superpower. Cutting right to the chase. "What's happening with your magic now, and the amount at your fingertips, is a lot. Difficult to learn control, or for you, relearn control, so fast and under pressure. But learn you must if you don't want them to win."

"I've been trying." She raised a hand. "I know *trying* isn't control." She'd heard the refrain before. "But… Even if I can control it, before they've pushed me too far, this will make turning back impossible, won't it? If I *use* this magic, it takes me farther away from being able to reverse this melding. Doesn't it?"

"It will." Esmerelda nodded, her gaze distant.

"But if I do cut off the magic now while I still can," Angie said, "if I can't open portals anymore, all the problems these people have with me go away. I'm no longer the threat Morty fears. I can't be the crutch to the hunters that Jacob fears. And whatever Carmen wants from me will be moot."

"You'll also no longer be in a position to save hunter lives by doing a thing they have trouble doing. And you might be less able to protect your family if they need you to."

Stating the very reasons Angie still hesitated. If she hadn't learned that she was actually a benefit to the hunters last night, though, she'd be here to turn that demon witch power off. Now. Before things went any farther. She'd take the damage to her witch power, if necessary, and learn to get by in whatever way she could.

But…her skill saved lives. Would it be selfish to stop helping? Wouldn't she be making things worse for the hunters if she could no longer open the portals?

"I don't know what to do," she said quietly.

"You could learn to control it all so they can never push

you into doing something you don't want to do," Esmerelda said.

"That doesn't end the threat they're all worried about. And I might be playing right into Carmen's hands. Whatever her real goal is."

"Control will end *your* worry, though. Control will ensure *you* know you won't unleash demon plagues or bring down storms. Unless you mean to."

And that was her other worry. All this power under her skin, waiting to jump out, to *do* things. She was terrified of what it could do. And had always been scared of it. Easier to see in hindsight. She really had been hiding from most of her magic for her entire life.

Hiding was easier. But it wasn't proving safer.

"I could still unleash a demon plague, on purpose, if…if emotionally pushed to it," she said, thinking of the threat to her family. "That danger doesn't go away with control."

"Yes, it does. If he pushes you, by going after your loved ones, you will have the magical power to fight back without unleashing the demons. You will have other ways to exact revenge, if you like. You won't need demons at all."

Angie blinked a few times at her mentor. Who'd just suggested she "exact revenge" on someone using her magic. Which…went against the "harm no other" basis of all her teachings. Angie opened her mouth, closed it again. Watched Esmerelda raise her brows.

"You don't *need* to seek revenge," Ezzie said. "What I'm saying is, you won't need demons to get revenge. So you won't have to worry about unleashing a plague in your anger.

If you give in to your anger, you can just use ordinary witch magic for that."

More blinking. That was…strangely reassuring. And she was a little appalled by just how reassuring it was.

"I don't want to give in to my anger," Angie said. "But knowing I could control the method I used, if I went crazy, is… Better?" It was better. It shouldn't be better.

Esmerelda gave her a little smile. "Life is full of choices. Better to have more than less. And for you, that means full control." She pursed her lips, tapping the fingers of one hand against the back of her other where they still rested across her stomach. "Unfortunately, I'm not sure you have the time. You won't learn to control the breadth and depth of your powers this afternoon. You have a confrontation waiting for you tonight."

"I can just not go to that meeting. It'll anger everyone, but I can stay away, focus on keeping my family safe…"

That still wouldn't give her much time. A delay of one night, maybe. Hell, Morty might come after her family tonight if Angie didn't show up where he expected her to. She might not gain any reprieve at all.

"We'll see what's happened since yesterday, first," Esmerelda said. "Some exploration at least. The rest is a worry for hours from now."

Angie only wished pushing her worry aside for later were that easy.

CHAPTER SIXTEEN

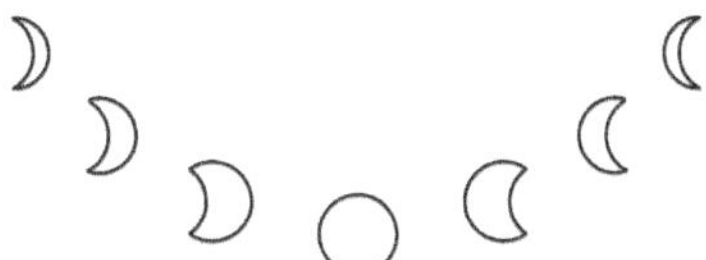

ngie felt delicately along the threads of her web. In the real world, she was aware of sitting inside a protective circle with Esmerelda on the hardwood floor near the sliding glass door at the back of Ezzie's house. She was aware that Sebastian was nearby, guarding them from outside the circle. She was aware of the lingering scent of tea and the earthy smell of Ezzie's garden coming inside on a warm breeze. But that awareness was peripheral to her main focus.

Her web of power.

The purple blending of magics had spread, but not as much as she'd worried earlier that day, after the confrontation with Carmen. She could almost feel her own anger when she allowed herself to delicately touch those threads of melded magic. Anger, but also an absurd amount of power. If she let herself relax, really feel it, it felt like she could do anything with all that magic. Not just open portals to demon realms, but break open reality if she really wanted to.

Which she did *not* want to.

"That's why we're here," Esmerelda's voice filtered through her mind, an echo, a calming breeze that rippled across the delicate lines of Angie's web. "So you can *choose* how to use this power. When to use it."

"It feels like my anger," she murmured, not sure if she was speaking out loud so that Sebastian would hear, but knowing Esmerelda would. "Maybe that's why it reacts when I get mad?"

"Power and anger can feel…similar. But you need to differentiate. It isn't your anger. Your anger is separate. This is just power, to be used as you see fit, at your command. Not your anger's command. It is no more an embodiment of your emotions than either the blue threads or the red thread. It is simply a different…flavor of magic. But your anger will call to the power."

"To the purpling threads? Is that why I keep calling storms?"

"Your anger defaults to the witch skills. That's why the storms. But it will call to any thread. Whichever you give it access to."

"So, is this witch magic or demon witch magic?"

"It's all *you* magic. The full web is yours. What makes you. And if you can embrace it *all*, you can command it all."

She still wasn't sure she wanted to embrace it all. Wasn't sure she wanted anything to do with any of the magic that wasn't blue.

And she supposed that was the problem. The reason she didn't have control over the other parts.

She couldn't ignore them anymore. Especially when she reached for them instinctively when angry or under stress.

So in the safety of Esmerelda's protective circle, she trailed a delicate mental touch along the blue threads, centering herself inside the web. Letting the light of it fill her mind. All of the light. Each color. Then carefully, she passed a touch along the purple line again, while still holding the balance of the blue. The lights swirled in her mind, the threads vibrating. Like a fly had flown near her web. Nothing landing, but the possibility was there.

Potential.

Yes. It felt like potential.

She felt the power swelling through her, surging suddenly, and watched as the light along the purple thread pulsed, in waves, moving toward her where she sat at the center of all that magic. She felt the energy like ocean waves lapping over her feet, her legs. Ebbing and then rushing forward again. Gentle at first. A soft rhythm.

But the longer she sat with her mind touching that power, the stronger those waves got.

"It's part of you, Angie." Esmerelda's voice. Deep. Booming through her mind. "Yours to control."

"It's too much." She wanted to pull away as another wave of power rushed up the threads to hit her harder, the storm of power growing.

"Not too much. You wouldn't have it if it was too much for you to control. That's the trick." This last almost a whisper. "You *can* control it because you would never have *more* than you can control. That's the secret no one says out loud. No witch ever has more power than they are capable of controlling. It's whether they choose to control it or not. Choose to *believe* they can control it."

No. That didn't seem right. There was so *much* here. Too much. More than she'd ever imagined. How could she control this? It was impossible. Not right. Not hers. The blending… That wasn't right.

The waves got stronger, harder.

"Nothing is wrong with your magic," Esmerelda's voice again. A bark this time. Sharp and annoyed. "Not now. Not ever. There is nothing wrong with you. You are not broken. This is as it should be. And you *can* control it."

But it felt so overwhelming. The waves battering her now. The pulses of light hammering into her, stealing her breath, drowning her.

She gasped, in the real world and in this realm of her magic.

Angie had always relied on balance, a core tenant of her magical practice, to sit on top of that needle point and balance all her natures. But now, she felt like she'd been pushed off that center. And she was falling. And the web would shatter and break apart.

Oh. What happened if the web disintegrated, tore to pieces like a real spiderweb?

"Then you will reweave it around you," Esmerelda said, quieter and less annoyed now. "The web is a mental metaphor. Any would do. But this image helps you see all your potential. The threads come from you, though. They *are* you. And if this image pulls apart, you rebuild. From you. The lines reforming. Another beautiful web. Stronger than the last."

Esmerelda's words washed over her even as she watched the threads start to pop and fray. Start to fall apart. And without trying, without thinking, she cast out a new thread. This one pure blue witch magic, straight out into the darkness of the mystical plane. And then another line of blue, catching the frayed pieces, rebuilding the web. She cast a new thread, feeling that power in her chest, flowing from her, stabilizing another section of the web. The threads with melded purple color snapped back into place as another blue thread spun out from her to catch them.

As she respun her web, mentally taking hold of it, of its structure and shape, rebuilding what was falling apart, she realized the pattern of it was changing. Still a circular web, still the cross threads zig-zagging around her over the radiating threads. But the colors…

Still a single red line. Right out from the center of her chest, pulsing with heat. But some of the threads around it were blue again. And the purple threads were in different parts of the web now. Things unto themselves. Not demon witch magic, and not a bleeding of that magic into her ordinary witch magic. Something…separate.

The red thread was its own distinct thing again, too. Solid and firmly a part of the new web. A strong radiating thread holding much of the structure together.

She sucked in a gulp of air, her chest hurting as she

realized she'd been holding her breath. When she released the air slowly, settled herself, she took stalk of the new shape of her web.

"What have I done?" she asked quietly. "What effect will this have?"

"You're in more control of it all now," Esmerelda said with a bit of a snort.

The sound shivered over her web and made Angie smile.

"You'll have to test the effects," her mentor continued. "But as you can see, none of this is outside of your control. The magic is all yours to command. Hiding from it will only cause you pain and grief. When necessary, you simply rebuild the shape, my little spider."

The pet name forced a surprised chuckle from Angie, even as a deep tiredness swept through her.

"You'd better rest now," Esmerelda said. "A cup of tea will help."

"I'm not going to pass out now, am I?"

But she didn't feel that kind of exhaustion. The kind that had taken her under all those months ago when she'd first touched the magic in this web. Now, as she ran mental hands across the threads, all she felt was the subtle vibrations of energy there, the potential. And an ordinary tiredness.

Which was good because she couldn't afford to pass out and sleep for the next twenty hours when Carmen and the others were still out there.

As if the thought of Carmen drew her into Angie's space, an image of the woman appeared, just at the edge of Angie's web, standing inside it, staring at Angie, her little smirk in place. Angie paused to stare back, felt herself frown in the ordinary realm.

The image of Carmen shifted, changed, until she was sitting in the center of a web. The lights around hers fuzzy and indistinct now, but a web. And then shrieks in the distance. Carmen smiling. Opened her mouth.

A flood of blood poured from her, spreading in rivers across her web, moving into Angie. Angie felt the flood like the heat from a lava flow, so intense she gasped. Then pain slammed into her. Another shriek. This one Carmen's. And in the background, just under the pain, Angie heard…

Chittering. Demons chittering.

Someone screamed. The heat intensified. The river of flowing blood filled her mind, wiping out the image of her web. Carmen was still there. But now they stood in a hellscape, a demon realm, surrounded by belching volcanos under a deep red sky. The ground crackled beneath them, cooling glass, a river of lava flowed between them. The taste of sulfur coated her tongue. The stench of burning meat and rotten eggs sizzled inside her nose. Sweat trickled down her cheeks.

Carmen was still bleeding, but this time from her chest. Angie looked down at her hands. Covered in blood.

She looked up again.

And a demon screamed in her face.

CHAPTER SEVENTEEN

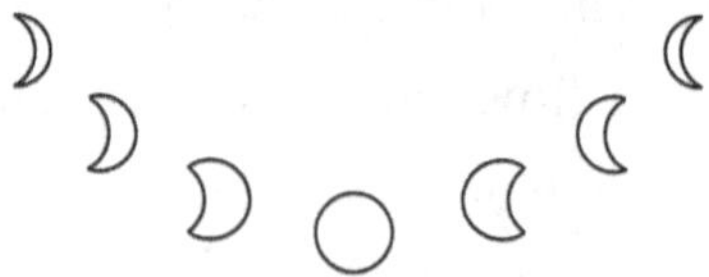

"Angela!"

Esmerelda's voice snapped into the vision, and Angie blinked hard, suddenly back in the real world.

The house. The hardwood floor. The protective circle reinforced with salt. The open sliding glass doors. Esmerelda's garden beyond. A soft warm breeze and the smell of growing things and tea.

Everything normal. The real world. Not a hellscape. Everything calm and peaceful and…

Not a hellscape.

Gasping, Angie folded forward, her hand to her chest where here heart pounded hard enough to hurt.

What the hell was that?

"A vision," Esmerelda said, but also asked.

"I… I don't know. Something similar happened when I first discovered the web of magic, during that supposed clear thinking spell. But… It wasn't this. This felt more…visceral. More real."

"Not your usual kinds of visions either," Esmerelda said.

She was right. Angie's visions weren't usually quite so overwhelming. And they didn't happen while she was sitting still, not touching anything, deep in a magical meditative trance. Her psychic visions required touch. She hadn't been touching anything. At least not in this realm.

She had been touching her web, though.

"A real vision or just…a fear manifest?" She stared at Esmerelda as she asked. There'd been a lot of fear in the vision, but only because it showed her her worst nightmare. Being trapped inside a demon realm, the demons approaching…

She'd been there once. Felt the slice of glass-like rock on her palms as she'd desperately tried to crawl away from those chittering demons. Their claws on her clothes, tugging to get at her skin. The panic…

She swallowed hard as the memory swept through her. Not a vision, that. An actual moment she'd lived through.

A nightmare.

"Ang?" Sebastian's quiet voice from outside the circle.

He'd remained remarkably silent throughout the session. Allowing her the space she needed. She was a little surprised it took him this long to speak.

"I'm okay," she said, still staring at Esmerelda. "At least physically." But mentally she was still in that horror place, trying to claw her way free.

She tried to focus on the details of the vision, around her fear and the memories of that other time. Something in it, something trying to get through to her. "A warning?" she asked Esmerelda.

"Possible. Possible your psyche's fear of all that magic you're learning to control defaulting to one of your worst fears, trying to prevent you from embracing the power."

Angie let out a half-chuckle, though there wasn't much humor in it. "You sound like one of my college professors. Psych one-oh-one."

Esmerelda rolled her eyes. "Are you ready for me to cut the circle?"

Angie dragged in a deep breath and let it out very slowly as she took stock. She felt in control of her magic. She hadn't opened a portal. And there were no demons looming and ready to break loose.

She nodded. "We can cut the circle."

ANGIE WAS SITTING ON THE BACK PORCH, SIPPING TEA AS SHE processed the images she'd seen when her phone dinged with a text. She scrambled for it, worried about her parents.

But the message wasn't from her parents.

Need your help. C

Given what Angie had just experienced in her vision, the terse message from Carmen jumped her pulse rate. She carefully set her tea mug down on the stone-topped table with a gentle click. Her hands were shaking as adrenaline that had just started to ebb ratcheted back up again.

Sebastian reached for her but didn't touch her. After what she'd experienced in the circle, she'd asked him not to for a short time, while she got herself settled. She was grateful he didn't touch her just then either. She wasn't sure her nerves could take it.

"Carmen." She showed him the text.

She'd told him about the images she'd seen, since he hadn't been able to see into the magical workings or even reach them through the protective circle. He, of all people, knew exactly what that image of being trapped in the hellscape would mean to her. He had nightmares of his own from those terrifying moments.

Sebastian had understood instantly why she was so shaken as she stepped out of the circle. He'd understand why she was shaken now, too.

"She can't be trusted," he said, holding Angie's gaze. "You know that."

"I know. And this could mean anything. She could need my help getting directions, for all I know. Or she's trying to make me come to that rendezvous with Morty, knowing I don't intend on showing up."

But Angie's adrenaline didn't calm at the logical explanations. Her heartbeat and the nervous energy running through her didn't slow.

Esmerelda came out of the house, her expression troubled. "You have to go," she said.

She couldn't have any idea what text Angie had gotten, so the fact that she wasn't asking a question, hadn't even really looked at Angie when she spoke, had Angie sitting up straighter. "Esmerelda?"

Her mentor turned her deep brown eyes on Angie and said, "Yes. You need to go. But I need to give you something before you do." She turned and went back into the house.

Angie exchanged a look with Sebastian. Esmerelda wasn't psychic the way Angie was, but she had a sort of instinct that went beyond any psychic skills. Her instincts left no room for interpretation either. If Esmerelda said Angie had to go, she had to go.

While she waited on her teacher, she texted Carmen. *Where are you?*

C: *desert. not sure.*

A: *Morty?*

Carmen didn't answer right away. After a few minutes of no response, Angie cursed under her breath. "She's in the desert somewhere but not sure where. She won't say, or can't say, if this is to do with Morty or not. I'm not sure where to find her. And this feels like a trap because that's what Carmen does when she's trying to push me into something. She forces the issue."

"You think she's lured Morty somewhere other than the place she'd planned to?"

"Possible."

Carmen had wanted them to be in an area surrounded by trees, though. So Morty would think Angie was about to unleash a plague. The desert wasn't a useful location if that was still her game.

"Possible she got the tables turned on her trying to follow

her original plan," Angie said with a frustrated shrug. "Possible this is nothing to do with Morty, and she's got some other nefarious plot. Or she could genuinely be in trouble. And until we find her, there's no way to know. But since Esmerelda thinks I need to go, I need to go."

Sebastian nodded, but he was frowning as he did. And the red in the depths of his dark brown eyes brightened briefly. "We'll go in assuming it's a trap. Doesn't even matter who the trap is for, just that this is some kind of trap. That's best with Carmen."

"Where, though? 'Desert' could be anywhere. Could be anywhere in this part of the country." Though unless someone had teleported her somewhere, Carmen couldn't be more than a few hours outside town. There hadn't been enough time for her to drive to—or be driven to—somewhere too far away.

Angie rang her mother—if she was in the garden, she wouldn't see a text, maybe not for hours—and just as she answered, Esmerelda came back out of the house.

"Mom, just making sure everything is okay there." She frowned a little as Esmerelda placed a box on the table in front of her. A cube a bit larger than her palm, silver and plain, an ordinary cardboard present box with a lid set on top but not tied down with ribbon or tape. The box didn't have any decoration or adornments outside of the pleasant silver color.

"We're all good," her mother said over the phone, pulling Angie's attention. "I talked Christopher into coming over and spending the day helping me move heavy things so dad wouldn't have to. He knows it's an excuse, but he's tolerating my protectiveness. At least for now. How are you? What's happening?"

"I'm good. We're fine. Had a weird session with Esmerelda. I'll tell you about it later." She hesitated, then, "I'm probably not going to be back for a few more hours. Don't worry if you don't hear from me. Okay."

"Of course I'll worry. But do what you have to do. We'll be safe in the house. You won't need to worry about us while you're dealing with whatever it is you have to deal with."

Angie let out a shaky breath. "Thanks," she murmured.

After she got off the phone with her mother, she gestured to the box and asked Esmerelda, "What's this?"

"A guide," Ezzie said.

"Guide?"

Angie lifted the small silver lid, releasing a puff of lemony-pine scent, like copal incense had been burned next to the box before closing it. Inside, on a soft bed of blue silk, sat a silver medallion. At the top of the circular charm, a small hook attacked to a long silver and turquoise chain coiled around the medallion in the box. The silver coin winked in the dappled light as Angie lifted it out to look more closely at the patterns etched into the charm.

On one side of the coin, the image of an owl, sitting on a tree branch, staring straight ahead. Every detail of the feathers, beak, eyes, taloned feet were all exquisitely rendered. Angie ran her finger over the owl, feeling the raised contours of the image. Smooth, but with a few rougher ridges, a texture that made her skin tingle. Or maybe that was some of the magic in the medallion.

She flipped it over to study the back. This side had an elaborate butterfly image etched into the silver, the creature also sitting on a tree branch with its wings raised above its back in a sort of offset V-shape that allowed both inside and outside patterns to be visible. Even with only the silver coloring, the tiny pattern carved into the butterfly wings was stunning and elaborate. So detailed, it looked as if the butterfly could flutter up off the coin at any moment.

Angie looked up at Ezzie. "It's beautiful. What's it for?"

"It will guild you to where you're going. This Carmen woman is dangerous. This could be a trap. But she could also need help. This will take you to her."

"A guide," Angie said, staring down at the medallion again, brushing a finger over the raised image of the owl. "Thank you. I'll return it—"

"No. This is more than just for today," Esmerelda said, wrapping her hand around Angie's free one. "This will guide you on the journey ahead. You have much to navigate. Like the pentagram brings you balance and an awareness of yourself, warding off your fears. This will guide you through the coming days and months. A gift. Freely given."

Angie's heart ached, gratitude and fear in equal measures. "Thank you."

Ezzie smiled and patted her hand. "You're a good woman, Angela Jordan. Remember that when they try to convince you you're not. And remember you are in control of all that power. You wouldn't have it if you couldn't control it."

Angie felt those words in her soul. She hoped, when the time came, she could believe them.

She held the silver medallion on the palm of her hand, lifting it a little closer to her face. It started to vibrate against her palm, the tickling sensation making her gasp. The vibration also created a little edge of…restlessness in her. Like she needed to move.

"How do I direct it?" Angie asked. "I mean, how do I trigger it to guide me to Carmen specifically?"

"Think of the person you wish to find and it will take you there," Esmerelda said. She settled back into her seat, taking a heavy breath, and folding her hands over her stomach.

The signs of exhaustion around her eyes and mouth momentarily distracted Angie. "You're okay? Should I call someone to come…"

Ezzie waved her away. "I'm fine. I need a nap and the sunshine makes me sleepy. You have things to do. While I am old and can nap when I want to."

Angie chuckled, though her worry remained a low-level ache in her gut. But Esmerelda was right. She had to check on whatever it was Carmen was up to. Trap or in trouble, either way, Angie knew she had to go.

She'd only just risen, when Sebastian went suddenly alert, his shoulders straightening, his entire body stilling. She frowned a question at him, but his attention was turned inward. Ah hell, she knew that look.

He was being called to the hunt.

And if he was going to have to track down a demon on the verge of escaping, she was going with him. Carmen would have to take care of herself.

He blinked and looked at her, holding her gaze for a beat, before turning to brush a kiss on Esmerelda's cheek. "Thank you for all you do for her," he said to the older woman.

"Thank you for the kiss, handsome man," Ezzie said with a cheeky grin. She patted his face, then shooed them toward the sliding glass doors. "Go go. I'm tired and you're both too tall to keep looking up at."

Angie kissed her cheek too, then hurried out to the rental car, handing Sebastian the keys without question. He was the one with the instincts guiding him.

She waited until they were buckled in and the car started before she asked, "Where are you being called?"

"I have to go there immediately," he said, without directly answering her question. Which meant he didn't know exactly. He'd have to follow his instincts and just drive and turn as those instincts directed him. "Doesn't feel like there's a lot of time." He frowned. "I'm surprised I haven't been feeling this tug for longer. The breach feels…like it's happening fast."

"Other things on your mind? Or just a rapidly deteriorating situation?"

"Both." He pulled away from Esmerelda's, driving to the nearest highway and heading south. "We could go back to your parents' house first," he said. "You don't have to come with me. Carmen…"

"I'm going with you. Carmen will have to wait."

Still, she lifted the medallion from the box again, holding

it on her palm as she thought of Carmen, just to see what would happen. The vibrating on the palm of her hand buzzed, a tickling that made her want to clench her fist to make it stop. But there was a sort of direction to the buzzing, as if one part of her hand buzzed more than the other. As she moved her hand around, the direction of that buzzing changed. Almost like a strange sort of compass. Only it didn't point north.

It pointed the direction they were driving.

"Oh, oh," she murmured.

"What?"

"I think where you're being called is the place I need to go, too."

"Carmen? She's summoned a demon?"

It was possible. And wouldn't be the first time. Carmen was enthrall to a Molder demon for a time. At least, she'd given the impression of being enthralled to one. Carmen was such a con artist, it was hard to tell what was real and what was part of an act. But she'd seemed to be at the command of the Molder when they'd first met. So it was possible she was enthrall to another. Or maybe she was in touch with the original demon again.

Angie had sent that demon back to its realm through a portal the demon had forced her to open. And Carmen had escaped, even though the demon hunters claimed they'd take care of her. Angie had assumed this whole time that Carmen had broken off contact with the Molder after it was banished, that she'd have had trouble summoning it again, and maybe wouldn't have wanted to since she'd failed it in its aims.

But it was possible Carmen was still enthralled to the Molder and was still summoning it into this realm. Which would be very bad. Sebastian had been called once when the Molder was about to escape Carmen's containment circle. It was terrifyingly possible that if Carmen was summoning it again, it was about to break loose from her control.

Angie shivered despite herself. Thanks to a demon relic, the bone lantern, that demon had been able to occupy Angie's body. Take her over. Send her consciousness sinking down toward a void where she had no control over what she did.

And what the demon had done with her body was open a breach to its realm.

Sebastian had brought her back to herself, sending her some of his own phenomenal will to help her force the Molder back out of her body. Just like when he'd reached into a demon realm for her, he'd managed to drag her back from the brink of disaster.

The nightmares she had about the Molder's possession were as horrible as the ones she had of being trapped in a demon realm. Though, she no longer felt the need to run away from Sebastian because of those nightmares.

If Carmen was summoning the Molder again, though, Angie and Carmen were going to have words.

Except…

Why would Carmen text Angie for help if the Molder was the problem? Why not say she needed Sebastian? She wouldn't have even had to text if she was having trouble with a demon. Carmen knew exactly how to lure Sebastian to a specific location. Knew all it would take was a demon on the verge of escaping to get Sebastian to wherever Carmen wanted him to go. She'd done it before, went so far as to set up a situation where a demon could escape its summoner, knowing that situation would lure Sebastian in.

There was no reason for Carmen to text Angie for help.

Unless, of course, it really was a trap.

"What the hell's going on?" she muttered.

Sebastian didn't comment, but when she glanced at him, his jaw was tight and his hands clenched the steering wheel so that the skin over his knuckles was pulled taunt.

No answers. But a lot of questions.

And a lot of terrifying possibilities.

CHAPTER EIGHTEEN

oth Angie's medallion and Sebastian's instincts led them off the highway, down a side road moving deeper into the high desert. A few turns, a dirt road, and a dead end, and Sebastian's instincts were still tugging him onward. Her little medallion's vibrations increased as they parked the car and got out.

"Out into the middle of the desert, then?" she asked Sebastian and her medallion at the same time. She glanced overhead. The sun was low in the sky, the day still lingeringly warm, but this time of year, once the sun set, the desert got cold. She didn't have a jacket with her. And she only had two plastic bottles of water in her purse.

Not great for a desert hike.

"'Fraid so," Sebastian said. He looked around. "No other cars. Either used an offroad, or hiked in from a different direction."

"Carmen's car was not an offroad." Not that that meant much. But Angie had been expecting to see the little red sportscar here somewhere. What did it mean that it wasn't around? Had they simply come in from a different direction? Or was it something more nefarious.

Sebastian lifted his chin toward the medallion still resting in her open palm. "It's still leading you this way?"

"Still leading me in the same direction. Whatever is calling you is also where Carmen is."

"Then we keep going." He narrowed his eyes at her. "You're still not feeling the call, are you?"

She shook her head. Even after months, even in a new setting, nothing had changed.

She wasn't meant to be a demon hunter.

"We'll worry about that after," he said.

After. Definitely a worry for after. But the high desert at night, without a jacket, with very little water, with a demon about to break loose, and a woman with mysterious plans and nefarious plots possibly in trouble—or leading them into a trap…

Yeah, none of this was good. And Angie was more than a little worried there wouldn't *be* an after.

Not the first time they'd faced the unknown and run into a demon fight together. Not even the first time she'd followed Sebastian to a fight here near her hometown. Still. This time felt different. Scarier. And she couldn't pinpoint why.

Maybe because she knew, deep down, this wasn't an ordinary hunt.

Sebastian rounded the car and lifted her chin until she

was looking him right in the eyes. "I've got you," he said. "We've got this. I won't let anyone hurt you."

"Same," she said. "But I'm going in as a witch. Not a demon hunter. This time… This time, I can't pretend. I have to go in as me."

He brushed his thumb over her jaw. "Then we'll definitely be okay."

The compliment surprised a little smile from her, which made him smile in return. He brushed her lips with a soft kiss, gentle enough to make her sigh. Then they faced the desert, and the pull toward danger.

As they walked, the little medallion started to shiver in her palm, and to her surprise, it rose up over her hand, hovering, leaving the turquoise and silver chain dangling through her fingers, almost like the string of a balloon. The owl face of the coin pointed out toward the desert, moving that direction now, not just vibrating.

"That's…interesting," Sebastian said quietly as they continued to walk, careful over the loose sand and rocks, keeping an eye out for snakes.

"Interesting. Yeah. That's the word."

She wished she'd had more time to ask Esmerelda about the charm. What all it was capable of. How it worked specifically. What spells it was infused with. She hoped they'd survive so she could go back and get all her questions answered.

Her gut tightened, but she kept pace with the medallion, never letting it speed so far ahead that it left its position over her open palm. But she did hold the chain in her fingers, worried the medallion would sprint off before she could stop it if she wasn't careful.

The sun dipped lower in the sky, casting deep shadows across the desert. There were no city lights glowing here, so night settled in deeply around them. Leaving the sage brush and occasional tall cactus as darker shadows against the growing darkness. At one point in her life, she'd have come out to someplace like this on purpose, with her small telescope, just to watched the stars. The darker it got, the brighter the dense line of the Milky Way stretching overhead. A sight she usually loved.

Shame she couldn't just enjoy stargazing with her boyfriend tonight.

As the evening deepened, a faint orange-red glow appeared in the distance. The flickering flames of a campfire.

Not a demon. At least…she didn't think it was. Yet Sebastian had been called here because he'd felt a demon escape was imminent. She'd expected more than a campfire.

They slowed their pace as they neared. The desert was wide open, only the scattered tall cactus to hide behind, and those didn't provide much cover. Whoever was at the campfire would see them coming. There was no way to get around that.

Which, she supposed, was probably the point.

The fact that there were no trees around that she could use to open a realm breach was not lost on her.

She considered asking Sebastian if he could will whoever was ahead not to see them approach. If he was doing that already. But she realized he might not be able to spare the energy, especially if someone with a strong will, like Carmen —or a demon hunter—was out there. Somewhere ahead, even if she couldn't see it yet, there was a demon, inside a circle, on the verge of escape. That was going to take all Sebastian's will.

And besides, whoever had lured them here already knew they were coming.

She did build a shield, though. One she held up in front of her and Sebastian as they approached the campfire. She had to manage the amount of magic she used going into a fight, same as Sebastian had to manage his will, but this part— spells and magic—was the part she was good at. Felt confident in her skills. More confident now that she'd worked a little with Esmerelda and knew a bit more about the stronger power coursing through her.

The shield was strong, a magical barrier to withstand most magic. And though it took longer to create, and took more power, she added the layers for protection against mundane weapons. Carmen wasn't above using a gun when it suited her purpose.

Since they had no idea if Carmen was actually here in trouble, or had simply been the bait, Angie wanted to prepare for any contingency.

She tucked the medallion into the front pocket of her jeans, now that they had a clear destination, and called up the magic, mouthed the words to the shield spells, twined her fingers together in the set patterns she'd spent years mastering and memorizing. But the spell felt somehow… different. Stronger? There was more magic flowing into it.

But that didn't feel draining. The magic was there. Plenty of it. Even for the extra shield layers. And when she was finished, shield firmly gliding a foot in front of her and Sebastian, she realized she didn't feel even a little tired.

Didn't notice the magic used, even though it had felt like she'd used a lot.

She murmured to Sebastian, "Got a shield up. Foot in front of you. I can drop it when you're ready."

"Against magic?"

"And mundane weapons."

"You sure you should have used that much power."

"In this case, yes." She nearly explained all the extra power she felt, all the magic just waiting there for her to tap, but they were too close to the campfire now. And sound traveled in the open desert.

If her enemies didn't realize how much magic she had at her disposal, all the better.

The closer they got to the campfire, the easier it was to see the area directly around it. Two people sat on stools or rocks next to the fire, on the opposite side to Angie and Sebastian's approach. They were within a few hundred yards before Angie could be sure Carmen was one of those two people.

The other was…

Jacob.

The man who'd warned her away from joining the hunters. The man Carmen claimed thought Angie was weakening the hunters by doing what she did.

The one who'd warned Sebastian that Morty was going to kill Angie soon.

He was not who Angie had been expecting. Even a little bit.

Jacob was an Asian-American man of medium height, his black hair cut in a loose style around a handsome, sharp-featured face. Dark eyes, the red glow in their depths easily mistaken for a reflection of the campfire light. The last time she'd seen him was more than six months ago. On the street outside her apartment building. He'd worn a suit then. Tonight, he had on jeans and a light windbreaker that Angie vaguely envied as the temperature was dropping fast now that the sun had set.

He sat beside Carmen, but his attention was on Angie and Sebastian. And he held a handgun in his lap.

The gun was pointed at Carmen.

Angie wasn't a gun person. She didn't know what kind of gun it was. But any kind looked big and ugly and dangerous to her. And this one was no exception, with the firelight glinting off its silver and black surface.

Jacob looked quite comfortable holding the thing.

"This isn't good," Angie whispered, her attention fixed on Jacob and his gun.

"Nope," Sebastian murmured.

"Did you expect him here?" She lowered her voice as much as possible.

"Didn't," Sebastian said.

Good. She wasn't the only one surprised.

She hadn't trusted Jacob from the moment he walked into

her work all those months back. But frankly, she hadn't pegged him as the gun-toting bad guy. She was very glad she'd added that layer against mundane weapons to her shield now, though. A good use of power. In the circumstances.

They stopped a few feet from the fire, staring across the flames at Jacob and Carmen. Outside of changing her thigh-length sweater for a leather jacket, and her bun a bit disheveled now, Carmen looked the same as she had that morning. No obvious injuries that Angie could see. This close, it was obvious she was irritated as all hell—her mouth pinched, her eyes narrowed—but she was sitting perfectly still with her hands in her lap, her gaze on Jacob instead of Angie and Sebastian. And she didn't speak.

Jacob gave them both a nod. "Knew you'd come. You were quicker than I expected. Thought it would take a little longer for you to find us, given…" He gestured with his free hand to all the open desert around them. "Not exactly an easy location to reach." He flicked his gaze to Angie. "I can see why you moved. Dry as hell here. How do you keep your skin from flaking off?"

"I like it. Desert heat is better than New York in August."

"Well, that's true." He smiled a little. As if this was normal small talk and he wasn't holding a gun on someone.

Angie really hated guns.

"What's happening, Jacob?" Sebastian asked. "I was drawn here. What have you done?"

"Stopped her," he said. "She was summoning a demon."

Carmen's mouth tightened and her hands clenched tighter on her knees, but she still didn't comment.

That was enough to set Angie's suspicions on high. She hunted around the fire with her peripheral vision, opening to the lines of magic around them. Looking for signs of a protection or containment circle. They hadn't come up against one. She'd have felt that. But that didn't mean there wasn't one around the fire.

When she didn't sense anything, she frowned a question at Carmen, but the woman was focused on Jacob and his gun.

Something was definitely wrong with this situation.

"If you'd been called to the hunt," Sebastian said, "I wouldn't have been. Why was I called if you're here?"

Yes. That was the problem. Hunters weren't called to the same hunt hardly ever. There just weren't enough of them to go around. Protégés and their mentors hunted together sometimes, even after the protégé was no longer in training. But other than that, hunters weren't called to the same hunt. Not unless there was a minor apocalypse about to happen.

Angie really hoped this wasn't a minor apocalypse situation.

She kept searching the immediate area around the fire with her senses open, looking for signs of magic, of anything they might be missing. With only campfire light and the slash of Milky Way stars overhead, there wasn't enough light to see far beyond the fire. At least not anything physical. But she'd be able to "see" magic.

There didn't seem to be anything there.

"No idea why we were both called," Jacob said. "That's why I had Carmen send the text. How else to get you here?"

"Yeah, that raises more questions than it answers," Angie said. "Why are we here? What's happening, Jacob?"

He settled his attention on her, smiling faintly. "You finally met Morty?"

She nodded. "Still adjusting to a bad guy named Morty," she admitted.

"He doesn't see himself as a bad guy."

"I know. Doesn't make him a good guy."

"He threatened your family."

She noticed the lack of question in that comment. "You knew he would?"

"I know he's ready to push the issue of you losing control. He's convinced it's only a matter of time, so why not sooner rather than later."

"How would you know that?"

Jacob shrugged. "He's not the only one with connections that help him gather information."

"Which is why you went to Sebastian and warned him?" But...why? Jacob sat with a gun pointed at Carmen. Had gotten Carmen to send the text that lured Angie here. Had ensured Sebastian would be here instead of back in New York. Why?

Jacob studied her over the top of the popping, crackling flames. "No one has hurt your family yet."

"No. And they won't."

"Or else?"

"Or else," she said with a nod. "But that will involve my magic. Not a demon plague." She hoped. But Jacob didn't need to know that she was worried.

"There's something wrong with your magic, though," Jacob said quietly. "Isn't there? That's why you're here. Back to training with a witch mentor. Something is wrong with your magic. And it's this woman's fault."

Angie frowned. "No."

She didn't clarify what the no was to. Because frankly, it was Carmen's fault that Angie had broken open these new skills and started the process of blending her magics together. Carmen had set up tests, and pushed Angie, until Angie had been forced to access the demon witch magic. It was thanks to Carmen's machinations that Angie learned she could open a portal without a tree.

And because of all that, there *was* something wrong with Angie's magic. Or at least there was something wrong with her ability to control it. One session with Esmerelda trying to convince her she was in control of all that power, because she wouldn't have it otherwise, was not enough to fix Angie's control issues. She trusted Esmerelda to be right, but she didn't trust herself to wield all that power yet.

None of which she was going to admit to Jacob.

The less he knew—or rather, the less Angie confirmed of his knowledge—the better.

"I'm sorry your magic has been affected by all this," Jacob said. "It's your true calling. You should have been left to it."

"Couldn't agree more," she said, but half distracted as she continued to hunt the immediate area with her magical senses open.

There had to be something here. Sebastian wouldn't have

been called if there wasn't a demon involved. And if Jacob had banished the demon before it escaped, Sebastian wouldn't have continued to feel the call all the way here.

"What will you do?" Jacob asked. "If you lose your magic?"

"Go into private practice as a counselor," she said without missing a beat.

If she'd had no magic, that or astronomy would have been her career choice. It's why she studied psychology in college. And she'd only chosen psychology over astronomy because she wanted to keep astronomy a fun hobby. She'd always felt a need to help others. Psychology felt right. But she much preferred her work using her psychic skills to help people over a more mundane practice with office hours. Switching to a mundane practice wasn't a choice she wanted to make. It was just her backup plan.

Jacob seemed a little startled by her firm and quick answer, but nodded. "You'd have been a good counselor."

Angie did not miss the past tense of that statement. "Why are we here, Jacob?" she asked again. "Why did you have Carmen send me that text?"

Sebastian took a step closer to her, but left room for her to move if she needed to. She sensed his tension in the little gap between their arms. Cold desert air brushed her back, raising goosebumps along her skin, but tension had a trickle of sweat running down her neck. The heat from the crackling fire was a sharp contrast to the cool night. The usually pleasant scent of the wood fire couldn't offset Angie's rising fear.

Something was happening. She was sure of it. Something was going on just beyond her ability to see it.

But what? Why had Jacob lured them here? Why did he have a gun pointed at Carmen? Why was *she* here?

Angie still couldn't see or sense a containment circle. She couldn't spot any magic happening anywhere nearby. But her skin prickled with warning, and anxiety crawled through her stomach.

Carmen flicked a glance at her, her gaze narrowed, but she turned her attention back to Jacob and his gun before Angie could understand what the other woman had been trying to communicate.

Almost unconsciously, Angie folded her hand up to the little dime-sized pentagram pendant dangling from her bracelet. She rubbed the charm between her thumb and forefinger, letting its calming, grounding influence settle her so she could think around the growing worry.

"We aren't…ready for the devastation you'll wreak," Jacob said, sounding resigned. "Morty will push you to give him an excuse to kill you. He'll hurt innocent people, just to force your hand, make you lose control. He wants an excuse to kill you. Wants to *prove* you're a threat, so he'll be vindicated. But he doesn't understand, doesn't realize what your real threat is."

"What is it?" Angie mentally hunted through her battery of spells, looking for something that would help here. Something that could get Jacob to point that gun away from Carmen so they could stop whatever was happening. She had a heat spell… If she could concentrate it on his arm, away from the gun so she didn't accidentally melt the gun and set it off…

But if she caused pain in the arm holding the gun, he might fire on accident.

The other arm then. Something that distracted enough for him to drop the gun…

"You've made the hunters weaker," Jacob said.

A comment that brought her out of her thoughts. Her full attention back onto Jacob's expression.

"We were already having trouble," he continued. "Fewer and fewer humans with the will to overcome a demon. Now, we have you." He smiled faintly. "And you make the hardest parts easy. We let you handle those situations, when demons escape and are on the loose, and we don't have to hone our will to handle those freed demons." He sighed and raised his free hand in a shrug. "That leaves us weak. Without the will to overcome escaped demons. We *rely* on you. Like a crutch. And make ourselves more vulnerable in the process. That can't continue."

Carmen had said that was Jacob's worry, his reason for wanting Angie away from the hunters. But hearing the confirmation from Jacob was…well, not better. None of this was good. But this meant Carmen hadn't lied about everything that morning.

"I tried to stay out," Angie said.

"I know. It's not your fault. They pushed you. Carmen pushed you." He raised the gun and pointed it more solidly at Carmen's chest. Carmen's gaze narrowed and she leaned back just a little.

Angie swallowed the jump of panic that raced through her and returned to directing her heat spell to one part of Jacob's free arm. Silently, she began mouthing the spell, twining her fingers in front of her in as subtle a way as she could manage while holding Jacob's gaze.

"All of them," Jacob continued. "Forcing you into work that was better left to the hunters. Trying to turn you into something you're obviously not."

"Obviously," Angie said, with no little sarcasm. In her mind, she continued to form the words of the spell, directing the pointed heat to a spot high on Jacob's left arm. His gun hand didn't waiver. He was too close to Carmen to miss. But most of his attention remained on Angie's face.

"And now," he continued as if she hadn't spoken, "because of what they've done, they've forced my hand, too. We can't afford to have you around."

"Tell that to the council," she murmured. Most of her concentration on the spell now. So much so, she only barely noticed the brief flare of red in Jacob's brown eyes. But the part of her brain that did register that flare gasped.

He continued to ignore her comments. "But Morty's answer isn't the right answer either. He'll endanger us all. He'll kill innocent people, just to get to you. He wants an excuse to kill you and he wants us all to know he was right about you. He's too power hungry. Too dangerous to be proven right. And you losing control… We can't fix that. Not as we are now. Because of you. Because you've left us without a strong enough will. It's a viscous circle."

"Terrible," she agreed as she formed the final hand

gesture of the spell and paused, waiting for a good moment before murmuring the last word to trigger it.

"Forcing you to lose control will get too many other people killed, and give Morty too much power among the hunters. That weakens us as much as you do."

"So what is it you intend to do about all this?" she said, flicking a glance at Carmen, whose full attention was on Jacob's gun. "You keep telling me all the problems you've got." Most of which she knew already. "What's your solution?" She triggered her spell.

Jacob shifted positions slightly, rolling the arm where she'd directed her spell. But he didn't lower the gun. Carmen moved a little to one side. Jacob adjusted the gun to track her without looking away from Angie.

He didn't react to the heat spot in his left arm again. Damn it. Not strong enough. Angie didn't want to actual burn him. Just distract him into lowering the gun or even dropping it. She started the spell again, making it stronger this time.

"What do *you* want out of this?" Sebastian asked, stepping in to draw Jacob's attention, which let Angie focus on her spell.

Jacob glanced at his fellow hunter. "I want to ensure the future of the demon hunters, to ensure our ability to keep overcoming demons. That's all I want. All any of us want."

"Any of us?" Angie asked, because the comment distracted her.

"I'm not the only one who feels this way," he said.

"You're the only one holding a gun on someone right now."

He smiled. "I notice you didn't call her an innocent someone."

"She's not. She belongs in jail."

Carmen snorted at that, but fell quiet when Jacob's gun lifted a little, aimed at her head now instead of her chest.

Angie went back to her spell, focusing most of her concentration to ensuring the spell was balanced between inflicting a low level of pain and not actually catching Jacob on fire. From her peripheral vision, she could see sweat trickle down the side of Carmen's face. Despite the woman's defiant expression, there was a lot of tension in her hands where they fisted against her thighs.

"Do you want to save her?" Jacob asked turning to look at Carmen, his brows lowered, his expression quizzical.

"Yes." Angie answered without hesitation. She cast her spell again, watching Jacob as he watched Carmen. Waiting.

"Why?" he asked quietly.

"Because I don't want anyone here to die. I'd like us all to walk away."

"A nice dream. Bit like world peace. Won't happen. But it's nice to imagine it could." He rolled his left shoulder again, his jaw tightened. Then he looked back at Angie. "I'm a hunter, Angela. I can will away the pain. You'll have to hit me with something more damaging if you want that to work. And if you hit me with something more damaging, I'm going to shoot her." He lifted his gun just enough to make his meaning clear.

Angie wanted to curse. Fucking demon hunters. She should have known something subtle wouldn't work. Of *course* he willed away the pain. Damn it. She should have realized. Should have considered…

The anger at herself and the situation sent a rush of adrenaline through her system. And that adrenaline triggered the rise of her magic. A rise that sent it bubbling up under her skin, a rapid burst of tingling sensations running through her nerves, making the hair on her arms prickle.

Filling her with…potential.

And for once, she decided not to suppress that potential. Not to tamp down the rising magic. In the distance, the sound of thunder echoed across the open desert. Clouds scuttered across the star-bright night sky.

"Don't hurt her, Jacob," Angie said, her voice deepening with the rise of her magic. "That will not go well for you."

Jacob glanced briefly at the sky, before settling his attention on her again. "What did Morty say? When your power rose like this?"

"Nothing."

"He wasn't nervous?"

"He was. Are you?"

"You're calling a storm," Jacob said. "We're out in the open and there's lightning in the distance. I can will a lot of things. But there is a very basic human instinct to worry about lightning."

"Good instinct."

"Are you worried?"

"Not about lightning."

"There are…other things in the desert."

And there it was, that flare of the red in his eyes. Easier to see in the darkness. Someone who didn't know about hunters might still confuse it for a reflection of the firelight, but Angie knew better.

"What have you done?" she asked.

"Why was I called here?" Sebastian asked right after her.

"She was summoning her former demon master," Jacob said.

Angie flicked a glance at Carmen.

"You know he's lying, right?" Carmen said, trying to sound defiant. But there was a tremor in her voice that belied her attempt. And that wobble was more disconcerting than the thought of Carmen summoning a Molder demon.

Jacob sighed. "I'm afraid there's no other choice now. I can't let you continue to weaken the hunters. And I can't let Morty kill you or involve innocent people like your family. I can't risk Morty being right about you."

"How do you intend on preventing any of that?" Angie asked as the storm rolled in closer. Lightning flickered over the dark desert, lighting up distant patches of sand and cacti. The power under her skin felt like a starburst, waiting to explode. She just needed a focus, an opening.

She didn't want to kill Jacob. But she didn't want Carmen to die either. And Jacob wasn't giving up.

He glanced out at the desert as another lightning strike zinged from the sky, followed by the clap of thunder, closer now.

"Impressive," he murmured. "Can you control it? Or is it controlling you?"

"End this now, Jacob," she said. "I won't ask again."

"You're not asking now. You're threatening."

"You started it." Which was true, so she didn't even feel petty for the childish comeback.

"No. Morty started it. Geraldine started it. The council with their infighting and conflicts started it." Jacob shrugged. "I'm just going to end it."

The words were barely out of his mouth when something behind him flickered.

And then, out of nowhere, like stepping through a rip in reality, a demon appeared just behind Jacob.

Angie didn't step back, but it was a close thing, her reaction only checked because her anger had left less room for fear. But the fear rose fast.

Not a Molder demon. That should have been a relief. It wasn't even a little bit.

This was a Shilv demon. A horrifyingly classical demon with skin a red so dark it was nearly black in the campfire and eyes glowing red in a sharp, pointed face. It had horns on its head and under its chin like a strange sort of goatee. Huge bat wings spread out behind it. Two thick, muscular goat legs covered in red curling fur. And very sharp talons tipped its four hands. A thick tail covered in scales and topped by three long, sharp spikes curved up over the top of its head.

Shilv were intelligent enough to be dangerous, voracious enough to be killing machines, the type of demons that old religions imagined lived only to punish humans. That wasn't why they existed. But that didn't mean they didn't enjoy the torture and fear of humans as they devoured them alive.

All demons were terrifying. All were deadly. Most were horrible and cruel.

A Shilv ranked at the very top of the truly horrible and cruel creatures.

Angie blinked up at the demon as the magic under her skin spiked with the fear-fueled adrenaline that raced into her bloodstream.

The demon smiled.

And a horrifying reality finally sunk in past Angie's fear. A reality that made her heart hammer so hard she was nearly sick.

She hadn't missed the containment circle earlier. There wasn't one.

It wasn't inside a containment circle.

That demon was free.

CHAPTER NINETEEN

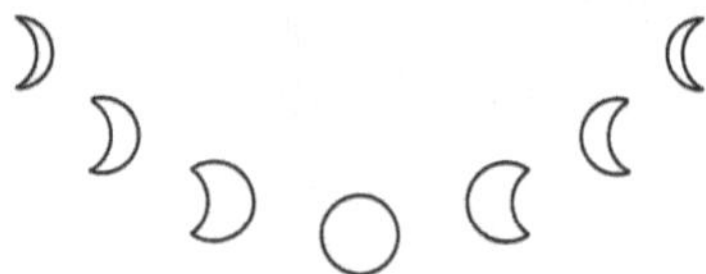

ngie could barely believe what she was seeing. A freed demon. One either Carmen or Jacob had to have released. Out in the middle of the desert when there were no trees around for her to open a realm breach so the hunters could force it back.

In the moments of shock, questions ricocheted through her, so fast, she almost couldn't catch any of them before the next one pinged off the last. But under most of them was the underlying *Why?*

Why the hell was this happening?

Jacob didn't move from his position sitting on a rock across the campfire from them as the demon stepped up behind him. Carmen shifted positions to stare at the demon, but Jacob still had his gun pointed at her. Sebastian took a step forward, moving almost, but not quite, in front of Angie to block her from the demon.

And Angie stood there in shock, as the scent of sulfur blotted out the more pleasant scents of campfire and desert sage, not having enough sense to even move. Too horrified that a demon hunter would free a demon into this world.

Of course, this could be Carmen's doing. But Carmen also knew Angie didn't need trees to return a freed demon. And she knew just exactly how dangerous a freed demon was. Angie doubted Carmen would free a Shilv without a plan. This situation didn't feel like a Carmen plan.

It felt like a Jacob plan. Especially with no trees in the area.

"What...?" She couldn't quite get the question out. What did Jacob expect them to do now? What deal had he made with the demon? Had he made a deal? A *demon hunter* collaborating with a demon was just...appalling.

The approaching storm settled, the lightning no longer flickering in the distance. No thunder sounded. Her shock overwhelmed her anger and the building magic under her skin settled down so that only fear had a place along her nerve endings.

And as that reality sank in, the demon lunged.

Angie gasped, instinctively reaching toward Carmen even as Carmen threw herself sideways, falling off her rock seat and landing dangerously close to the fire. She scrambled from the fire and the demon, crab walking backward to put distance between her and the beast.

But the demon didn't get more than a half foot forward before it froze in place. It stood with his claw-tipped hands outstretched, all four of them reaching for Carmen, snarling but not getting any closer.

Angie glanced at Sebastian. He full attention was on the demon, his focus absolute, his body tall but relaxed, his jaw loose.

The red in his dark brown eyes flared.

The demon snarled at him. Sebastian said, "No." And the demon slid backward the half foot he'd lunged forward.

Jacob smiled. He rested the gun on his thigh, no longer pointing it at Carmen. Which might have been a relief to Angie if she'd been able to think.

She still couldn't gather her braincells enough, though. That ability was returning slowly. Too slowly really. She needed to think. To focus. To do…something.

"I'm glad to see your will is still as strong as ever," Jacob said to Sebastian. "Even though you've worked closest with her." He tilted his head to one side. "Is that because you love her and if your will fails, she might get hurt? That makes sense. A motivating factor the rest of us wouldn't have. Makes sense." The last few comments he said mostly to himself.

"Why?" Angie managed again.

The demon howled, a sound that made her jump. Sebastian said, "No," again and the demon slid another few inches backward.

But to get it back to its realm…how would Sebastian do that? How did Jacob think he should do it? Jacob had set this up so that Angie had no trees to help. She didn't need a tree anymore. But Jacob didn't know that. He expected Sebastian to send the demon back the way hunters did when she wasn't around. Through a challenge.

"A test?" she asked Jacob. "Why? Sebastian isn't the problem here."

Jacob held her gaze, though she had a hard time looking at him and not focusing all her attention on the demon standing a few feet behind him. The months of training with Sebastian had gone out the window in those moments along with her ability to think. She should have been gathering her will, reinforcing his with her own to hold the demon in place.

Or better yet, she should have been gathering her magic and sending the demon back in her own way.

Even as that thought occurred to her, she instinctively reached for her magic, for the spiderweb threads of power that surrounded her in the magical realm. She mentally grabbed at the blue threads first. Avoiding the purple, which she struggled to control, avoiding the red, which she wasn't ready for yet. But the blue was familiar, in her control, and helped settle her. Gave her a place to focus. Returned her ability to think.

She balanced herself in the center of that web of power and let it flow into her, let the comfort and familiarity of it all wash away the shock.

Her shield was still in place. That was something.

And her anger was rising again. Which was probably dangerous. But she didn't care in that moment knowing a *hunter* had freed a demon into this realm.

"What's your deal with the demon?" she asked Jacob and she heard the deepening of her voice.

Jacob's eyes narrowed. "Why do you think I would make a deal with a demon? Go against years of training like that? I'm not her." He gestured at Carmen with the gun. "I didn't turn down the job to seek revenge. I'm not the one who is turning their back on what the hunters are and are supposed to be."

"I didn't free a demon," Carmen hissed, then scrambled back from both demon and fire a little more before climbing to her feet. She looked around the open, dark landscape, as if she might run.

"You won't get far," Jacob said, barely glancing at her. Most of his attention was on Angie. "If the desert doesn't get you, the demon eventually will."

"Not if we send it back," Angie said. This was one of the few times she didn't care if Carmen ran away from a situation. One less person Angie had to worry about falling victim to the demon.

Though, Sebastian did seem to have the creature under control. It snarled and hissed and spit, but it didn't move any closer to anyone. Angie risked a glance at Sebastian. He didn't *look* to be straining, though twin lines of sweat did trickle down his temple and over his jaw. But that was the only outward sign he was exerting himself. And that could have just been the campfire.

Another cold desert wind blew across Angie's face, cooling her own sweat. She let more of the magic fill her, let the familiar tingling sensation push down her fear.

"We?" Jacob said. "You can't send it back." He lifted his

free hand. "No trees. And not enough will to do it, even with Sebastian's help. This has never been your calling."

"No," she agreed. "But I'm not helpless in this world." A reminder to herself as well as him. She was far from helpless. This wasn't the first freed demon she'd faced.

And she didn't need trees anymore.

"This is for him," Jacob said. "If he can send it back, without your help, then there's hope for the rest of us. It's better this way."

Angie stopped listening to Jacob. A surprise test for Sebastian against a freed demon was a shitty move anyway. And she did not intend on standing by and watching Sebastian fight the demon on his own, just because Jacob thought it was a good idea.

She focused fully on her magic, trusting Sebastian to keep the demon controlled. Just as he trusted her to do her part now. Delicately, carefully, she touched a mental hand to one of the threads coursing with purple magic. A rush of power surged into her, jolting her. That melding of her two magics so strong it took her breath.

In the distance, thunder rolled again.

"Do it," Carmen urged.

That she hadn't run away already surprised Angie. She'd have expected Carmen to take her chances with the desert, snakes, and dehydration instead of waiting around to see if Angie and Sebastian survived a freed demon. It might have crossed Angie's mind to worry about that, to worry that Carmen hadn't run, but she didn't have the attention for that sort of analysis.

Most of her attention was on her magic, on the thick surge of power filling her.

Ah, it felt good. Too much and yet…just right. Esmerelda had said she only had what she could control. Could she really control all of this? *All* of it?

So much of it.

She delicately ran her fingers down the purple thread, gasping as another surge of magic slammed into her. Gripping that purpling thread more fully, she concentrated on the lightning in the distance, on *controlling* the strikes, rather than them happening as a reaction to her rising emotions.

Calm this time. Controlled…

Strike.

The thunder boomed moments after she'd dropped the line of lightning into the desert sands.

She smiled.

Around her, she was aware of the others. Her eyes weren't completely closed, though she realized they were half closed as so much of her attention was in the magical realm. But she could see Jacob glancing toward the desert. She was aware of Carmen off to one side. And she was aware of Sebastian, standing right next to her, his will holding the demon in place.

But he wasn't forcing the demon back to its realm on his own. He wasn't challenging the demon to a fight. At least not out loud. They were locked in a pure, push-and-shove match of wills. If he did nothing else but that, he could hold the demon, but he wouldn't be sending it back to its realm.

He was trusting her to do her part. Not wasting will or risking lives to challenge the demon on his own.

Angie intended on earning that trust.

She dropped another lightning bolt into the desert, still more than a mile away. But the exercise made her feel confident she had control over that surge of elemental power.

Then she reached out a mental, metaphysical hand for the red thread. That single line of her demon witch magic imbedded in the rest of her web of power.

She hadn't done this since Carmen had forced her to six months ago. Because being able to scared the shit out of her. And she'd never tried this while also tapping the new blended purple threads. Only with the blue and the single red before this.

But the balance of using all three sources of power felt… right. Angie's witchcraft was all about balance.

And the three had a symmetry that appealed to her on a fundamental level.

That made her feel like she could do this.

She touched the red thread carefully at first, a delicate brush of mental fingers over the power. The feeling shocked another gasp from her. The rush of heat making the hair on her arms lift and her shoulder blades tingle.

Then she gripped the thread.

Her body bowed as all that combined magic slammed into her, hard, stealing her ability to breathe or think. It took precious seconds to regain control. Precious seconds to wrangle the feeling back to something she could work with.

Across the fire, Jacob said something she didn't hear.

Beside her, Sebastian took a step away. One single step. Giving her room to work. Beyond the fire, the demon roared what she thought might be a denial.

The night air cool Angie's cheeks, a contrast she used to keep grounded in the present, even as she opened herself fully to the power surging into her.

Before, she'd opened one portal on accident, and one with so little control she'd had a hard time closing it again.

This time, she focused on control. On only doing this when *she* commanded it. Not when the magic surged.

The demon lurched forward, stopped in its tracks again. Sebastian's deeply voiced, "No," echoed across the campfire. The demon screeched, loud enough to blot out most other noise. Loud enough to make Angie's ears hurt.

"Do it!" Carmen shouted, her voice somehow getting through the noise from the demon.

Angie nodded, though she wasn't sure she did it physically. She was as much in the metaphysical world now as she was in the desert outside Albuquerque. And with the magics surging through her in a swirl of circling power, she watched the threads of her web vibrate, felt the balance of all that magic.

Hers to control. To use.

To open a portal.

A rip in reality opened a few feet from the demon.

Revealing a hellscape beyond.

CHAPTER TWENTY

The sounds of the hellscape washed over Angie first, the hissing and crackling of lava rock cooling. The bright red lines of lava running across the landscape, the deep red sky above a plain of black rock and volcanos and rivers of glowing heat. The scent hit her next, smacking her in the face with the rotten egg stench of sulfur, the underlying metallic flavor like blood. Coating her tongue and making her gag.

But it was the chittering in the distance, that sound of demons moving through the hellscape. Demons that could notice the rip in reality. Demons that would use that rip to escape into this world.

Except she already had a demon in this realm. One that needed to be sent back.

The demon could see the opening into the hellscape and screeched in denial. No one else should be able to see the rip.

At least, when she did this with a tree, no one else saw what she did. But in that office building at Halloween, Carmen seemed able to see the rip, or at least saw the demons trying to break back out of it into this realm. Sebastian hadn't seen it, though. Angie had asked him. So likely Jacob couldn't see it.

But the demon's screams of denial no doubt gave the game away.

"What's happening?" Jacob asked. "What have you done?"

He bolted up from his perch on the rock next to the campfire and spun to face the demon. The first time he'd paid the beast any attention.

"The demon goes back," Angie said, her voice so deep she barely recognized it. "Now."

"Send it through," Carmen shouted, though Angie couldn't see where she was now.

Angie's full focus was on holding open the portal. That hadn't taken effort the last time she'd done this. And it didn't take effort now. The effort would come with closing it. Easier to do with the portals between tree trunks. She just had to turn away—though pulling her gaze from the hellscape wasn't always easy. She only had to look away from this portal, too. But this was more…connected to her. And dragging her gaze away last time had not been easy. At least at first.

She couldn't turn to look at Carmen, though. Or anyone else. She had to focus on keeping the portal open, keeping her gaze on it, so Sebastian could will the demon through.

She'd opened the breach right next to it, and between Sebastian's will and the creature's draw to its realm, it stumbled toward the hellscape, despite its shouts of denial.

"Back to where you came from," she murmured, sending a shove of will toward the demon to aid Sebastian.

But her will wasn't as strong as her magic. Not in the demon hunter sense. The demon resisted her shove, resisted the drag of the hellscape.

And then another push of will. That brush of strength she knew so well. Sebastian's will, so powerful it was a kind of magic all on its own.

"Back, beast." Sebastian. His voice a boom of command echoing around the campfire. So full of his will the feel of it raised goosebumps along Angie's arms.

"What's happening?" Jacob shouted again.

"Shut up and leave them to finish this," Carmen said, her voice hard.

"Impossible." Jacob again, but sounding strangely hoarse.

The demon hit the portal, its arms dragged inside even as it resisted. More screeching. More shouts of denial.

Because Angie's focus was on the demon and the hellscape, she was only vaguely aware of the flash of light to her right. The flickering of firelight over metal.

Carmen shouted a warning.

And the next thing Angie knew, Carmen raced past her, in front of her, nearly drawing her attention from the portal before the demon was through.

The demon pulled its arm back out of the hellscape.

Angie refocused on the breach. More will poured

through her and the demon lurched back into the demon realm, halfway through the portal. The sound of a gunshot. Shouts and curses. Something digging into the dirt behind her.

The demon's scream. The chittering beyond in the hellscape.

The demon's tail lashing out as more of it disappeared into the portal.

A scream.

And to Angie's horror, the demon dragged someone into the hellscape with it just as Sebastian's will forced it all the way through.

Another scream.

Carmen.

The demon had dragged Carmen into the hellscape.

"Hold it open," Sebastian shouted.

And then he was through, too.

He couldn't even see it, but he dove past the barrier. Racing to save Carmen.

Panic and fear swamped Angie. She held the portal open even as her heartbeat hammered. This was her nightmare come to life. Again. Only this time, she wasn't the one dragged into the hellscape. Carmen was there. And now Sebastian. And if she closed the breach, they'd be lost.

The chittering beyond increased, piercing her ears, sending her adrenaline surging. "Hurry, hurry," she muttered under her breath as terror caught her throat, squeezing so tight she could barely breathe.

She could see the approaching demons in the distance

now. The line of darker shadows against the bright red sky, moving toward her break in reality.

And somewhere in there, both Carmen and Sebastian.

Fuck. Fuck. Fuck.

She moved closer to the breach. She wasn't sure why. To keep it open, but also maybe to reach in and help pull them through. She wasn't thinking that clearly.

Sebastian was in there. Every other thought got submerged under that reality. Sebastian was inside the hellscape.

And there were demons approaching.

She neared the breach, the stench of sulfur gagging her. Fear choking her. The sounds of chittering beyond the portal scraped across her nerves until she felt like her skin was being flayed. She heard Sebastian's voice. Then Carmen's scream.

Oh goddess. She had to help. How could she help?

Keep the portal open. Keep it open.

But she couldn't let the other demons overwhelm Sebastian.

The line of the approaching beasts was closer now. The chittering louder.

Angie heard thunder rolling in the distance behind her.

Yes. Lightning. She couldn't call water in the hellscape, but she could call lightning. Had done that before.

She pulled all her focus toward those elemental sparks inside the demon realm. Called the lightning. Held tighter to the threads of her magic.

The flash and sizzle of bright white electricity cut through the red-hued hellscape, slamming into the distant line of approaching demons.

She smiled in satisfaction as the demons screeched and the line of racing beasts scattered and broke apart. She slammed them with lightning again. Lines of flashing brightness in the shadowed realm. A wall of defense, keeping the creatures away from her portal.

Away from Sebastian.

She heard him shout again. Couldn't make out the words.

And then…behind her.

"Close it."

Jacob's voice.

Even over the chittering from beyond the realm breach, she heard the click of the gun behind her.

"Close it," Jacob said again. "Before anything gets out."

"Sebastian and Carmen will be trapped." Her voice as harsh and gravely now. She pulled more of her magic into her, tightened her hold on the threads.

She still had the shield raised, but it wasn't behind her. If Jacob shot her from behind, he'd kill her. That would trap Sebastian and Carmen. Sebastian would die, too.

Intolerable.

Impossible.

"It's too late for them," Jacob said. "Close it. Now. Before it's too late."

She heard the panic in his voice, even though he was trying to hide it. Trying to sound confident and assured. Trying to channel his will.

Yes, she realized. He was trying to will her to close the breach.

And his will had no effect on her. None. She felt it like a distant buzz. The vibration of a fly on her web. Nothing more.

"No," she said. "I won't let them die there."

"You'll kill us all if you don't close the breach. You'll unleash more demons!"

She sent another jagged line of lightning into the approaching beasts. More screams. "I will not."

"I will shoot you to prevent this disaster," Jacob said. "I don't want to. But I will."

"No."

Her shield wasn't in the right place. But all the power pouring through her, into her, all that magic…

She reformed the shield at her back. The words of the spell spilled out of her at the same time as she sent another bolt of lightning into the demons in the hellscape.

Nothing she'd been able to do before. Casting two spells at once. Speaking both at the same time, hand gestures for one completed as the other boomed in the distance. But the magic flowing through her, the *power*… She could do so much more than she'd thought.

She heard the zing and ping of a bullet clicking off something. The sound made her jump despite herself. A part of her hadn't thought he'd really shoot. Not with a fellow hunter still inside the hellscape.

She'd underestimated Jacob's fear.

Another bullet pinged against her shield. And then she

felt a shove. Jacob's will. A push hard enough to move her sideways a step before she braced again.

She did not take her gaze off the portal breach. Sent another rapid, multi-pronged row of lightning slamming into the ground beyond.

Sebastian. He came into view. But where was Carmen?

There. In Angie's peripheral vison. Sebastian had a hand on her arm, pulling her close even as something dragged at her.

She had to help them. Had to help Sebastian.

She took another step closer to the breach. Reached inside. Heat seared her skin.

"Sebastian," she shouted. "Take my hand."

He reached for her. She gripped his palm. The feel of his hand in hers washed relief through her. She tugged.

Then a shove from behind. Hard. Hard enough to make her stumble forward.

And Angie fell through the portal.

Into the hellscape beyond.

CHAPTER TWENTY-ONE

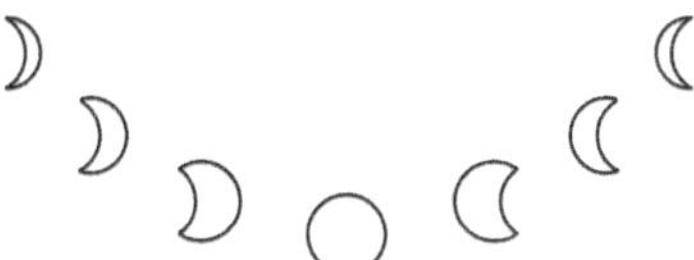

$\mathcal{A}$ngie came up hard against Sebastian as the heat and dryness of the demon realm closed in around her. Sebastian caught her, holding his balance so they didn't both go tumbling to the ground. But that was the only saving grace. Because once Angie got her feet under her and her balance back, the enormity of where she was, what had happened, hit her.

She'd been shoved through the portal. She was *inside* the demon realm.

And she'd looked away from her portal because she'd been shoved forward.

That last sent a jolt of adrenaline through her blood so fast she nearly couldn't breathe. She glanced behind her, hoping she was wrong, hoping the worst hadn't happened.

All she saw was the black rock and lava river expanse of the hellscape spreading out around her. No glimpse into the cold desert she'd just been in. No sign of Jacob. No sign of the human world.

Just crinkling rocks, the stench of sulfur and brimstone.

And the chittering of approaching demons.

This was the nightmare Angie had been running from for two and a half years, the nightmare that haunted her sleep and tortured her memories. The nightmare that had been so overwhelming, she'd tried to leave Sebastian to make it stop.

Not only had the nightmare not stopped. She was once again living it.

She was *in* a demon realm. Only this time, the portal wasn't still open and a few feet away. There was no portal. She was stuck in the hellscape with no exit.

Terror rolled her under. Fast. Hard. Taking all her common sense, all her ability to think. A panicked horror that wrapped a fist around her throat and squeezed. She gasped, panted to drag in air, drowning in her fear. She clung to the only solid thing she could reach.

Sebastian. He was here, too.

He was trapped, too.

She met his gaze. No!

The chittering of approaching demons got louder, sounded closer.

No, no, no, no, no! Sebastian was here. And demons were approaching. And there was no portal.

They were trapped. And demons were closing in on them.

The lightning spell formed in her mind before she even considered what she needed, what she could do. The spell just popped into her mind. And in the metaphysical realm, she grabbed one of the purpling threads of her power. Not a choice. Just the thread she grabbed first.

The words of the spell spilled out of her. She felt the static of electrical energy rising around her. She didn't look away from Sebastian's beloved face as she cast the spell.

In her peripheral vision, she could see the bright, flickering strikes of lightning pummeling the ground around them. Close enough for her to feel the electricity along her skin.

Someone screamed. Not Sebastian, not her. A demon?

She dropped more lightning across the rocky plain, in a circle of destruction. The chittering demons screeched. The boom of the thunder claps shook the ground. Rocks cracked. Someone shouted something.

Angie never took her gaze from Sebastian's. His arms were around her, steadying her. She didn't need to worry about her physical body. He had her. So she moved more fully into the metaphysical realm to grab more of her power, dragging in that raw energy, letting it fill her every cell.

And she used all of it to rain lightning out of the red sky, pummeling the landscape with deadly flashes. She didn't consciously aim. Beyond Sebastian, she didn't care what the lightning hit. Could only think of keeping the demons away from him.

The sounds of thunder booming again and again battered her ears so that it was the only thing she heard.

But she noticed when Sebastian spoke to her, even if she couldn't hear it at first. She watched his mouth move. Knew he was trying to tell her something. He didn't look panicked.

Calm and serious. His arms tightened around her and he said something.

She read the word on his lips. *Enough.*

Another drop of lightning and that word sunk in past her terror.

She blinked, finally looking away from Sebastian. The rain of lightning had left the lava rock landscape dotted with pockets of sizzling holes. Some starting to fill with lava. Others just smoking pock marks in the black-glass ground. Gray dust like ash filtered through the sky, giving the red horizon a sort of orangish glow. The stench of sulfur was nearly overwhelmed by the sharper sting of burnt ozone in her nostrils.

And there were no more demons racing toward them.

Now that she'd stopped dropping lightning, that the thunder had ceased, she recognized there were no more chittering sounds either. Just the silent pop and crinkle of cooling rocks and, in the distance, the deep rumble of a volcano.

She blinked a few more time. Her brain didn't really want to work, didn't want to accept she was standing inside a demon realm. Definitely didn't want to recognize that they were trapped here.

Carmen stumbled up beside them, and it was the first moment since getting shoved into the demon realm that Angie remembered Carmen was here, too. That the entire reason Sebastian had jump into the realm was because Carmen had been dragged in by the Shilv demon.

And that memory made her gasp, look around again.

"It's gone too," Sebastian said quietly, as if reading her mind. "You hit it with the first volley of lightning."

"And almost got me," Carmen said sourly. Then, more grudgingly, "But thank you. That strike saved my life."

Angie nodded. She was glad Carmen was safe. No one, not even the worst of the worst, deserved the sort of death a demon dealt out inside the hellscape. And Carmen wasn't the worst of the worst. Just not a very good person.

"What happened?" Sebastian asked her quietly.

"Jacob tried to shoot me while I was holding the portal open for you."

Sebastian's eyes narrowed dangerously.

"I put a shield in the way," she said, so she could get the rest out before he lost his temper, "but I was distracted with the lightning bolt spells, and he managed to…shove me. I'm not sure with will or physically. Just… I was pushed through the breach right after I grabbed your hand." She looked behind her where she knew there was no portal back. "And because I fell forward…I stopped looking at the breach."

"We're trapped," Carmen said, her voice high and tight. "He trapped us here."

That Carmen, of all people, wasn't blaming Angie for the portal closing—even though Angie considered it her fault—struck Angie as significant. Telling.

And more reassuring than it probably ought to have been.

"Not permanently," Sebastian said, though his gaze was on Angie.

Angie blinked. Her brain was slow, sluggish. Terror and adrenaline had somehow deadened her logic rather than sharpened it. Or maybe that was the expenditure of power she'd released in the moments after landing in the hellscape.

It took her a long few moments to realize what Sebastian was talking about.

Her eyes widened when she finally did. "I can open another one. We aren't trapped. I don't need a tree anymore."

That hadn't been an option the last time she'd been dragged into a hellscape. At least not one she'd been aware of. And the only reason she knew she could do this now was because Carmen had forced her to discover it.

The bitch had saved all their lives by forcing Angie to learn her own powers. That was an irony that did not make Angie happy.

Carmen visibly slumped. And for the first time since Angie had met the woman, Carmen looked shaken. Scared. There was no smirking or bravado or arrogance. Just a terrified woman whose gaze kept darting out over the inky plain, her skin pale, her eyes wide, her jaw tight. Her thick brown hair, which had been up in a bun, was askew and falling over. Her leather jacket had a hole ripped in the sleeve. And, Angie realized belatedly, she was bleeding from a gash on her thigh.

"You're injured," Angie said. "We need to bandage that."

"Get us out of here first," Carmen snapped. "I'll worry about the rest in our realm."

Angie nodded. But when she tried to stand away from Sebastian, her body trembled so hard she dropped back against him again.

And she finally recognized the damage she'd done to herself, accessing and loosing that much magic all at once.

The exhaustion wasn't as bad as the very first time she'd touched the line of her demon witch magic, that first time she'd discovered the spiderweb image of her powers. But this was close. Her whole body felt weak and drained and ready to collapse.

They were inside a demon realm. She couldn't collapse. She had to get them out of here.

"Shit," she muttered.

"How bad is it?" Sebastian said.

That he didn't ask what was wrong, that he understood, filled her with a kind of desperate relief. He knew her so well. And she was grateful for that understanding because she didn't have the energy to explain.

"Not as bad as it's been in the past, but I'm…tired."

An understatement. Her body felt leaden, weighted down with a need to sleep. She blinked hard a few times to stay awake. She didn't *think* she'd pass out. Goddess, she hoped not. But she was absolutely exhausted.

"Get us out of here," Carmen said. "What are you waiting for?"

Angie let out a slow breath, trying not to panic herself. "Not sure I can yet. I need to…rest."

"We don't have time for you to rest," Carmen snapped. "This is a *demon* realm. There are *demons* everywhere. And sexy here—" she jutted her chin at Sebastian, "—can't kill them in this realm any more than he can kill them in ours.

We're trapped. We're vulnerable. And there are *demons* everywhere."

As if she'd summoned them, a sound in the distance, like a raven's caw, pierced the air. Far off, over the top of a belching volcano, dark shadows rose over the lava flows, winged beasts circling the caldera. Angie cursed. More demons. Distant. But these flew. They'd be here soon. As soon as they noticed the humans standing in plain sight in the middle of the crackling black landscape.

"We should hide," she muttered, cursing the weakness swamping her limbs.

Carmen was right. They didn't have time for her to be weak. But she wasn't sure they had a choice. Her body demanded she give it some time to recover. She'd never used that much power before, not all at once. Even if Esmerelda insisted Angie could control that much magic, it didn't mean using it didn't take a toll.

"How long do you need?" Sebastian asked, his attention on the dark shadows circling the top of the distant volcano.

"I don't know. At least a few more minutes." She closed her eyes and tried to touch her spiderweb of power, but the image didn't rise in her mind. Nothing but a black sleepiness. "Shit. I think I'm going to fall asleep."

Panic crept back in again. She wasn't sure she'd ever felt like she *couldn't* access her power. But…it wasn't there for her at the moment. Just the weight of exhaustion pulling her under.

"You can't," Carmen said, her voice squeaking out again. "We have to get out of here. Sleep on the other side."

"I can't access the power I need to get us out yet," Angie said. "I need to recover. At least a little bit." She blinked hard some more, trying to keep herself awake.

"You need food, if you can get anything down," Sebastian said.

Goddess, he knew her so well. The stench of the hellscape made her stomach roll at the thought of food. But she had a few protein bars in the depth of her purse, still hanging at her hip, so she dug them out. There were the two bottles of water at the bottom of her purse, too. She took a huge gulp from one before passing it to Sebastian. He barely took a sip before handing the bottle over to Carmen.

Angie forced down one of the two protein bars, barely tasting the chocolate coating. The bar was half melted—whether from being in the hellscape or from hanging against Angie's hip while she expended all that magic, she wasn't sure—so she left a bunch behind in the wrapper, but that hardly mattered. Getting water and some sustenance in would help her energy return faster.

If she couldn't regain enough energy to access her magic, she wouldn't be able to open a portal. They'd be trapped here indefinitely. And there were demons in the distance. They wouldn't survive long against another swarm.

"This way," Sebastian said, drawing her toward a pile of black rocks she hadn't noticed. "We can stay tucked against the rocks and I'll keep the demons at bay until you've recovered enough." He nodded at Carmen. "We'll deal with your wound while we wait."

Carmen snarled, glanced back at the demons in the

distance, cursed under her breath, and hurried to the pile of rocks. She limped as she went, and continued to swear in Spanish almost exclusively.

Angie wanted to swear again, too. She hated feeling weak and she was terrified she'd burnt something out and they really were trapped here. If she couldn't recover enough to open a portal, they were fucked.

And if she'd somehow managed to burn out her magic…

No. She wouldn't think like that. The magic was still there. She was just exhausted. She'd be fine soon. They'd all be fine soon.

The distant demons let out that cawing sound again, a screech of noise that echoed over the plain.

Mocking Angie's hopes.

CHAPTER TWENTY-TWO

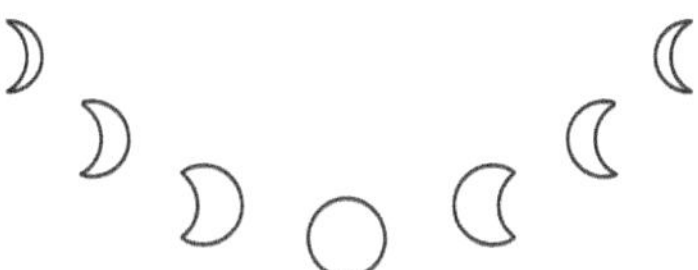

Angie stumbled over the black lava rock to the outcropping of larger boulders, the crinkling as the rocks cooled making it sound like she was walking over glass shards. The visceral memory of her hands scraping over those shards as she tried to escape a hoard of demons descending on her made her want to throw up the protein bar she'd just stuffed down.

She was living in a nightmare. Not dreaming. Actually here inside the hellscape. And there was no open portal with a view home.

The winged beasts in the distance still circled one of the belching volcano tops. No chittering of approaching demons stabbed her ears. And Sebastian's arm was warm and secure around her waist as he half carried her to the sheltering rocks. Even having Carmen here, having another human face, helped ground Angie.

She had to let herself relax and rest. She had to get enough energy back to access her magic again. That was the only way to get them out of here. Even with his impressive will, there was only so many demons Sebastian could hold off on his own. Carmen had enough will to summon demons, to deal with the clever, powerful beasts. And if Jacob's insinuation had been true, Carmen had a will strong enough she could have been a demon hunter at one time. But even that wasn't enough to hold off a hoard of them.

Without her magic, Angie couldn't even call the lightning that had kept the beasts at bay, driving them away so they'd have breathing room.

But how long would it take to replenish her strength? She didn't think they'd have the hours she probably would have taken in her own realm. Hell, she wasn't even sure how time worked here.

Sebastian helped her ease down behind the clump of black rock so she was sitting on the hard, sharp ground. Careful of how she moved so she didn't cut herself on the rocks, she adjusted her purse to one side and contemplated Carmen, who still stood, her gaze scanning the wide, rocky plain.

"I'll check the immediate area," Sebastian said. "I won't go far," he hurried to assure when Angie opened her mouth to protest. "Within shouting distance. I just want to make sure nothing is hiding close by, ready to pounce. I'll be right back."

Angie nodded reluctantly. Watching him walk away was one of the harder moments of her life. She sucked in a breath, snarled at the horrid taste of brimstone on her tongue. Goddess, would she ever get that flavor out of her mouth? She'd rather suck lemons.

Carmen paced behind their rocky cover, her gaze tracking constantly. But blood leaked down her thigh, darkening her jeans, and she limped as she moved.

"Come here," Angie said, her voice harsh and hoarse. "We need to stop the bleeding."

Carmen waved that away, but Angie said, "You want to attract demons with the scent of your blood? I'd rather not add that to our troubles."

Carmen pursed her mouth. Then reluctantly joined Angie, easing down beside her. She hissed as she stretched her leg out in front of her and examined the cut through her torn jeans. "What can you do about it? You aren't a healer."

Angie opened her purse and proceeded to pull out a small portable package of wet wipes, a ziplock baggie with a handful of band aids of various sizes, and a small bottle of hand sanitizer. She set the package of wipes on the ground, but the heat in the rocks made it steam so instead she put everything onto the sturdier leather of her purse.

Carmen scowled at the haul. "You sure you don't have kids?"

"Why?"

"You have the purse of a mother. Prepared with snacks and band aids and all that shit."

"Not a mother," Angie said with a definitive nod. "Never want to be one."

Carmen raised her brows. "That surprises me."

Again, she had to ask, "Why?"

"So prepared." She gestured at the purse. "Got that protective thing going. You look after kids when you're around them."

Angie didn't think it was a very wise idea for Carmen to remind her of how they'd first met, how Carmen had endangered a child and nearly gotten her killed because Carmen wanted to destroy the girl's father. But Carmen ignored Angie's scowl.

"You seem like the type," she finished with a shrug.

Angie flattened her mouth. "I'm not going to get that lecture where you tell me I'm being selfish not having kids, am I? Not from you of all people."

Most people didn't lecture her to her face, at least not the people who mattered to her. The people close to her didn't even question her choices. But there'd been a few people from her father's church who thought a woman's only mission in life was to procreate, and they'd made sure Angie knew their feelings on the topic. In return, Angie had made sure their food tasted funky the rest of the day.

Carmen snorted. "No lectures from me. I never wanted kids either. Prefer being an aunt."

"Are you one?"

"I am. Much better for all involved."

Angie's turn to snort.

"You're an aunt now. How's that?"

That Carmen knew about her family, in any kind of detail, irritated the hell out of Angie. She didn't even know Carmen's real name—a fact Carmen had taunted her with a few months back—and yet Carmen knew about Angie's newborn niece.

"I adore my niece," she admitted, grudgingly giving Carmen a truthful answer. "She's adorable, sweet to hold, and sleeps better than my brother deserves. Though I'm glad she sleeps for my sister-in-law's sake. And I am very content to be the aunt." She frowned, studying Carmen through narrowed eyes. Then let out a huff of a breath. "I really don't like that we have something in common. You know that, right?"

Carmen smiled. Not a smirk this time. A genuine smile. "I know. It's funny actually. How much you hate it. But we're more alike than you'd like to admit, chica."

"No. We are not." She leveled Carmen with a look that put an end to the conversation and handed her the hand sanitizer and the wet wipes. "Clean around the cut. Then dump as much of that sanitizer over it as you can stand. No telling what sort of deadly microbes there are here. It'll sting but there's enough alcohol in it to kill most things."

Carmen hissed, her jaw tight when she dumped the sanitizer onto the jagged cut in her thigh. Her nostrils flared and she cursed through her teeth as she dabbed the viscous goop into her wound.

Angie scanned the area as Carmen worked on bandaging her cut, ripping her jeans further to get at the injury better, using the band aids like butterfly stitches to hold the jagged edges of the cut together as best she could.

"Little surprised you don't have a stitch kit in that bottomless purse," Carmen said through her teeth.

Angie glanced at her. "I do have a small sewing kit. But the thread isn't strong enough. Or sterile."

Carmen's harsh chuckle cut off abruptly on another hiss of pain. "You think sterile matters here? If we can't get out of this place, none of this will matter."

"We'll get out." She had to believe that. She had to or she'd go insane.

As the immediate panic ebbed with her adrenaline, other things crept through her mind to worry her. Like the fact that while she was here, she couldn't get to her parents if Morty showed up. The fact that Jacob might go to Morty to say Angie was dead. Would Morty leave her parents alone then? But what if Jacob didn't go to Morty? What if Morty had no idea where Angie had gone?

Being stuck here meant Angie couldn't help her family. And it meant her family didn't know where she was. If she didn't get back, she doubted Jacob or Morty would tell her parents what had happened to her. They'd be left to wonder, only knowing she'd disappeared.

The thought of them being hurt that way was intolerable.

If survival hadn't been enough motivation in and of itself, worry for her parents would have driven Angie to find a way home.

She scrubbed her hands over her face, then back up through her hair, loose and damp from sweat. Irritated by the curls crackling with static in the dry air, she pulled a hair band out of her purse and knotted her hair into a small bun at the base of her neck. Better not to give the demons something to grab onto anyway.

When she finished, she glanced up to see Carmen staring at her. "What?" she asked, her tone sharp.

Carmen shrugged. Then without looking at Angie, she said, "Thank you. For coming when I texted. I wasn't sure you would."

"I don't like you. That doesn't mean I want you to die."

"I don't want you dead either. You know that, right?"

"I know. You want to use my demon witch skills for some nefarious purpose."

"Maybe," Carmen admitted, with a little shrug. "It's a handy skill."

"I'm not doing anything that would make you happy," Angie said. Then relented a little. "Except for getting us out of this hellscape. I'll do that as soon as I can." It was like pulling teeth to admit this, but she said, "I hate with every fiber of my being the way you went about it, but… I'm glad you forced me into learning about this skill. We'd be dead otherwise."

Carmen gave a little nod that could have meant a lot of things.

They fell silent, scanning the plain as they settled into their uncomfortable truce.

The ground rumbled as one of the distant volcanos erupted and spewed strings of lava into the sky. The glow of the red viscous liquid against the black stone under the red sky left Angie's eyes sore, and she found she had to focus on the rocks to keep from seeing spots.

Slowly, the details of the surrounding landscape penetrated her initial impression. She was surprised to see signs of plant life, scrubby gray grass and twigs, popping up between some of the rocks. And now that she looked more closely, she realized there were some shapes like trees scattered over the plain. Nothing like trees in her realm. These were more like collections of spikes and thick vines twisted together to rise above the ground in the vague shape of a tree. Nothing with a V in it, though. At least that she could see.

Would that even work on this side of reality? Even if there'd been actual trees here, would she be able to use one to open a portal? Learning there were things like trees was a revelation, but that there might be trees she could use…

Easier than trying to open a portal without one. She didn't have to tap the demon witch magic directly. All she had to do was look between the V in a split trunk and the barrier between realities thinned. No effort at all. In fact, when she was exhausted, she was even more likely to accidentally open a breach because she wasn't as cautious in those moments.

What would happen if she could do that? Would that portal bring them back out into the desert? Somewhere else in the human world? Out into a space without any trees, the way breaches opened through trees on her side spilled out into open air on this side?

All things she'd never considered before, or even wanted to consider. Being nearly trapped in a demon realm once had been bad enough. She'd hoped to avoid doing this again. And honestly, she'd assumed if she'd somehow landed back into a demon realm a second time, she wouldn't live long enough to give the landscape much thought.

Sebastian returned as she stared at one of the spike and vine twists that bore a passing resemblance to a tree.

"No demons nearby," he said. He nodded at Carmen were she still sat on the ground near Angie. "Did you get the bleeding stopped?"

"Mostly. Best I can manage for now. Your girlfriend didn't have any convenient butterfly stitches in her purse."

Angie snorted, almost a laugh, and the sound drew Sebastian's questioning gaze. She shook her head slightly, letting him know she'd explain later. "Did you see anything else?" she asked, leaning against the rocks at her back, carefully, so she could look up at him more easily.

"Lot of rocks and lava and a few tiny creatures that scattered when I got too close. Think they're afraid of me."

"Well, you are the alien here."

He chuckled faintly. "In a land full of predators who eat whatever they come across, I suspect the little things scatter from anything larger than a pebble."

"Good instinct here," Carmen muttered.

"How are you feeling?" Sebastian asked Angie, his voice low.

"Still tired. The protein bar settled, though. The water helped. But I'm still dopy, like I could sleep." She didn't dare. Not here. This wasn't the sort of place a human took a nap if she expected to wake up from that nap. But her body would have appreciated some sleep. "Sitting is good. I should be good enough soon." She hoped.

Recovering from burning too hard too fast magically-speaking had usually taken her some time in the past, though.

She might have access to more power than she'd ever thought possible, but she also hadn't practiced with it enough yet. And she was, frankly, still a little scared of what she'd been able to do earlier.

In the middle of this mess, being afraid of her own powers wasn't a good place to be. She had to figure out how to embrace them all.

If she could access them again.

She knew she hadn't burned out complete, in the logical part of her brain. But she was trapped in a demon realm. Their only way home her ability to open a portal. And if that magic was gone…

No. Thinking about it didn't help her recover. She would recover. "Maybe some more water," she muttered and pulled out her second bottle.

"How much shit do you have in that bag?" Carmen said with a head shake. "It's like a bottomless pit. A magical bag with a hole back to your apartment that you're just reaching through to get shit."

"Wouldn't that be the perfect purse," Angie said on a sigh. She'd love something like that. Unfortunately, her purse was no such thing. Just an ordinary bag. Fully stocked. "I like to be prepared."

"With water and snacks and bandages?"

She shrugged. "Never know." She gulped down a third of the bottle then passed it to Sebastian. He only took a few sips before handing the bottle to Carmen.

Angie scowled at him. "You have to drink more than a few sips. We need the full strength of your will here, too."

"I'm fine, love. I promise." He leaned in to brush a kiss over her head.

Carmen rolled her eyes as she drank half of what was left in the bottle. Then she handed the rest to Angie. "Drink the rest. Your portal is our only hope."

Angie finished the water, let out a long sigh, and leaned her head against the rocks at her back. They were warm but not as hot as the ground under her ass, and sharp, but not cutting her through her clothes or snagging her hair. She closed her eyes and listened to the crinkling of rock cooling over lava and the distant sounds of demons.

Goddess, how could she even close her eyes? She wasn't sure. She was so overwhelmed being here, so exhausted by the magic she'd burned through, it was like she'd resigned herself to this realm already. Even the terror was weirdly banked now, just a sort of low-level tightness in her gut, but not enough to keep her hypervigilant anymore.

They were in really big trouble if she'd exhausted even her fear of the hellscape.

No immediate chittering of approaching demons, though. The winged beasts seemed to be content circling the volcano caldera. She could take a moment.

Just a moment…

She blinked her eyes open when she felt a gentle touch on her shoulder. She expected it to be Sebastian, but he was leaning against their rocky cover, his back to her as he scanned their surroundings. The touch was Carmen. And she pulled her hand back the instant Angie's eyes snapped open.

"You fell asleep," Carmen said. "Hope that helped. How do you feel?"

"I fell asleep?" Wow. That was…not something she'd thought she was capable of. Not here. She considered how she felt, though. Not like she'd slept much. But…a little less exhausted. The nap seemed to have taken the edge off. "Still groggy but better."

"Can you access your power?" Carmen asked quietly, her voice low, her eyes wide.

"Not sure yet." Angie glanced at Sebastian. He was looking down at her, his eyes narrowed, the red glow in the depths of the brown brighter here. "I'm afraid to look," she admitted to him, ignoring Carmen.

"We'll figure this out, one way or the other," he said. "It'll be okay."

She wanted to believe him badly enough she didn't brush aside the reassurances. Instead, she sat up so she was no longer leaning against the rock at her back, and studied the plain stretching out around her. The rocky expanse, the red sky, the belching volcanos and streams and rivers of lava. That scrubby spike tree that looked more like twisted vines trying to imitate a tree.

"If this fails," she said quietly, "we need to hunt for more of those trees." She nodded to the weird spiked thing. "If there's one with the right shape… I might not even need to touch the magic directly. The portal should just open."

Just needed the right shape. She'd gone her entire life not having direct access to the demon witch magic and still opened portals easily—too easily. So easily she had to be very careful where she looked even walking past sidewalk trees in the middle of New York City. All they'd have to do is find a tree with the right shape.

She didn't let herself consider that the vines might not *count* as trees to her magic. Or that trees inside the demon realm might not serve the same purpose for her magic. This wasn't her place, her environment, her realm. She really had no idea how her magic would work here.

But she had to hold on to the hope, to the options, because if she started to believe they were really trapped here, she'd lose her ability to function.

And then the demons would take them.

CHAPTER TWENTY-THREE

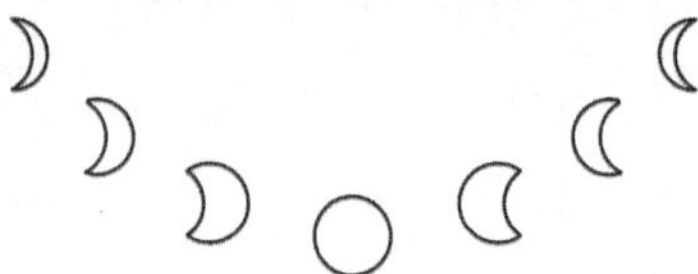

Bracing herself for the worst, Angie settled herself on the hot ground, crossing her legs and sitting up straight, taking up the same posture she used when in front of her altar because she thought any added reminder of who and what she was would help.

Sebastian remained in his position leaning around the rocky outcropping, so he could guard their backs and watch for approaching demons. But Angie could feel his gaze brushing over her regularly. She didn't turn to look at him again, because she wanted to focus. But his presence was reassuring and helped her settle further.

Carmen scooted away, too, giving Angie room, though Angie didn't really need the space for what she was about to do. Still, it was nice not having to worry about Carmen distracting her.

With her heart pounding hard, Angie took in a few deep

breaths, and finally closed her eyes, opening her senses, her inner mind's eye, to her magic.

Faint. The web was very faint. Blue lines so translucent they were difficult to see. The even fainter purple. And when she looked down at her chest…

The red thread of her demon witch magic.

That one was brighter than all the others, as if being in the demon realm had strengthened it. And, she realized suddenly, there were two lines now. Distinctly red. Not the blending of that red with her witch magic. Two strong red lines radiating out into the rest of her very dim web.

She brushed mental fingers over the threads, gasped at the vibration in her chest. It was hot. Sharp. She almost felt cut by the threads, like so much cheese. She glanced at her hands, or what passed as her hands in the metaphysical plane. Drips of blood landed in her lap.

That… That wasn't good.

A memory rose, so fast, she didn't have time to slow or stop it. Of Carmen sitting in the middle of a web, blood pouring from her.

Angie wanted to open her eyes, to flinch away from the memory of that vision. Instead, she allowed herself to remember, to *see* the vision again. Carmen, sitting in the middle of a web of blue, blood pour from her chest, her eyes. Her mouth open but no sound came out. Angie felt her physical body wince.

This wasn't a real vision, she reminded herself. Not her kind of psychic visions. She wasn't touching Carmen. She wasn't touching anything but her own knees and the rocky ground. This was a memory. Not a vision.

A memory of a vision. Still. Just a memory.

But what was her memory trying to tell her? What had the vision been trying to tell her? It had risen twice now. Once just that afternoon. In hindsight, the vision from the afternoon could have been warning of this moment, of being trapped in the hellscape. But that didn't explain why her memory pulled up the vision again, when they were already here. And it didn't explain the first vision.

No clarity came, just the memory, and another hot flush of not-quite pain as she touched the red threads again. Two now. What did that mean? Why the change?

Even as she wondered that, she saw a third thread spear out from her chest. Not an old thread turned red. Not the mix of demon witch and witch magic blending. An entirely new thread, as if she was weaving that new thread into the web even as she sat in the middle of the demon realm.

There was…power around her, she realized. Power she had access too. Power that resonated with her demon witch power. Out beyond her web, like a red mist. Did she dare touch that mist?

Most demons didn't have what humans thought of as magic, but they did have an energy, a power, that was similar enough as to make no difference. That power was, for all intents and purposes, magic. And some of them could wield a great deal of it.

The way demons used it was more like the way wizard magic worked. All brute force, tossing around fire and bolts of energy and pure, unadulterated power. Only the most powerful of demons used that sort of demon magic. Many of them were just physically vicious and violent, their terror, their deadliness arising from their delight in physically tearing into other beings.

But there were demons powerful enough to use this demonic version of magic. And for the first time, Angie saw that energy. She didn't see it surrounding other demons. She'd never seen it through the portals she'd opened. She hadn't seen it the one other time she'd been inside a demon realm. In fact, she'd never even looked, hadn't thought to look.

Had had no idea there was anything to see.

Now, as she tried to access her own magic, she could *see* all the other power around her. And, to her horrified shock, the demon witch magic reached out to it. Connected with it.

Used it to weave more of that magic into her web.

The instant she realized what her body was doing without her conscious thought, she stopped. She pulled back from that circling mist, from the way she was weaving even more of it into her own magic. It wasn't overwhelming the blue. In fact, as she watched the witch magic deepened, strengthened —and wasn't that a relief!—but in addition to that, she'd pulled in even more of the surrounding power. She'd *added* to her own power with demon magic.

That wasn't good.

But it meant she'd probably be able to open a portal.

Okay. Deal with the repercussions of accidentally absorbing demon magic later. The feel of her power, her strength rose with every passing second. She brushed the new threads again. A shock of energy went through her. Three full threads of demon magic.

She looked at her metaphysical hands. Her blood had dripped into the red mist around the outside of the web, bright red dots inside the fog. In the distance, she thought she heard a laugh. Then a scream.

And the scream forced her eyes open. She blinked hard, as the real world rushed over the top of the metaphysical one, like waking suddenly from a nightmare, with the nightmare still an afterimage in her eyes as she blinked.

Her reality was still a nightmare.

But Sebastian and Carmen were there, and neither was screaming. And no demons seemed to be rushing down on them. So…perspective.

She wanted to laugh but knew the rusty harsh sound clawing at her throat would worry Sebastian and he had enough to worry about.

"I can access the magic again," she said. She met his gaze. Held it. Trying to tell him there was more without saying anything aloud. She didn't want to talk about the demon power, the added energy she'd woven into her own magic without meaning to, in front of Carmen. Who would no doubt find a way to use that power for her own ends.

Sebastian's gaze narrowed slightly, but that was his only outward reaction to her stare. "Do you think you can open a portal now?" he asked quietly.

She rolled her lips into her mouth, let them out with a popping sound. "I think so."

She hoped so. She still wasn't sure what accessing the magic would do to her. That blood she'd seen on her hands in the metaphysical realm had to have meant something. She glanced down at her hands, resting in her lap. Her fingers felt...raw. Like she really had cut them. But there was no blood.

Good thing since blood attracted demons.

She looked at Carmen, at her leg. "How's your wound?"

"Be better when I can get back to our realm and find a doctor," she said. "Why are you stalling?"

"Scared it won't work," she admitted.

Given where they were, admitting that fear out loud didn't bother her, even in front of Carmen. Some things were just too self-evident to deny.

She pushed to her feet, using the rock to balance herself, and staying low behind the cover as best she could. Sebastian stepped closer, his hands hovering out as if he'd catch her if she fell. Which she appreciated since she wobbled. Her limbs still felt weak and tired. But the magic was there. She could feel it again.

She could also feel that demon mist, now, the energy surrounding her. And that she could access it still. That it was hers to use. The power there, all that strength was...terrifying in how tempting it was.

Was that the real danger for a demon witch? Learning that all *this* was within their reach?

Had other demon witches ever learned about this?

Shoving aside the concerns and questions, she focused inward on her own magic. She wanted to concentrate on the witch side of her power, to reassure herself she was still *her*. But that wasn't the magic that would get them out of here.

In the distance, the flying demons cawed. And the sound seemed louder now, echoing across the open plain. She glanced over the rocks. They were still flying over the caldera, but in the glow from lines of lava, darker shadows moved across the landscape now. A line of them. And at the edge of her hearing…

The chittering sound.

She hated those chittering demons. Hated that sound to the depth of her soul.

"Have they seen us yet?" she whispered to Sebastian.

"They've been passing for a few minutes," he murmured back. "Not long. Haven't see us yet. Won't be long before they catch our scent, though."

"Open the portal," Carmen said where she'd stepped up on the other side of Angie. She was also looking over the rocks at the passing line of demons in the distance.

"Yeah." Angie nodded. "Yeah." She had to try. She could deal with any damage she caused herself on the other side.

She turned away from the impending demon threat, though that took an act of will and made the hairs on her neck prickle, and let her eyes drift half-closed. She took hold of her witch magic to balance herself. And a surge of power flowed through her limbs.

Ah, that felt good. Right.

She allowed herself to grab a thread of mixed power next, knowing the strength in that would help. And here, more balance. The two magics propped her up and gave her strength. Coursing through her body, filling her exhausted limbs.

A faint glow rose around her. A pale bluish-purple color. Surrounding her. Faint but still bright in the weird light from the demon realm's red sky.

"Ang?" Sebastian asked.

"Yup. See it. Not sure why it's happening again." The same thing had happened in the pharmacy parking lot that morning, but Sebastian had been able to keep others from seeing it there. They couldn't afford for him to use his will on that here, though. "The demons?"

"Don't seem to have noticed," he said, his voice tight.

"Yet," Carmen added, panic creeping into her own voice. "Hurry."

Angie finally let a metaphysical hand hover over one of the three red threads, the original one that had always been a part of her—though how she was certain that was her original power, she didn't know. Instinct. So much of her magic required instinct. The demon witch power, more than any other. She hesitated a beat, then allowed herself to grab onto that thread.

The surge of strength and energy made her body bow, hit her like a hurricane-force wind. She fell back against the rocks and Sebastian reached for her. She shook him off. He didn't touch her, and she was thankful he understood her well enough to know how bad that would have been in the moment.

She focused all that pummeling power, wrestling it back under control. Esmerelda said she could, so she could. And she did. Though it took effort. The magic, all three threads of it, felt both wild, like they could swirl into a storm without much effort, and also balanced. All of her, all at once.

And so fucking strong now. So…powerful.

Letting that sense of strength fill her, she turned her attention to opening a portal. The portal hadn't opened automatically, the instant she'd touched the demon witch magic. Her training with Esmerelda had at least given her that much control. At least, she hoped that was what was happening here. She hoped she could still open a portal.

She put effort into calling it, into thinning that barrier between realms. Into breaching that normally impenetrable wall between realities.

A swirl of energy in front of her, circling open…

Revealing the desert beyond.

CHAPTER TWENTY-FOUR

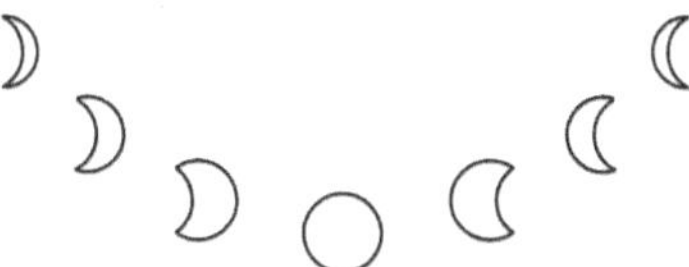

*A*ngie released a slow breath and her shoulders sagged as she looked on her realm again. She'd done it. They could get out. They weren't trapped forever.

The portal looked different from this side. A swirl of circular energy opening before her, surrounded by red. Not like the rips she opened from the other side, or even what happened when she looked through a tree. The *feel* of the portal was different from this side as well. This had felt more…controlled, maybe? She'd had to purposely call it. But not like in her own realm. This was more like… Like opening a door. Required effort, but a low level of effort that felt easy and natural. The door wasn't too heavy for her.

The difference was enough to momentarily distract her from the escape hatch she'd just given them.

It was not enough to distract Carmen. "Let's get out of here," she said, and more frantically. "Now, now, now!"

The terror in Carmen's voice brought Angie back to her surroundings. To the sounds of that nails-on-a-chalkboard chittering.

Getting closer.

The demons were coming. Shit.

"You can see the portal?" she yelled at Carmen.

"Yes."

"Then what are you waiting for? Go!"

Carmen stopped hesitating. But as she neared the portal, something swooped down out of the sky, a black shadow their only warning.

Carmen screamed. A cawing sound.

And Carmen lurched up into the air, demon claws on her shoulders.

Angie felt Sebastian's will flow out of him like a rough wind, snagging at the demon's wings. "Release her," he said, his voice deep, the command a physical thing.

The flying demon cawed a protest. It flapped its huge leathery wings, the stench of sulfur intensified in the wind. Its glowing red eyes were the only clearly visible thing inside a mostly shadowed form. Those eyes flared.

"Release her," Sebastian commanded again. His will so strong Angie found herself opening her own hands.

The demon cawed again in protest. And then it released Carmen.

To fall fifteen feet to the hard glass-rock ground.

Without thinking, in a sort of panic, Angie reached out to Carmen, and that sent out a flash of power that…caught her.

A cloud of oddly colored magic surrounded Carmen, slowed her descent. Until she settled safely on the ground.

Carmen gave her a look. Angie, her gaze still mostly on the portal she'd opened, shrugged. She had no idea either. But they didn't have time to figure it out.

Another winged demon swooped down over them. This time, Carmen stretched her hand out and swiped it to one side in a rough gesture. The demon jumped sideways and slammed into another winged demon, the two tumbling away.

Angie had nearly forgotten about Carmen's telekinetic ability. But that was handy.

A shadow passed directly over her, pulling her gaze up. Overhead, a half dozen winged demons circled. Within their shadowy forms she caught sight of long talons on hands and legs, a long tail, and the glowing red eyes in the center of horned heads. Their cawing echoed over the plain, a screech of sound that raked across Angie's nerves.

The sound of chittering from the other demons was right on top of them now, too. She didn't want to turn and see what was approaching.

"I've got these," Sebastian said, standing close to her shoulder, facing the plain at her back.

"Your sword?" He had a flaming sword he often pulled out of nowhere to use in freed demon fights. He'd never told her the story of the sword, how he got it, where it went when he wasn't using it, though she'd asked once. But it had to do with how he'd become a demon hunter, and he didn't talk about that day. So she hadn't asked again.

That sword would be very handy now, though.

"Can't use it here," he said, as the wind of his will blew past.

Angie didn't have time to ask him why.

Carmen flung another two winged demons into each other. "The portal!"

Carmen's shout reminded Angie she'd looked away from their escape hatch. Shit. She looked back.

Only to realize it hadn't closed.

A quick inner look confirmed she was still holding onto all the magics she needed to keep it open. But apparently, it didn't require her gaze from this side anymore?

"Go," she shouted to Carmen.

"I can't without bringing these bastards with me."

Even as she said that, Angie watched one of the winged demons arrowing toward the portal. She didn't have Carmen's telekinetic powers to throw it away. She didn't have the same will Sebastian was using to hold back a hoard of chittering demons.

But she did have all that demon magic at her disposal.

She didn't really think that thought consciously. She just felt herself reach out to the surrounding mist, and then she flung her hand up at the demon heading toward the opening to her realm.

A bolt of fire shot from her palm, slammed into the demon, and sent it tumbling backward, away from the portal, into two of its companions.

Angie blinked. That was…more like something a wizard did. Witches couldn't use energy bolts or wizard bolts, couldn't shoot pure energy from their palms like that. But even if she could, what she'd just used didn't look like a wizard bolt. It looked like the kind of thing a demon flung around. A stream of fire.

And it hadn't worked like her magic. No spells. No elaborate hand gestures. Nothing that was familiar. Just brute strength and a focused power.

Yet it still felt like *her* somehow.

She shot the same burst of fire at another demon as it swooped down toward her. The demon screamed. Spiraled away from them. And to Angie's utter surprise…

Exploded. Shattered into a rain of demon parts.

"Did you just…?" Sebastian muttered.

"You just…" Carmen gasped.

"I couldn't have," Angie said, her eyes wide. Humans couldn't kill demons. That was impossible. Demons could be banished, driven away, wounded by humans. But not killed. Only a demon could kill another demon.

And maybe demon magic could kill a demon…?

One more thing to worry about when they were safe. Carmen flung another demon into two swooping down toward her. The chittering at Angie's back had her hairs standing up. And the portal was still open even though she wasn't staring at it.

Angie flung more of her magic fire out of her palm, into the swirl of cawing demons overhead. The blast sent them scattering higher. Leaving the way to the portal temporarily open.

"Get through," she shouted at Carmen as she called down

the lightning again. The power that felt familiar and witchy. She zinged the flashes of energy behind her, dragging down a series of bolts to land into the chittering demons.

More screaming.

"Hurry!" Angie yelled at Carmen.

She refocused her gaze on the portal to ensure it didn't suddenly close. Taking her attention away from the surrounding demons took effort, but the last thing she wanted was for that portal to close suddenly just as Carmen tried to go through.

Carmen raced through the breach without looking back.

Angie let out a breath. "Now you," she said to Sebastian, still concentrating on holding the portal open. She still felt like she was exerting the same level of effort it took to hold open a door. Not much, but necessary so the door didn't close in their faces.

How the hell had she held it open without looking at it? How was that possible?

"Together." Sebastian stepped up closer beside her, still facing the chittering demons at their backs. The force of his will like a wall she could feel behind her.

She wanted him through first, to make sure he was safe, but she also knew he wouldn't leave her with her back to all those demons and no one to guard her.

She grabbed his hand. "Together," she said and walked them to the opening.

Only a few steps. But the sound of demons behind them, above them. The screams and chittering. The caw of the winged demons getting closer again. It took all Angie's focus not to look behind her to see how many there were closing in on them.

At the portal's edge, she heard something else, something new. A sort of rattle snake shaking, a hiss, a chittering entirely too close to her back.

"I've got them," Sebastian said, as if sensing her hesitance. "Step us through. I'll keep them back."

Trusting his will more than she trusted her own magic at that moment, she pulled him through the portal. Keeping her gaze on the desert ahead.

The cool rush of dry air made her gasp. Relief washed through her. The scents of sagebrush and creosote, a lingering campfire. The dark night sky with the thick band of Milky Way stars arching overhead.

Sebastian's hand in hers. Safely standing on the cool sand. No more crinkling black rock or red sky.

They were home.

She could still hear the chittering behind her, though. The hiss and screams from demons. She looked over her shoulder.

The portal was still open.

"Fuck." She faced it again.

She'd expected it to close automatically on this side, once she was through and no longer staring at it, the way it had closed when she'd been pushed into the demon realm. She expected it to work the way it always worked when she accessed it from this side.

But she hadn't opened it from this side, had she? She'd opened it inside the demon realm. Been able to look away while there and the portal hadn't closed.

Apparently, it didn't close automatically on this side either.

There was a pile of demons at the entrance, pushing against an invisible barrier. Not her portal's barrier. Sebastian's will. His hand on hers was clenched tight. She didn't want to distract him by pulling her hand free.

But she had to close the portal.

How, though? If removing her gaze didn't do it, how was she supposed to get it shut?

She'd had to put a little effort into opening this one, even after tapping the magic. She'd had to consciously swing open the door between worlds.

Which meant she had to swing the door shut again, too. On purpose.

She quickly turned to the metaphysical plane and realized she was still holding onto all the different threads of magic, all the different energies making up her powers now. She eased her hold on the red thread and, like calling the portal to open, she mentally commanded it to close.

The opening swirled and shrank.

The demons beyond screamed. A hissing that raised the hairs on her arms.

"Keep them back just a moment longer," she said, her voice deep and scratchy.

She eased her hold on her other magics, though the power continued to flow through her, feeding her with a strength she'd never experienced before. It felt like her, but her so much stronger.

And so much more controlled.

Without spell or hand gesture, with just a mental command, she closed the breach. Watching the circular opening whirl smaller and smaller. Watching the hellscape, and the screeching demons vanish.

Until the portal collapsed, winking out of existence.

Leaving only the vast expanse of desert and rocky hills stretching out in front of her.

CHAPTER TWENTY-FIVE

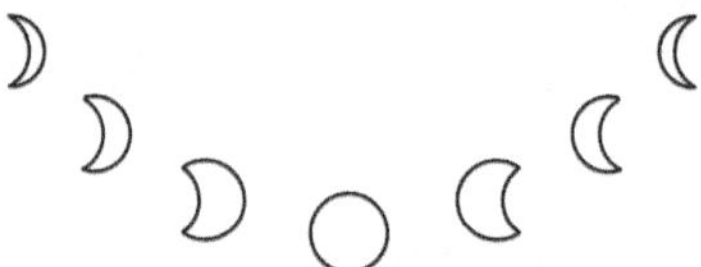

Angie finally blinked as the reality of what she'd done, what she could do, settled over her. The desert air brushed her hair across her forehead, cooling sweat she was only now recognizing as it trickled over her temples. The feathery touch of dry desert air and the familiar scent of creosote cleared the hellscape from her senses, slowly, as she reoriented to being back in her world.

Out of her nightmare, out of the demon realm.

But at what cost?

What had she done? What had happened to her?

She didn't have more than that moment to recognize the changes, though. No time to examine them.

A throat clearing. Not Carmen.

Angie swung around. To see Morty standing there beside a gaping Jacob.

The thought crossed her mind, *At least this isn't the*

hellscape. And that was a huge relief. But since Morty was smirking, the relief didn't ease her anxiety. All her relaxing muscles tensed up again. She found herself reaching for her magic without thought. Wrapping that power around her, even the demon witch magic, in a blanket of balanced energies.

With all the power coursing through her body, she took a step forward, putting herself slightly in front of Sebastian so she could protect him. Trusting him to have her back if Morty had brought anyone else.

"So," Morty said. "Portals without trees? I see you took the final step without any of us realizing. Smart, on your part, to keep that to yourself. I wouldn't have waited six months if I'd known we were here already."

The little speech had Angie's pulse thumping. Damn it, what did Morty know? *How* did he know this was possible when she hadn't?

Because he had access to all the records the demon hunters had on the demon witches, she thought with an inner sigh. And she hadn't been allowed to see those records. Despite multiple requests.

She nearly groaned aloud. Now she had a better idea why she'd been denied access to all that historical information. If they knew it was possible for a demon witch to open a portal without trees, if that was in the records, they no doubt wanted to keep that knowledge from her for as long as possible.

And Carmen had pushed Angie to discover that skill sooner than Angie would have on her own.

Carmen had also known it was possible.

Again, Angie wondered if Carmen had seen the demon witch records. And if so...who had been protecting her among the hunters? Who had allowed her access to those records when Angie herself couldn't get a look?

Even as she wondered this, she looked around for the other woman.

There weren't a lot of places to hide in the open desert landscape. The rocky hills were some distance away. They'd exited the hellscape exactly where they'd entered it. But there were no convenient hiding spots nearby. Not even a tall cactus or large clump of tumbleweeds.

Carmen had definitely left the hellscape and returned to this realm. Angie had watched her race through the portal. She had to be here somewhere. But where?

Angie wanted to ask what Morty intended, wanted to ask where Carmen had gone, but after a beat, decided this was a moment to keep her mouth shut and let the bad guys do the talking. Though she was very curious what was happening between Morty and Jacob, what she'd stumbled out of the hellscape into.

A fight? A meeting?

Enough time had passed in this realm for Jacob's campfire to die, but not long enough for the coals to be completely cooled. So not as much time had passed here as it had felt like had passed in the demon realm. At least, she didn't think so. It was hard to say. For all she knew, this was the next night and those were the coals of a different fire. But she doubted that. Her phone would be buzzing from the depths of her purse with texts from her parents if she'd been gone that long.

So how long had Morty been nearby? Had he been hiding close to the campfire during her entire conversation with Jacob? And if so, where? Was his will strong enough he could have hidden in plain sight from two skilled demon hunters? She supposed that was possible. But not likely. Sebastian in particular would have been looking out for that telltale use of will nearby.

The silence stretched as she waited for Morty. She didn't have to wait as long as she might have expected.

"You haven't asked about your family," he said, his eyes narrowing slightly.

"What should I ask?"

She flexed her fingers with the need to reach into her purse for her cellphone, to text and make sure her parents were okay. She hadn't been gone long enough for them to miss her, thankfully—she wasn't sure she'd tell her mother about this, mainly because it would worry her more than she already worried—but Angie had been gone long enough something could have happened to them while she couldn't be reached.

"They're fine," Morty said. "For the moment." He smiled and glanced past her, to the desert stretching out behind her and Sebastian. Waiting. When nothing happened, he said, "It's tempting, isn't it? To open that portal and force me through. Get rid of the threat."

"Not even a little bit," she answered honestly. In fact, that hadn't even crossed her mind until he'd brought it up.

The demon magic, the power she'd accidentally incorporated into her web of magic, still fizzed through her blood, a sort of charged heat under her skin. That energy made her feel powerful. But also scared her. Until she knew what that added strength and magic could do in this realm, what she could do with it, she didn't even want to tap it. She definitely didn't want to open another portal and have to face the hellscape again. She'd closed the portal in the face of a hoard of demons. Those demons might still be there. If she opened another breach between the realms, she risked unleashing those demons onto this one.

No, the last thing she wanted to do was open another portal.

Morty's gaze narrowed and a jump in his jaw muscle hinted at clenched teeth. "It's only a matter of time before it overwhelms you. Before the anger takes over."

"Stop pushing my anger, and that time extends out significantly. To infinity, honestly. You think having *just* escaped that realm, I'm eager to unleash those monsters here? You are as crazy as you seem to think I am."

"What was it like? Being there?"

Like all demon hunters, Morty had that telltale flash of red in the depths of his eyes, the side-effect of spending so much time dealing with demons. They absorbed some of the demon energy into themselves eventually.

That red flared briefly in Morty's eyes when he spoke of the demon realm now. A flare that made Angie frown.

"Terrifying," she answered honestly again. "What else would it have been like?"

"But…you can…resonate with the realm. With the energy there. All that extraordinary power. At your fingertips. I wonder, what did you bring back with you?"

"Nothing." A lie. She wasn't a great liar. But she'd been so bluntly honest up till now, she hoped she'd get away with this one. "Well, Sebastian and Carmen." She forced herself not to look around for Carmen. If the witch had taken off and was out of their hair for the moment, that was fine. That gave Angie one less worry.

"Yes." Morty nodded at her. "But your eyes are very red now. There's almost nothing of the green visible. You brought something more than your companions from the hellscape."

Fuck. Her eyes were red? That had happened when Carmen forced her to open a portal just before Halloween. When she'd dropped lightning into the demon realm while still standing inside her own. When she'd learned she had more control of the portal than she'd thought. But the color had faded by the next day and there wasn't a hint of it left. Not like a demon hunter's eyes.

"Side effect of opening the portal this way," she said by way of explanation.

But she knew it was more. Knew it was the magic she'd absorbed. Magic that still crackled under her skin. Like static electricity now, more than heat. The power was…settling. Which, she was a little worried, meant it was so incorporated into her own magic, it was becoming a part of her.

And that was not good.

"You sure that's all it is?" Morty asked.

"What's happening here?" she finally gave in and asked. "What are you trying to get at. Just spit it out. I'm not a patient woman."

Morty smiled and glanced at Jacob. "He didn't know what you could do. Thought he'd be safe out here in the middle of nowhere. He didn't know the portal without trees was an option."

"You're stalling, Morty. Spill."

"You're becoming what they all become in the end," Morty said. "So much of the demon witch curse is a predictable process. We've tried keeping the information from them. That fails. They discover the truth anyway and they lose control. We've tried giving them the information. The process just accelerates. You're heading for a cliff and you can't stop. You *will* lose control."

"No."

That was her only response to his little speech because she was reeling and she didn't want him to know. Teetering on a precipice. But what the fall would mean she had no idea. She knew she couldn't trust him. She didn't want to believe what he was saying—he could easily be twisting half-truths to justify himself. But…

He'd known about her ability to open a portal without a tree. He knew more about the demon witch powers than she did because he had centuries of historical data. He was absolutely telling her a truth as he saw it.

And she couldn't accept it. There was a catch. There was always a catch. Just like in deals with demons. There were loopholes and gotchas and ways of twisting a simple phrase to mean multiple things. Her brain insisted that what Morty was telling her involved a very carefully constructed selection of truths framed to send her spinning.

Given where she'd just been, what they'd just managed to survive, she was already reeling. A very good time to bump her further off balance.

And Morty would know that.

He wanted her to lose control. He'd been pushing for that since their first meeting. But what would that get him now? Out here? With only Jacob to help him if she did unleash a hoard of demons on this realm?

"Did you access the energy inside the demon realm?" he asked, almost kindly. "To escape, did you pull in power from the red mist?"

"I did what I had to do to get us out." She hadn't even been able to discuss this with Sebastian yet. She hadn't had a breath to understand what she'd done and what it had done to her. She wasn't about to give an enemy any more information than he already had.

"Yes, you did. Of course, you did. At heart, you're a good person. They were almost all good people. To start. They just couldn't stay that way."

"I don't know what you think you know about me," she said, very slowly. "You're making a lot of assumptions. And presumptions about who I am and will be. I'm not my ancestors and I'm not all the demon witches of the past. I'm not living some scripted process with no input. I was only inside the demon realm because he pushed me in." She jutted her chin at Jacob.

He didn't wince, or show any sign of regret, but then his expression had gone blank shortly after she and the others reemerged from the portal. And he hadn't so much as grunted during her conversation with Morty. So his thoughts were well hidden.

"An unforced error on Jacob's part. He thinks you're weakening the hunters, and that the council isn't paying attention to that weakening."

Jacob's expression closed up even more, but he did glance sideways at Morty.

"I know very well what's happening among the hunters," Morty said, to her, but she suspected to Jacob, too. "I know we are fewer and fewer every year. I know that having an easy option for disposing of freed demons is…tempting. I know why Gabriella continues to support you becoming a demon hunter even though we all know that's not going to happen. You aren't a hunter and never have been. You are something else. And that something else will never be one of us."

"What's Gabriella's end game then?" Angie asked, mostly because she was still so off balance, she needed Morty to keep talking while she tried to regain her footing.

Behind her, Sebastian had moved closer. His hand hovered at her lower back, like he'd catch her if she fell. Like he wanted to touch her but knew she couldn't take it.

In that moment, she couldn't. It was taking a considerable amount of her control to hold it together and hide how shaken she was by everything that had happened and everything Morty was telling her. The buzz of demon magic still hummed in her cells. The extra threads of demon witch magic in her overall blending of power made her *feel* different, and she hadn't had time to figure out those changes. Carmen was still nowhere to be seen. Angie might have actually *killed* a demon using the hellscape magic. And if anyone touched her right now, she was so unmoored she probably wouldn't be able to stop herself from reading them. That would swamp her already tender psyche.

And that would be bad.

Knowing Sebastian was there, that he had her back, was reassuring. Knowing he knew her well enough not to touch her in this moment was everything.

"Gabriella wants to change history," Marty said. "She thinks you're the answer to our waning numbers, not our ultimate destruction. You could do the work of multiple hunters, according to her, and ease some of the pressure on us. Except I don't believe history can be changed. You're our curse, not our savior. You will destroy us all. But not quite in the way Jacob fears."

"You psychic now, too, Morty?"

He smiled. "I don't need to be. I can see the demon powers overtaking you with my own eyes. Your eyes aren't just red, Angela. They're glowing red. Power is emanating off you in waves of heat. You will turn into the very thing we fight."

"I'm not turning into a demon," she snapped. "That's ridiculous and impossible."

At least, as far as she knew.

Demons were another whole *being*. Not of this realm.

Different *things* with their own range of different species and biology and everything. Morty might as well be telling her she was becoming an alien from Alpha Centauri, the idea was so absurd. Humans didn't *become* demons. Possessed by them, yes. Killed by them, often. Tempted and twisted into horrible people by them, absolutely almost every time.

But *becoming one*? Impossible.

She remembered the exploding demon. The way fire had coursed from her hand. How she'd killed a demon even though humans couldn't do that. Only demons could. A thread of fear moved through her gut.

No. No. There was another explanation. Something that made sense. What Morty was saying couldn't be true.

"Not precisely a demon," Morty admitted with a shrug. "But as close as to make very little difference. You are *tuned* to demon magic. You can use it, like a demon. In ways even some demons can't. And no human can resist the call of that much power. It is not in our natures." He shrugged, a pragmatic gesture at odds with what he was saying. "Humans are weak. We know it. Demons know it. That's the entire problem. Humans are weak and fallible. And that makes them susceptible to the lure of power, even when their intentions start off good."

Morty glanced at Jacob. "His intentions are good. In the grand scheme of things. Yet he was prepared to banish you to a demon realm. To banish another hunter. Both people who haven't *earned* that sort of punishment. As someone who knows what being inside a demon realm usually means for humans, one could consider what Jacob did quite evil. And yet, he did it in an attempt to save humanity. I've threatened your family, perfectly innocent people, the very people I'm supposed to be saving, in order to push you into unleashing your powers so we can destroy you. I'm trying to manipulate you so that I can justifiably kill you. Again, quite an evil plan. And yet, it is my attempt to save humanity. Good goals, from well-intentioned people, resulting in committing evil acts for a better end."

"That's a lot of bullshit and nonsense, and we both know it," she said. "A twisting of words to make a point that all people are like you and would do what you do. Even good people. Except that you're wrong."

At least, she hoped he was wrong.

But look at Carmen, committing evil in the name of revenge against evil. All around her, Angie could see the proof of Morty's perspective. If she looked at the world through a cynical lens. Through Carmen's lens.

Were they right? Would she fight this destiny only to lose because the power would corrupt her? Turn her to committing evil in the name of…pragmatism?

Angie believed in balance with her whole heart. And she believed in the witches' creed that what you sent out into the world, you got back. It was why she avoided curses. Why she was careful with her magic. Why she did the work she did and tried to help people. She'd always actively chosen *not* to risk sending out evil, even for the sake of ending evil, for the, ironically, pragmatic goal of not destroying herself on accident with that evil coming back on her.

Her own self-interest as well as her ultimate desire to do

good in the world went hand in hand and dictated the way she lived her life, the choices she made with her magic and her psychic ability. They'd even driven the way she used her demon witch magic.

The thought of giving in to evil, of the power overwhelming all her other impulses, was utterly terrifying.

And not who she was.

It was not who she intended to be.

CHAPTER TWENTY-SIX

"Y ou're not going to convince me to turn evil with words," Angie told Morty, holding his gaze as the desert breeze blew the hairs that had escaped her bun across her forehead. The night was so deep now, she could almost feel the dawn approaching. An hour maybe. But on its way. And with it, the light.

For some reason, Angie—a woman who loved the night because it gave her access to the Universe, to the expanse of stars that filled her with perspective—needed that coming dawn. That show of light cresting over the horizon and spreading like pink paint across the desert. She needed the reminder that she was in *this* world and here she was herself. Not a demon. Not even close.

Having access to demon magic didn't matter. Having the ability to open portals and unleash demons didn't matter. Being able to get out of the hellscape without needing trees didn't matter. Even being capable of maybe killing a demon didn't matter. She wasn't a demon.

She was a witch.

Instinct, perhaps some hint in Morty's stance, had her constructing a protective circle around her and Sebastian. Reciting the spell in her head, her hands moving in the subtle gestures needed to set the circle. All of it on instinct, without real thought behind the action. But when she realized she'd thrown up a circle to protect her and Sebastian instinctively, her conviction that she was a *witch* above all else intensified.

When pushed, she reached for her witch powers. When scared, when angry, when in need, she reached for that specific energy. Not the demon threads. Not even the new purple magic. She *defaulted* to the witch energy she knew and loved.

Feeling that power rise. Feeling all of the other magic she'd absorbed feed her base power, heightening her witch magic but not overwhelming it, made her release a deep breath.

No matter what Morty said, what he tried to do, she was not some pre-programed computer running through an inevitable series of predictable behaviors. She was herself. She was in control.

Just as Esmerelda had said.

She wove the added strength she'd gained from the other realm and from her heightened magic into the circle. And as it closed around her and Sebastian, she let her shoulders relax.

Then she smiled.

Morty's gaze narrowed. "What have you done?"

"Nothing, Morty. Nothing you need to fear. I'm not the one doing the threatening here." She shrugged. "Although, I will defend those I love. It really would be better for all of us if you'd just leave me alone." She glanced at Jacob. "Have you ever been inside a demon realm? Ever crossed that line?"

Jacob shook his head, but didn't speak.

"It's my darkest nightmare. The thing that wakes me up in a cold sweat. And that wasn't the first time it's happened to me. I've been there. Once before. Going back this time nearly broke me. Could have broken me." She looked at Morty again. "It didn't. And if that didn't, Morty… If that didn't…" She blinked as she realized the truth. "If I could come out of that without breaking, I won't break."

She still knew harm to her family would push her right up to that edge, right up to the dangerous point of losing control, of letting her anger get the best of her. But… But she could hit that edge without loosing demons onto this realm. Without succumbing to the fall Morty assumed was inevitable.

She might finally allow herself to issue curses, but she wouldn't default to demons.

No. What Morty really needed to worry about, what he should have been worried about from the very beginning, was what she'd do with her regular witch magic.

In the distance, thunder boomed.

Jacob flinched, subtly, but a flinch. And he glanced in the direction of the thunder.

Morty held her gaze. "Calling a storm?"

"Sending a warning. I'm not who you think I am. I will not be what you think I'll become. But that doesn't mean I'll roll over and let you kill me. Or anyone I love. I don't have to turn evil to stop evil."

"You sure about that?"

She thought of Sebastian, constantly stopping evil as part of his job, his life. Always going after the demons, rescuing even the idiots who summoned those demons if he could. And his mentor Aidan, who'd saved a five-year-old from herself in a church parking lot more than twenty years ago. Who always sent the demons back and had been walking this world for a very long time, doing good without succumbing to evil.

Protecting people, doing good, didn't require an ends-justifying-the-means approach.

And that was the difference between her and Morty. Between her and Carmen.

A good reminder for herself as well as everyone else.

"I'm sure."

Now that she was safely inside a circle, now that she felt like she could breathe, she glanced around for Carmen again. The woman had a phenomenal will. Maybe she'd pulled the hunter's trick and willed them all not to see her. She could be hiding in plain sight, standing in the darkness only a few yards away, remaining perfectly still and willing the rest of them not to notice her.

But Carmen was a survivor. A selfish survivor. Angie found it hard to believe the woman wouldn't have run away if she'd been able to.

But how had she gotten away from Morty and Jacob when they'd been just outside the portal?

They'd have to have let her go.

Again, Angie wondered what had been happening between Morty and Jacob before the portal opened, before Angie and the others had come through. The tension between the two men was obvious. What exactly was going on?

She called the distant lightning, letting it flash across the predawn sky. Smiled a little when she realized she wasn't bringing lightning out of fear or anger. She had control of this, too. Knowing her powers weren't getting the best of her was a relief. She should have known she could trust Esmerelda's assertion. She did trust her mentor. Still… She'd worried.

Not anymore.

Another sizzle of lightning brightened the desert landscape again. She glanced around in that flickering light. But she couldn't see anywhere Carmen could be hiding.

Finally, she gave in and just asked. "Where did Carmen go? Did you let her leave?"

She'd almost said escape. Except right now, Carmen wasn't the dangerous one. Well, Carmen was always potentially dangerous. And her machinations were complex. Angie still didn't trust the woman as far as she could throw her.

But justice for Carmen wasn't something either of the men in front of Angie were in a position to dole out. Not when they were little better than Carmen in their actions.

"Concern for the woman who killed a demon hunter?"

Morty asked. "That would seem to align you with the wrong side of this equation."

"Concern for another human being seems to put me on the *right* side of all this, Morty. It's you who keeps trying to justify murder."

Morty chuckled. A disconcerting sound given the conversation. "I'm sorry things can't be different. I find I quite like your spunk, Angela Jordan."

"Spunk?" What was she, three years old?

"Carmen has escaped the hunters' justice for a very long time," Morty said. "I haven't been the one helping her with that."

"Didn't think you were." Well, he was on the list of suspects, but that was only because she suspected everyone on the demon hunter council of duplicity. Even Gabriella.

"You could have left her behind in the hellscape. That would have been justice."

"No. That's not a fate for anyone. Ever." No one deserved what demons did to humans. No one.

"You realize her name isn't Carmen?"

"I do. Do you know her real name?"

Morty shook his head.

"You're not really one to cast aspersions on someone using a fake name, though, are you? Morty?"

His mouth twitched, but she couldn't tell if that was a smirk or not. "No," he said. "But do you wonder *why* she's adhering to an old demon hunter tradition of going around by a false name? Of not revealing her real name to a witch?"

"Some witches do that, too. Curses and such. Work better

with someone's real name." She narrowed eyes. "What are you getting at, Morty? What don't I know?" A lot. She was certain of that. There was a lot about all of this she didn't know. But her patience was getting thin. "What are you desperately wanting to tell me?"

"She could have been a demon hunter. At one point, we thought she might be. But her…will is corrupted."

Jacob had implied the same thing. And Angie had suspected as much, even before Jacob's casually tossed comment earlier that night. Carmen obviously had the will to have been a demon hunter. Instead, she'd used that will to deal with demons and seek revenge against those she considered evil. Taught horrible people how to summon demons and then let them be destroyed by the demons they called. But she endangered lives through her actions. Innocent lives. Children. She used unscrupulous people in her schemes. She'd made enemies of freed demons and their mobster pawns. She wasn't the good guy and didn't aspire to be.

But Angie had never heard of a will being corrupted and wasn't sure what Morty meant by that turn of phrase. It was too specific to have been an accident on his part, or just figurative. He meant something.

She was about to ask. But something about the way Morty's stance changed, the way he angled a little so his attention was divided between her and Sebastian and… another point on the opposite side of the nearly cold campfire pit.

Angie turned to face that spot. Only desert at first. Just

the sand and rocks barely visible beneath the deep dark sky, with only the starlight to provide illumination.

And then as if they'd been standing there all along… Carmen.

With a demon at her back.

CHAPTER TWENTY-SEVEN

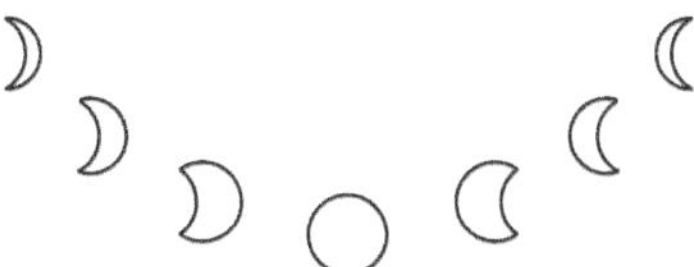

*A*ngie took a step toward Carmen but came up against the reality of her own protective circle and cursed. She'd have to drop the circle to reach Carmen. Her instinctive reaction to help the other woman pushed her to do just that, immediately. But a more logical part of her paused to study the situation before jumping in.

The true horror of it hit then. When she realized the demon behind Carmen was the very same type of demon Carmen had once called master.

Angie swore aloud and her own terror spiked.

The Molder demon was a thing of horror, like all demons. Gray, skeletal, ragged clothing fell from its body, tentacle hair and a rictus grin. Black eyes, with a pinpoint of red in the center. Limbs long and out of proportion to the body. Black talons tipping its long fingers. It fed on fear and reveled in terror. It snuck into nightmares and tortured humans for fun. It was sneaky, manipulative, and deadly.

And it had once taken possession of Angie's body, swamping her consciousness and nearly unleashing a demon plague using her powers. Sebastian's will had given her the strength to remember herself, to throw the demon out. But it had been close. So very, terrifyingly close.

Of all the demons she'd encountered in her life, of all the horrors she'd faced, only two types of demons truly hit her lizard brain with such raw terror it was difficult to think. The chittering demons that swarmed across the hellscape.

And the Molder demon.

Having one here. Now. Right after she'd just escaped from another of her nightmare scenarios, the horrible chittering sound still fresh in her ears… It was like all her nightmares from the last two and half years piled up against her consciousness all at once.

But the worst part, the absolute most terrible part…was that the Molder demon knew she was afraid. And savored it.

The beast's rictus grin widened. Revealing rows of sharp, black teeth that clacked together in a sound that raised the hair on her neck and made her gut tightened.

Angie reminded herself she was inside a protective circle. It couldn't get to her. And there was no bone lantern for it to use to possess her body this time. She was also stronger than she'd been at their last meeting. And not just in her witch powers.

She was stronger in her demon witch powers as well.

The memory of the exploding demon in the hellscape

came back to her. She wasn't sure she could do that in this realm, without being surrounded by the red mist of demon magic. And she knew she didn't want Morty or Jacob to know she'd done that. Didn't want to even hint that she was capable of it.

But the memory that she *could*, at the very least, cause damage to a demon now helped settled the overwhelming panic that swamped her brain and made thinking so difficult. She dragged in a few deep breaths, filled her lungs with the desert scents, the dry sand, the faint creosote. The lingering scent of the banked campfire. The faint scent of sizzling ozone from the lightning she'd called earlier.

She let her terror sink into the earth and wrapped the balanced energies of her powers around her again.

As she did, the surge of strength that flowed through her body further calmed her. She was peripherally aware that she was glowing again. Like she'd done in the hellscape. But she ignored it. It would give Morty more reason to fear her, she supposed. But at the moment, she was more concerned with the Molder demon.

And Carmen standing just in front of it. Not moving. Staring straight ahead. As if in a trance.

That was…bad. Very bad.

"They're contained in a circle," Morty said.

Angie could feel his stare on the side of her face but she couldn't look away from Carmen and her blank expression. The other woman blinked once while Angie watched but that was her only movement.

"I wouldn't release a Molder demon on this realm," Morty continued. "I'm not a monster."

"Beg to differ," Angie murmured.

"She walked into the circle," Morty said, ignoring her comment. "I had to scramble to close it so the demon didn't escape."

"And you did that without rescuing Carmen first."

"She's…collateral damage I'm afraid."

"Lot of you two using Carmen and then writing her off as collateral damage."

And it was really starting to piss Angie off. Even if Carmen was notorious for using others as collateral damage herself. Angie felt the lightning in the air, in the distance. But didn't call it this time. She didn't know what was happening here. She needed information first.

That her anger didn't automatically bring the storm, though, was a good sign.

"She's not a good person, you know," Morty said.

"Aware of that," Angie said, still staring at Carmen, into Carmen's eyes. Waiting for…something. Some sign that she was in there, hearing this, aware.

The focus on Carmen meant Angie wasn't staring at the Molder demon either and that helped her control her terror. The demon was inside a containment circle, but that hadn't stopped it from using an artifact to possess Angie's body. The memory of her essence, her very being, sinking into a void wasn't something she could easily set aside. And the Molder would scent that fear on her, know she was remembering.

Though…

It hadn't spoken yet. This wasn't necessarily even that same demon. There was more than one Molder demon in the realms. Unfortunately. But whether this was the same one or not hardly mattered. It didn't have to be to trigger her terror…

Which was maybe the point?

"Why a Molder demon?" Angie asked, with her gaze still on Carmen. "You didn't mean for Carmen to be in there with it. But you summoned a type of demon she used to work with. Why? Why *that* demon?"

She let her gaze move up to the demon hovering behind Carmen. It's smile widened as it met her gaze. She felt the drag of disorientation, but not strongly. Not enough to pull her over or drag her into the demon's thrall. Just an awareness that it would try.

"It triggers your terror, doesn't it?" Morty asked.

"Of course. Everyone here knows why, too."

"If I were to release it, or let it get its revenge on Carmen… What would you do?"

"Stop it."

"Send it back to a demon realm."

"Yes."

"Open a portal?"

"Whatever it took to rid this world of it."

Carmen blinked again, very slowly. But nothing else in her expression changed. Angie still couldn't tell if she was even there. Angie hunted the ground inside the circle. The demon hunters had taken the bone lantern—both bone lanterns since it turned out they came in pairs—and supposedly locked them away safely in a vault somewhere. Except Morty had access to that vault. Was there a bone lantern here? Was the demon actually possessing Carmen's body in that moment?

But no. Angie couldn't see anything inside the circle. And anyway, Carmen would have to be holding it for the demon to access her body.

There was a glowing red fog hovering inside the containment circle now, though. Thick and rolling around the desert sands, obscuring the ground and Carmen's feet. The fog gave Angie the outline of the circle. It wasn't a large one. Maybe six feet diameter. Enough to contain the demon but only barely. Only barely big enough for Carmen and the demon together.

Sebastian leaned close, without touching Angie, and whispered in her ear, "That's not the same demon. Same species but a different beast. Carmen isn't enthralled to it because it was once her master."

Good to know what she was dealing with. "No lantern?" Morty could well be willing her not to see it if it was there. Sebastian might be able to see through that sort of manipulation.

"Not that I can tell."

Okay. That was something. She didn't want to end up being possessed by a demon again. Not after…what she'd picked up in the demon realm.

"You know you're glowing?" Sebastian asked quietly.

"Yup. Can't help it."

Sebastian didn't comment. Not much he could say. Until

she had time to really study what she'd brought back in her magic, she couldn't explain all this. And she wouldn't have tried in front of Morty and Jacob anyway.

Jacob, who still hadn't spoken.

And Morty, who still hadn't explained why the hell he'd summoned a Molder demon.

When he thought Jacob had banished her to a demon realm. Before Morty had known she'd discovered how to open portals without trees yet.

The Molder was here *before* she'd opened a portal back to this realm. Before they'd escaped. Before Morty knew they *could* escape.

Morty had summoned that demon, but not for Angie or Carmen or Sebastian.

That had something to do with him and Jacob.

"What were you intending?" she asked aloud. "What was going on between you and Jacob before we showed up?"

Slowly, slowly, through the terror of seeing that particular demon, and the shock of seeing Carmen in its clutches, and the fear of what could happen, she'd lost sight of the fact that Morty had to have summoned the thing before he even knew the rest of them had survived the hellscape.

Morty had to have thought Jacob killed all of them. Including another hunter. Morty knew demon witches could open portals without trees, but he hadn't known *Angie* could yet. Jacob had seen her open a portal *into* the hellscape without a tree. But no one survives the hellscape for long. He probably assumed she'd be unable to open a portal back because she'd be unlikely to survive long enough to do it—especially when she didn't open one immediately.

Did either of them even know porting back from the demon realm was possible? Had Jacob told Morty what happened? What had been revealed before she and the others returned?

Her brain circled one bit of information—Morty thought Jacob had killed Angie, Sebastian, and Carmen. He had to have. Even if he'd known she could port back, no one survived the hellscape long. At least…not that Angie had ever heard. Going into the hellscape was a one-way trip for mortals.

Morty wanted Angie dead, so that shouldn't have bothered him—he wouldn't get his validation that she was a dangerous person who had to be murdered, but he'd at least be rid of her and any threat she posed.

He didn't care that Carmen was currently in danger with the Molder, which meant he wouldn't have been very bothered about her dying in the hellscape either. He wasn't the hunter protecting her. He'd said as much. Carmen had said he was a threat to her now. Obviously, Morty didn't care if Carmen died or not. He'd have released her from the Molder's grip by now if he was determined to keep her alive.

So that demon wasn't here because of anything to do with Angie or Carmen.

Did Morty care that Sebastian would have died in the hellscape with them?

Another rare—and very skilled—demon hunter lost to their cause might have bothered Morty. Maybe. Up to this point, he hadn't shown any interest in what happened to Sebastian. Hadn't mentioned it. Hadn't said much to her about Sebastian and her relationship with him.

But…

Fucking hell, what if more of this had to do with Sebastian? Not just killing Angie to eliminate the threat of a demon witch, but…but doing it so that the hunters didn't also lose Sebastian?

The thought came from nowhere. The hunters had been such a burr in her side, so focused on either dragging her into the fold as a hunter or eliminating her because she was a threat in some way—either a threat by weakening the hunters or a threat because she might lose control and unleash a plague of demons—that she'd just assumed all this had been because of her.

Even Sebastian hadn't considered that any of this might have had anything to do with *him*.

But what if it did? What if…

What if more of this was, in some way, about Sebastian?

She had no real reason to consider that possibility. Wasn't even sure where the idea had come from. But now that she'd had it, it nagged at her. Something in it, something… important.

She finally took her gaze off the Molder, trusting Sebastian to keep an eye on it, and faced Morty. "What was really going on here, Morty? Why did you summon a Molder demon when you thought I was dead? This—" she gestured at the demon, "—wasn't about me."

She turned to really look at Morty, at Jacob. Jacob who

stood without talking, his expression closed and unreadable. Morty giving nothing away. Not even a blink. That neutrality made her hackles rise. Something was definitely not as it had seemed.

She narrowed her eyes at Morty. "What is this really about?"

CHAPTER TWENTY-EIGHT

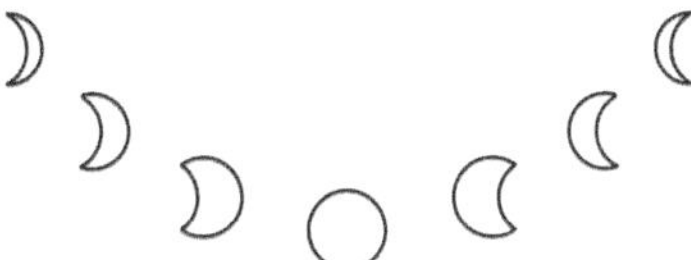

Morty considered her, his expression still neutral, and for the first time since Angie had returned to this realm, he wasn't smirking at her. She knew at least some of all this was to kill her. She *knew* that. She believed him when he said he considered her a threat. She believed he was a threat to the people she loved, and he would do whatever it took to eliminate her.

But…

Until Carmen had run through that breach and back into this realm, Morty and Jacob both had to think Angie and the others were dead.

The Molder demon didn't make sense if it had to do with Angie. Or even Carmen.

The idea that this had more to do with Sebastian than she'd thought took on more weight. Got stronger.

But she didn't say that out loud. She wanted to hear Morty's excuse.

The silence stretched as the desert breeze brushed across her cheeks and whisked away the sweat on her temples. Though everything was still night dark and the stars still shone overhead, the feel of the approaching dawn crept over the landscape, just waiting to burst free.

Angie could see the faintly glowing halo surrounding her. Impossible to pretend it didn't exist in the dark. White light. Not blue or red or even the purplish color that had surrounded her inside the demon realm. She had no idea what that meant. Why she was glowing from inside her protective circle where she was technically safe from all current threats. But it was the least of her concerns in that moment.

"You've met a Molder before," Morty said. "You know what they're capable of."

"You know I have and I do."

"You know they're…good at manipulation."

"All demons are good at manipulation."

"Molders are also extremely difficult to put back once they're freed. It's why Carmen didn't risk freeing her master. Why she used the…barrier, I suppose you'd call it, of the bone lanterns. A way for the demon to walk around without having to give in to freeing it."

Except that Carmen had still almost lost control of the demon at one point. Sebastian had been called to stop that escape.

"You could return a freed Molder demon," Morty said. "Especially now that you've taken the step to opening portals without trees. But as far as we knew, you were dead in the hellscape."

"Exactly," she said.

His mouth ticked up at one corner, but this half-smile still wasn't his usual smirk. "Sebastian could banish a free Molder demon. He's one of two active demon hunters capable of that. Only him and his mentor Aidan. Before you... There were only four or five hunters left who could banish any of the freed demons. And only Sebastian and Aidan are capable of overcoming the wills of the strongest demons. Like a Molder. But some... Some were even too strong for them. We've had to make arrangements with some of those demons. And not all of us are happy with those arrangements."

She'd known that last part, about arrangements having to be made, and thanks to Sebastian's revelations about freed demons the other night, she knew some of the more powerful demons had been given sanctuary to save lives. She knew Gabriella, for one, didn't like those compromises even a little bit. None of that was news to Angie.

But the part about Sebastian and Aidan...

She'd known Aidan was a legend. She'd seen Sebastian in action and knew he was a superb hunter. But... Of all the demon hunters, of *all* of them, only Sebastian and Aidan could banish the more powerful freed demons? Only two of them left who could do that?

How was that even possible? Only two of them?

How was the planet not overrun with freed demons with only two lone humans to fend them off?

Well, because they made deals with the ones they couldn't send back, she thought with a wince. And because the hunters worked hard to reach the demons *before* they broke free.

Angie had assumed, after last night and Sebastian's revelation, that he'd been called to all those demons because of *her*. Because she'd be able to help him. That they saved other hunter lives by her working with Sebastian, but also that having her in his life meant Sebastian was called more often to those freed monsters. She'd worried that being with her put him in more danger than if they'd never worked together.

But…but what if he'd *always* been the one called to those freed beasts? He and Aidan. Always the ones called to take care of the worst and most dangerous demons who broke into this realm. Had either of them even realized? Did Sebastian know he and Aidan were the only ones left who could handle something like a Molder demon? Did he realize even before her that he'd been called to freed demons when other hunters weren't?

Only two of them to handle all of that.

Goddess, no wonder Jacob and Morty and Gabriella were worried about the future. All of them with different ideas of how to save the hunters, but all of them aiming to protect the others, to protect the world.

And Angie was just starting to recognize how difficult the problem was.

With only Sebastian, Aidan, and maybe two or three other hunters capable of banishing freed demons, if Angie really did lose control one day and release a plague… There wouldn't be enough of them to stop it. Just as Jacob had said.

Did Jacob know how dire the situation was? Was that why he was so determined to strengthen hunter wills? How much of this had he known?

Maybe not all of it. Maybe not the part about Sebastian. Because while Jacob might have taken away the threat Angie posed by banishing her to the hellscape…he'd also nearly eliminated one of the few hunters who could stop freed demons. Not something any of them would want.

"Was the Molder meant as a punishment for Jacob? For killing Sebastian?" She started when she realized she'd asked those questions aloud. Her brain was whirling through all this, tumbling over each new bit of information as the chaos of it all refused to settle into something she could grab hold of, something she could fully understand.

"The Molder can…see into many of the demon realms," Morty said. "One of its unique skills. If you can get it to do what's asked, without losing your soul, it can tell you what's happening on different planes."

"You were trying to see if Sebastian could be saved." She blinked hard a few times as that sank in. As the… implications of it all sank in.

"Since it was already here, I thought I might as well see if he could be rescued."

Wait. Already here? But that would mean… "Jacob or Carmen?"

And why had Jacob been hiding the demon from her and Sebastian after they'd arrived? Had to have been Jacob willing them not to see the beast, right? Especially after Jacob had gone to the trouble of *freeing* another demon. Why risk having a Molder demon here as well? One that the other demon might have freed?

Morty glanced at Jacob, who was looking straight ahead. "He hadn't intended on freeing that particular beast. But he needed a way to get Carmen here. Knowing that would bring you. The other already freed demon was to lure Sebastian here. Though why he bothered, I've no idea. Where one of you goes, so goes the other. You two can't be separated. At least not for long."

Angie thought about the two years she'd tried to stay away from Sebastian. Two years he tried to give her the space she needed. No. No, they couldn't be separated for long. Even when they tried.

But why did that annoy Morty so much?

Because she was a demon witch, and a threat, and Sebastian was apparently a rare hunter the council desperately needed. She rolled her eyes at herself.

"So the Molder was a lure for Carmen," she said slowly, looking at Jacob as she did. "To get us all here. Where there were no trees. So you thought you'd be safe from me."

"Carmen linked herself to a Molder demon," Jacob said, his first words during the entire exchange. "Any of their kind can tug at her now. It's one of the many reasons to avoid dealing with the bastards."

The Molder inside the circle chuckled. A sound like a key scratching metal. Angie winced.

"The perfect demon for the perfect job," Morty said.

"You hid the Molder, though," Angie said to Jacob. "Freed a different demon to force Sebastian into a fight."

"Even Jacob wasn't stupid enough to free a Molder," Morty said. "If he wanted to test Sebastian, he needed something…manageable. Something Jacob could manage."

Jacob said, "Banishing a freed Molder demon is…"

"Impossible," the Molder said, its voice sliding through their group like a boa constrictor ready to wrap them all up and choke them.

Angie tried not to look at it, but caught its wide, teeth-baring smile from the corner of her eye. Carmen still hadn't moved. How the hell were they going to get her out of there without freeing the demon?

"Not impossible," Sebastian said to the Molder. And the force of his will washed past her.

The Molder snarled, but slid back a step, away from Carmen. Shoved, Angie realized, by Sebastian's will.

"But very difficult," Morty said, in an almost placating tone. Angie couldn't tell if he was trying to placate a now snarling Molder demon or Sebastian.

"So what now?" she asked Morty. "Sebastian is alive. You want that. I'm alive. You don't want that. But as you can see, even facing one of my most primal terrors, I'm not in a hurry to unleash a plague. I *understand* why I scare you. I *understand* why Jacob wants me to stay away from demon hunter work. But none of what either of you are doing is *helping*."

Morty's jaw tightened, a crack in his normally calm exterior. "In the end, what Jacob wants and what I want are the same. We want the hunters stronger than the demons. We want to keep the demons at bay. And we both know there are not enough hunters with strong enough wills to do that anymore. We *need* Sebastian with us."

She narrowed her eyes, frowning. "You're fighting me, fighting my relationship with Sebastian because of what I am and what I could do, but... You know he's a big reason I would never unleash a plague. Outside of the usual not-wanting-to-end-the-world reasons. I would protect Sebastian with everything I had. You realize that, right?"

"You'd protect him even with your life?"

"If necessary."

"But you see, that's the problem."

"You want me dead, why is that the problem?"

"Because he would do the same for you," Morty hissed.

Angie sucked in a sharp breath. The truth hitting her like a slap.

She couldn't argue with Morty, couldn't deny what he was saying, because in the depths of her soul, she knew he was right. Sebastian had reached into a hellscape to save her. With his will alone, he'd pulled her from the void that a Molder demon tried to push her into. Sebastian always had her back. And she knew without doubt he'd protect her with his life, the same as she'd do for him.

"History will repeat itself with you," Morty continued, his tone softer now. Resigned. There was no more smirks or smugness. "You can't stop it. But killing you... Unless Sebastian accepts the need for you to die..." Morty let out a sigh and shook his head. "Trying to eliminate you as a threat while at the same time keeping Sebastian among the hunters, keeping him loyal to us and working with us… Once you two got involved, things got infinitely more difficult. Hunters getting involved with anyone romantically is always…complicated. Almost impossible. Your relationship caused even more complications."

"So…" She swallowed. "So trying to get me to lose control…" Angie paused as the information fully sank in, as the real reason Morty kept pushing her really hit home. "You weren't doing that to justify killing me to the other hunters. Not even to the council. You've been trying to prove to *Sebastian* that I need to die."

The full weight of that came crashing down on her. The… horror of Morty's plan left her breathless.

"Never," Sebastian snarled. For the first time since they'd stepped from the hellscape, he moved in front of her, standing between her and the other hunters. "I will never allow you to kill her. There is nothing you can do that will justify that to me."

"And that's our problem," Morty said.

From inside the circle, the Molder demon began to laugh. Because Sebastian's focus was on the hunters, Angie turned hers to the demon. It hadn't returned to standing just at Carmen's back, but it seemed to have grown taller while she'd been reeling from Morty's admission. The thick tentacles of its hair waved in an invisible breeze and the red pupil in the depths of its black eyes flared briefly.

"Hunters fighting amongst themselves?" the Molder said.

"What a beautiful thing. Leaves this realm…weak. I like weakness."

"Not weak," Angie said. "Not while I'm here."

"You are a mere vessel. My brother captured you. How strong could you be?" The beast flicked its gaze to the spot where Angie had opened a breach into a hellscape. "You will be our doorway, won't you, tiny human? You will free us to feed on your world."

"No," she said, and her voice came out very deep. The white glow that had surrounded her when she'd wrapped herself up in all her magics had faded during the conversation with Morty but now it flared again. Bright enough she could see it clearly in her peripheral vision.

The circle she'd put around her and Sebastian protected them, even if the Molder got free. But Angie didn't want to test Sebastian's will so soon after he'd been in the hellscape and had to hold off an entire hoard of demons. She trusted him. She didn't trust the circumstances. But she needed to get Carmen out of the demon's containment circle.

How? How?

Another circle?

In the distance, thunder echoed across the desert.

Using all her magic, including what she'd brought with her from the hellscape, she built a circle outside the Molder's, adding an extra foot of space for Carmen to hide in. Building containment circles took time. Normally. And normally, she'd use only her witch magic. But with this one, with all the magics combined, it happened quickly. The circle flared a faint red instead of the usual blue. And not just in her mind's eye.

Jacob hissed in a breath. "What have you done?"

"Carmen," Angie said, ignoring Jacob. "If you can hear me? I need you to step close to the edge of the red circle."

Carmen didn't move. Fuck. The other woman seemed captured in some trance. And if Angie couldn't break that trance, her vague circle plan wasn't going to work.

She couldn't reach inside the circle with her magic. That was really the point. No magic in. No magic out—specifically no demon magic out. Only will. Her will. The demon's will.

And her will had never been strong enough on its own against a demon.

She'd always needed her magic.

But now…some of that magic was demon magic.

Frowning, she focused on those three lines of power inside the mental web of her magic, let the energy of them resonate until she had at least some feel for it. It was still hot, and sharp, and felt like it would draw blood if she wasn't careful, even though that blood letting would only be on the metaphysical plane. She hoped. Still, to fight a demon, using demon magic seemed…obvious.

But how to use it to break Carmen's trance?

First, she tested it against the Molder. Holding the power of that magic in her mental hands, gently, she turned to her will, the method of fighting demons that Sebastian had been trying to train her to. She used the demon energy to reinforce that will, and then she shoved at the Molder.

She felt the force of its will slam up against hers the instant she pushed at it. But it still slid backward a step.

Unfortunately, so did she. Dammit that thing was strong.

"Ang?" Sebastian asked quietly.

"Carmen," she muttered. A shorthand she hoped he'd understand.

In the next instant, Sebastian's will slammed into the Molder. She *felt* the weight and strength of it flowing past her. And the Molder snarled a denial even as it jerked up against the edge of its containment circle. As it touched against that barrier, it hissed. And for a moment, Angie thought they could do this.

But then the beast smiled. And its will hit Angie again.

She leaned into the shove, refusing to move backward this time. But the suddenness of the attack, focused on her instead of Sebastian, took her breath away.

The pressure cut off abruptly and Angie sagged, almost stumbling forward. She straightened and narrowed her eyes. Then focused on Carmen. On the link between Carmen and the Molder.

Most of what Angie did had a visualization element to it. She *pictured* what she was manifesting, her psychic insights came as visuals most of the time, even opening portals involved an aspect of seeing. She had a visual image for her magic now that she used to manipulate her various powers. *Seeing* lines of magic and power was how her particular magic seemed to work best.

So she wasn't entirely surprised, once she focused on it, that she could *see* a line linking the Molder to Carmen. A faint, glittering line of blackness that could easily be mistaken as a shadow. The shadow line linked the Molder's chest to Carmen's back. A flickering of energy flowed through the shadow like starlight.

In the back of her mind, Angie hated that she found that energy pretty. Something so insidious shouldn't also be pretty.

She heard Sebastian grunt.

"You okay?" she whispered.

"Fine. Can you break Carmen free?"

"Think so." She reached out with her will, but instead of shoving at the Molder, she wrapped her will around that shadow line connecting the demon to Carmen. Her will… strengthened by the demon energy she'd absorbed.

The connection felt…delicate. But strengthening the longer Carmen remained connected to the Molder. Angie tightened her will around it. And she felt the connection shiver.

The Molder snarled and a surge of countering will pulsed through the shadow line, hard enough to loosen Angie's will. She scrambled to tighten her hold again, and in doing so, dropped all pretense of delicately testing that link. She gripped it. Hard.

And it shattered in a flare of power that actually sent her stumbling backward.

Sebastian caught her before she fell on her ass, then released her the instant she had her balance. The physical contact left her nerves ringing, but she hadn't accidentally read him and for that she was grateful.

"You okay?" Sebastian asked.

"Get ready," she said. She didn't have time to explain.

By the time she had her feet, she could see Carmen blinking and looking around.

"Dios," the woman muttered and stumbled away from the demon. Crossing the demon's containment line.

Breaking the circle.

"No!" Morty snarled.

He and Jacob turned to face the Molder. She could only assume they were both working on the containment circle because she couldn't feel their wills the way she could feel Sebastian's. But even as they worked, she did feel Sebastian's will, flowing past, flowing into the Molder as it tried to surge forward.

Carmen scrambled back a few more steps and came up against Angie's secondary circle, hitting it and hissing as she moved away instantly. She rubbed at her arm where steam rose from the sleeve of her leather jacket. "What the hell?"

Angie wasn't sure. She hadn't realized there'd be heat in her containment circle.

"Get ready," she shouted at Carmen.

Carmen looked at her through narrowed eyes, but didn't argue or even comment. She held herself balanced on her toes, her gaze jumping between the Molder and Angie. Waiting.

"The inner circle?" Angie asked Sebastian.

"Not holding," Sebastian said. "The Molder is fighting Jacob and Morty's attempts to rebuild it." He cursed. "And

I'm having trouble distracting it enough to give them the time they need."

"Your will," she muttered, so low she hoped no one else heard.

"Being tested," he admitted.

Of course it was. There was only so much a hunter could do before they had to rest. There was only so far even a powerful hunter's will could go before they exhausted themselves.

And Sebastian had *just* been inside a hellscape holding off demons at their most powerful. Fighting demons inside their own realm. With just his will.

The inner circle had to be rebuilt before she could lower the outer one to let Carmen out. Otherwise, they risked letting the Molder escape. But if the hunters couldn't rebuild that inner circle before the Molder left it…

They'd be no better off than they were now.

Even as she thought that, Morty cursed. Jacob stumbled back a step. Sebastian dropped to his knees.

And the Molder demon stepped out of the inner circle…

Rising above Carmen once again.

CHAPTER TWENTY-NINE

Carmen turned to face the demon now looming above her as Angie looked on. Angie had no idea what to do now that her vague plan had failed. The beast had escaped the inner containment circle. It was still contained inside the secondary circle she'd built. But Carmen was still trapped with it, and because she'd once tied herself to a Molder, this particular demon could overtake Carmen's will.

And all three demon hunters were on the edge of collapse.

"Sebastian?" Angie dropped to her knees beside him. He was breathing hard, sweat dripping down his temples. She was afraid to touch him, but she desperately wanted to, wanted to feed him some of her strength the way he often did for her. She just didn't know how. "What can I do? How can I help?"

"Too worn out after…everything." He pulled in a deep,

gulping breath. "Don't know how to get her out without releasing the demon."

The demon in question chuckled from its place in front of Carmen. It wasn't watching her, though. It was watching Angie and Sebastian.

"You can't beat me," it said, the sound of its voice raking over Angie's nerves. "Weak humans. So weak." Its gaze settled on Angie. "You are different. Still only human. But… You and I could make a deal."

She opened her mouth to say no. She didn't deal with demons. There were always loopholes, always unseen ways to die. But she had to stall it while she considered her options.

"What kind of deal?" she asked, as she frantically searched for a way to get Carmen out.

She could try another secondary containment circle. But the failure of the first attempt when all three hunters were trying to reinforce the original circle didn't bode well for a second attempt with only her to rebuild the broken one this time. There was no way to bring Carmen across the line of the new circle without breaking it and freeing the Molder.

Really the only option to save Carmen was to banish the Molder back to its realm.

Which would require opening another portal. Onto the hellscape they'd only just escaped.

And what if the Molder dragged Carmen in with it, the way the Shilv had? Sebastian was in no shape to fend off a hellscape's worth of demons a second time. The rescue would be entirely up to Angie.

She did not want to face the hellscape again. She didn't want to open another breach when she still wasn't certain what the demon magic had done to her. But with the hunters unable to help…

What choice did she have?

It would mean dropping the circle around her and Sebastian, though. The one that had been protecting them from Morty and Jacob.

"I will release the woman," the demon said. "In exchange for one touch."

The demon's offered bargain broke through Angie's rapid-fire thoughts. "One touch of…what?"

"You."

"No," Sebastian said, his voice a boom despite his exhaustion.

The Molder slid back a step before stopping itself and snarling at Sebastian. "Stay out of this hunter. You are not strong enough to stop me now."

"Why?" Angie asked, frowning at the demon. Did it know she was a touch psychic? Could it…take some of that from her or use it?

She had no intention of touching the demon. That would involve getting inside the circle with it. She couldn't just reach across the line to let it touch her—she'd break its containment doing that, and she'd just get sucked into its deadly hold. She wasn't stupid enough to make this deal. But she was very curious why the Molder was attempting it.

"You have survived the hellscape. Humans do not survive the hellscape. I want to know hoooowwww…" It drew out the *how* like a hiss as it wove around Carmen to the edge of the faintly red containment circle. Its black eyes dragged at Angie, disorienting her despite the barrier of two different magical circles separating them.

"Luck and Sebastian," she said, shaking her head and shifting her gaze to the demon's tentacle hair so she wasn't making direct eye contact. "Simple. You have your answer. No touching required. Now release Carmen."

"We haven't made the deal yet. And your answer is… incomplete."

"No deals," Sebastian said again, more of his will shoving the demon backward. But every effort cost him.

From the corner of her eyes, she saw his hands trembling where he had them flat on his thighs, his shoulders rising and falling with his pants. She wanted to touch him, to reassure him, to do something to help…

But the only way to help him, the only way to help Carmen, was to banish the Molder.

"My answer is all you get," Angie said. "No deals that involve touching. What's your second offer." There were always alternative ways a demon might try to trick a less than leery human. She was sure this one had another offer at its taloned-fingertips.

She was not disappointed.

"No touch, then," the demon said, its voice slipping into a mesmeric rhythm. "Just approach the circle and let me get a good, clear look at you. Without the barrier of your magic between us."

Ah, a tricky deal that. Because she could easily assume it

meant her own circle. Except that the containment circle keeping it out of her realm was also made up of her magic. The deal would rupture the integrity of the containment circle, probably the instant she dropped her own protective barrier.

"What good does a look at me get you?" she asked, hoping it would think she was considering this counter offer. She did stand and move closer to the edge of her own circle, a little in front of Sebastian. She couldn't open a portal inside the containment circle while still inside her own protective haven. She did have to drop this circle. She was afraid that would leave her open to the Molder's manipulations, though.

Carmen wasn't the only one susceptible now. A Molder had occupied her body, too. That left Angie more vulnerable to that species of beast.

There was no good answer here.

Especially because she had to hope neither Morty or Jacob got it into their heads to interfere with the exchange between her and the Molder. Or try to kill her while she was dealing with it. She *hoped* they realized her circle was the only thing holding it, and killing her would free it while every single hunter capable of banishing the Molder was too exhausted to do so. She *hoped* their own sense of self-preservation, their desire to keep Sebastian alive, all of their stated goals of not destroying the world with a demon plague, were stronger than their need to put an end to her.

"A look at that pretty pretty red color in your eyes will tell me a lot," the Molder said.

Direct eye contact without the barrier of two full circles

between them would be bad. It had managed to throw her off balance even with all the magic between them. So, yeah, no, she wasn't doing that.

"Seems to me you can see my eye color just fine from there. Not seeing how this benefits me." That was the rub with demon deals. They had to at least pretend the deal gave the human some sort of reward.

"You will get your companion returned," the Molder said, and there was a slight narrowing of its eyes when it did.

Angie went with a hunch. "You're asking for more than that in exchange. Her life isn't an equal reward."

As she spoke, she desperately hoped Carmen would not dispute that comment. Of course Carmen's life was worth more than the demon getting a good look at Angie. But the demon wanted something with that look, something that was important to it, and Angie had a feeling, that something far outweighed Carmen to the demon. That was something Angie could use. But only if she didn't have to waste time arguing with Carmen about her life's value.

Fortunately, Carmen did keep her mouth shut—a master manipulator herself, hopefully she understood Angie's gambit.

"What would you like in exchange for something as harmless as a close look into your eyes? That is nothing. No cost to you at all. And in exchange you receive your companion unharmed."

The offer of giving over Carmen unharmed was…telling. Up to now, the Molder had offered to release Carmen, to return her, but *not* to return her unharmed. Not even alive, now that Angie thought about it. Just "release her" or "return her." That wording, to a demon, had a lot of potential loopholes in it. Nothing in that wording required the demon to "release" Carmen alive.

Fucking demons. Angie really hated their manipulative machinations. But the last six months of supposedly being a hunter had honed her skills in dealing with the sneaky bastards. That had been one of the few things she'd been able to learn and get better at during those months.

"You claim a look into my eyes is no cost to me, but you're looking for something there. Something you're desperate enough for, you're willing to deal with me, even though I'm not the one who summoned you."

"You are the one currently containing me," the Molder said. "You are the only one here to deal with."

True as far as it went. However, "I didn't summon you. I didn't call for a deal. You want something from me. Something more than what I want from you."

"You dismiss your companion so easily? I don't believe you care so little. You've gone through a lot of trouble to keep her alive. To try and rescue her. You came all this way when she sent you a message." The Molder flowed closer to Carmen again, stopping within a foot of her.

Carmen took a single step away, but that brought her back against the circle's edge. She hissed and stepped away from the circle again. A reaction that made Angie frown. That containment circle was putting out heat. None of Angie's circles usually did that, not to humans. That was the effect of the demon magic. And it wasn't a welcome addition.

"I never claimed I didn't want Carmen alive and out of that circle," Angie said. "But the value of that to me is less than the value to you of getting a close look at my eyes. I want to know what you hope to gain from that look. I can only offer a suitable trade if I know what I'm giving you."

So much bullshit might have made her wince only a few months ago. She didn't flinch or blink as she felt the Molder's gaze moving over her face. She didn't meet its eyes, of course, but she shifted her gaze to its chin instead of its tentacle hair. *Almost* looking at it in the face.

"One of the weak hunters…," the Molder started, its voice low and rhythmic, "the one who didn't call me… He thinks you've brought something back from the hellscape with you. That red in your eyes… He said you are becoming like a demon?" The Molder laughed.

And from the corner of her eye, Angie caught both Morty and Jacob wincing. They'd been remarkably quiet during the exchange. No comment or warnings or trying to intervene. She wondered at that. Were they biding their time, or unable to intervene?

Or just waiting to see what she was capable of?

"Ridiculous idea," Angie said. "I agree."

"You are human. You cannot be a demon, even should you want to be. Humans before you have tried."

That was interesting, almost distracting. Who? *Why?* Though she suspected the why had something to do with greed and power. The usual motives. "I don't want to be a demon so what's your point."

"You may not be becoming a demon," the Molder said,

"but you could be…more. If you wanted. I could help make you more."

She had to roll her lips into her mouth to keep from laughing out loud. Wow, had the Molder gotten a wrong read on her if that's what it was offering. She didn't want what she'd brought out of the hellscape, hadn't even had time to discover the full implications and damage she'd done to herself. And the Molder thought offering her more of the same was a good idea?

If it had really wanted to get to her, it would have offered to *remove* the demon magic she'd absorbed. Now that…that would have been tempting.

But then, demons didn't think getting *less* power was motivation for anyone. And she supposed most humans who summoned them were looking for more. She just wasn't one of those humans.

The offer might have just been a lure, but she also wondered if the Molder knew what the demon magic was doing to her, what *exactly* she'd absorbed and how it would affect her human body. It was only just occurring to her that the absorbed magic might, possibly, be something that could kill her. The demon wouldn't tell her that unless it thought that knowledge would help in the deal.

So should she admit to anything aloud, while Morty and Jacob were listening? Or keep playing it coy?

"What do you know that I don't?" she asked the demon. So hard to get information from the bastards, and she didn't dare reveal anything until she knew more.

The bargaining was just a stall, biding her time in hopes

she'd figure out a way to get Carmen out safely without releasing the demon. Figuring out a way to banish it without having to open a portal. The demon magic fizzed through her body, in her veins. She was *aware* of it there. And that made her hesitant. Worried anything she did would backfire.

All made worse trying to see through a demon's machinations.

"I know that what you brought back will consume you," the demon said, this time hitting her fear dead center. "I can help you to control it, help you use it so that it does not kill you."

Fuck. The demon had figured her out. And after only one false guess. Only one misstep. That was the lure. The temptation. The thing that could get *her* to deal.

She wasn't going to. But the fact that the demon had gone from misreading her completely to such a perfect, bullseye shot at her fear was irritating.

"You're offering to save my life in exchange for giving me Carmen's life? That's an…odd sort of bargain, isn't it?" she asked. But now that the fucking demon had her number, she needed to switch gears. Focus less on the bargaining, more on how to get Carmen out of that circle.

Unfortunately, her only real solution was to open a portal. Without the hunters to help, she had no other way of banishing a Molder. She just so *so* didn't want to open another portal.

"It's the one you want, though," the Molder said, rising a little higher over Carmen, its smile widening to show its sharp black teeth. "You want the knowledge I have. And I will share it with you. I will release your companion and share my knowledge."

"In exchange for?" She was out of options and out of time.

"One long look into those pretty pretty eyes."

"Do not try to stop me," she murmured to Sebastian. "Please." She glanced down at him. "Trust me," she mouthed.

His jaw clenched, but he nodded.

The Molder laughed, but Angie ignored it while she held Sebastian's gaze.

And dropped her protective circle.

CHAPTER THIRTY

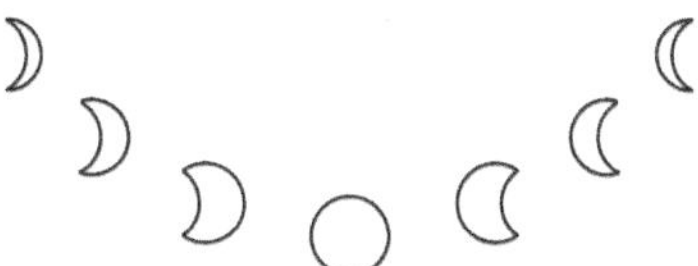

The Molder's laughter echoed across the open desert, grating and horrible in its smugness. Angie held Sebastian's gaze for a moment longer, trying to tell him without words not to panic. He didn't rise from his knees, but she could see his struggle in the tightness across his shoulders and the way his fists clenched against his thighs.

Thanks to everything else that had happened that night, he didn't have the will to fend off a Molder demon. Not yet. The only way to end this was for Angie to end it.

The night breeze fluttered over her cheeks, a cool, mild contrast to the fear pumping in her blood. On the horizon, sunrise approached, leaving the landscape almost darker now than it had been in the middle of the night.

Neither Morty or Jacob commented when she lowered her circle. They didn't argue with her. They hadn't spoken at all since the demon bested all three hunters. When she could drag her gaze away from Sebastian, she finally glanced at the other two. Both stared at the Molder demon, still safely inside Angie's larger circle. But the stare looked…

Involuntary. Like they were in a trance. Or maybe not a trance, but that same state that the Molder had held Carmen in before Angie broke the connection.

The realization startled her enough she turned to look at the two men fully. How could the Molder do that from *inside* a containment circle? Could it control them that way because it had broken Jacob's circle? Was Angie's not strong enough?

That thought was terrifying. Especially since she was about to step up close to that circle.

Carmen had been inside with the Molder when he'd captured her. Angie had been able to break that link using the demon magic coursing through her. She needed to break the link the demon had on Morty and Jacob, too. And hope they wouldn't interfere with what she had to do next.

But if she broke the link, would that weaken her circle further, or give the demon more strength somehow?

So many unknowns. So much she couldn't anticipate.

She did look for the connection between the two hunters and the Molder, to see if she could learn anything from it. To see if it was visible the way Carmen's link had been visible to her.

But… She couldn't see the shadow line this time.

Shit. What was happening with Morty and Jacob then? If not a link to the Molder, what was keeping them in that trance-like state?

This complicated what she had to do next. But she couldn't stall and she couldn't wait any longer. Time was up.

Pushing aside the problem with Morty and Jacob for the moment, she approached her circle. The undulating heat of it rising in her mind's eye as she neared, the faint red glow of it visible in the real world. She'd never built a circle like this one. And the thought of breaking it made her jittery. The thought of standing next to it and it failing made her heart hammer.

The demon stopped laughing as she approached, but its smile grew. Those rows of sharp black teeth clacking together as she stepped up to the very edge of the barrier. Then it flowed close enough to look her in the face, ducking low.

She didn't meet its gaze yet. "We haven't made the deal," she said, her eyes lowered and hooded.

"But you want to," the Molder said quietly, much too close now. Its nearness made Angie's skin crawl. "You want to know what I know. You want to save your companions."

The *s* on that companions felt like a slip. The demon was right. She wanted to save everyone. But they'd only been negotiating a bargain for Carmen's life and safety. Not all her companions. The *s* implied the others *were* in danger from the Molder in that moment.

That Morty and Jacob were somehow in the Molder's thrall.

Did that mean it could capture Sebastian now that the other circle was down?

She didn't dare turn her back on the Molder, not when

standing this close to it. It couldn't reach through her containment circle—she didn't think—but since the barrier was made up of demon magic as well as her own, she wasn't certain enough to risk it.

And she hated that she didn't know.

"I do want all my companions safe," Angie confirmed. "And I want you back in your own realm."

"But why when this realm is so…rich. So full of bad people for me to…take care of for you. We could do that. You and I. Eliminate the bad people." Its voice dropped, lulling and tempting and insidious.

Angie wasn't tempted. She wasn't Carmen, despite what Carmen thought. Angie believed in the consequences of her actions. And using a demon for vigilante justice had so many consequences she didn't even want to think about it.

She saw Carmen flinch from the corner of her eye. The Molder's offer was something Carmen would have been tempted by. *Had* been tempted enough to make a deal with a Molder. Angie wondered if the flinch was because Carmen was still tempted, or because she was remembering all the horrible things she'd done in the name of the deal?

Was there any regret there at all for the way she'd gone about things?

"The last one of you I dealt with didn't want to leave its realm for this one," Angie said. "Wasn't prepared to lose that much power. It found alternatives. You are prepared to sacrifice so much power just to be here?" She gestured around at the open desert.

"The other one had a limited vision. Mine is bigger." Its hands rose, almost but not quite pressing against the barrier of her circle. Red fog covered the ground around its feet, thickening and swirling as the demon moved. "And I wouldn't have to lose power if you opened a portal to let me through. We only weaken when we come through a broken circle."

"That's not true," Angie said. "And we both know it."

At least, she was pretty sure that wasn't true.

She'd never let a demon through on purpose. On accident, once. And she'd sent demons back to their realm through a portal many times. But so far, she hadn't released any into this realm, not since she was five. Coming into the human realm always cost a demon power. The more powerful they were, the more power they lost getting here. A sort of safe-guard for vulnerable humans.

That didn't stop a lot of the demons. And the chittering beasts that roamed the hellscape never hesitated to try and get into the human realm. Even a weak demon was more powerful than most humans, and this place was full of the fear and food they loved best.

Most of the time, though, the demons attempting to break into this realm and wreak havoc weren't the most powerful because the most powerful didn't want to weaken themselves that much.

The previous Molder she'd dealt with had used the bone lantern relic to ride human hosts. It wasn't quite like typical possession—which was harder to accomplish and usually killed the host quickly—and it didn't require the Molder sacrifice power to get here. They could still affect things in this realm without all the other costs.

That Molder had also tried to use Angie to loose demons on this realm through a portal. Not itself, though. Just other demons.

She didn't *think* her portal changed the rules of demons coming into this realm. She didn't *think* they'd maintain all their power coming through. But…she wasn't entirely certain. She'd never thought to ask Aidan, after the church parking lot, if those demons were weaker for breaking into this realm through Angie's breach. She'd been too young and scared and hadn't know anything about demons to even ask the question.

And it hadn't occurred to her to ask the question since either.

But, she reminded herself, demons lied. And manipulated facts. And she couldn't trust anything the Molder said.

She also couldn't trust it not to be using the truth to manipulate her.

The Molder smiled. "You're not so sure, are you? If you freed me, you could…test my word."

"No." That wasn't the sort of test she was prepared to run.

"I can help you. If you opened a portal to let me into your realm, I can help you learn to control…everything."

She hadn't met its gaze yet, let it look into her eyes, but she realized the Molder knew more about what she'd brought back from the demon realm than she wanted it to. At least, it was hinting it did. Morty and Jacob would learn the truth soon, too, if the Molder kept talking.

"No thank you. All I want is my companion returned uninjured. That's all we're discussing."

She touched her powers, delicately, allowing the various energies to flow through her.

The additional red lines inside her web didn't blend in with the witch magic when she touched them. But the image of Carmen with blood pouring out of her jumped into Angie's mind's eye again. Then the memory of the blood dripping from her own hands as she handled the demon threads for the first time inside the hellscape.

So much blood.

The power surged, heating, coursing through her limbs. And as she stared at the Molder, she wondered…

Would it bleed?

The Molder straightened back from the edge of the circle, and even though Angie wasn't meeting its gaze, she saw the way its features tightened, the way its smile dropped.

From the corner of her eyes, she noticed the glow again. Brighter. And not white now. Not the purplish-blue from the hellscape either. But…red?

Hard to tell in her peripheral vision. Didn't matter. What mattered was getting rid of this demon and getting Carmen out of the circle alive.

She moved her hands in the precise set of gestures, murmured the spell under her breath, watched it form in her mind's eye. The Molder watched her, snarling now, but she focused on the magic as she wove all of it together into her spell. The power built into the patterns.

When she spoke, her voice was deep with all the magic coursing through her. "There will be no Molder demons inside my realm. You will not enter. Now. Ever. You will return to your realm and never enter this realm again. They will summon, and you will resist. You are done here."

"No!" the demon screamed.

And surged forward...

CHAPTER THIRTY-ONE

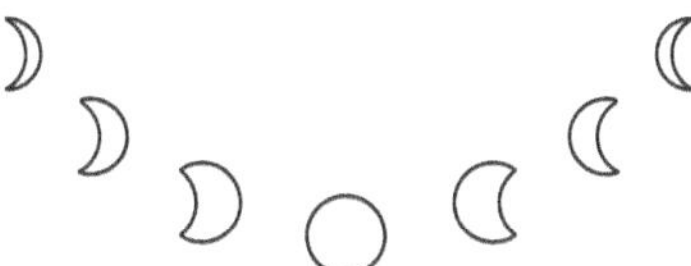

$\mathcal{A}$ngie watched, almost dispassionately, as the demon rushed toward the edge of her containment circle… only to slam up against the smaller circle she'd formed inside the large one. A circle that isolated the demon from Carmen. She'd never tried to do anything like that before. A part of her was a little surprised it worked. A containment circle inside an already established circle instead of outside…

Something she'd keep in mind for future reference.

Though, she thought this might have been possible only because the demon had been summoned into a smaller circle originally. Or maybe it was because Angie was weaving together demon magic, witch magic, and her special demon witch powers into the energy to form the containment circle. It flared a bright red when the demon slammed against it, a red that wasn't just in the metaphysical plane. So definitely not her usual sort of circle.

But then the larger one hadn't been either.

The demon roared. "No! This is not possible! We were bargaining. You cheated."

She almost laughed at that last. "Pot calling kettle black," she muttered. "And we weren't bargaining. You were bargaining. I was stalling. Those are different things."

The demon slammed its fists against the edge of the containment circle. Angie felt that hit and winced. Not quite like being punched, but close. She was more tied to this circle than she realized. And she hadn't thought to put up a barrier between her and it. Mistake. Especially with this kind of spell.

But the circle held.

The demon hissed and slammed the invisible barrier again. Angie winced, but took the hit with little more than a grunt. She wasn't finished with the demon yet.

From behind her, Sebastian said, "Ang?"

"I'm fine," she said. "The Molder is leaving now."

"No!" It slammed its fists on the circle again.

This blow felt like a slap. Angie absorbed the shock with a quick indrawn breath.

"Let me out of here," Carmen said, her voice frantic as she pushed up against the larger circle's edge despite the hiss and smoke rising from her leather jacket.

"Once it's gone," Angie said. She didn't want to drop any of the containment protections yet. Over her shoulder, she said, "Morty? Jacob?"

She didn't want to look away from the Molder to check on them. But if they'd been linked to the Molder somehow, sending it back into its realm while they were still tied to it could be…bad.

She'd cut a tie made between a human and a demon before, when the demon was back in its realm and the human was suffering in this one. That tie had been forged on purpose with the human and demon, though. She hoped this situation would be less horrible since, if there was a tie, the two hunters hadn't formed it voluntarily. Though, how the demon could have done that through the circles, she still wasn't sure.

"Fine," Sebastian said. "Finish this."

He sounded better than he had a few minutes ago. Not recovered. But recovering faster than she'd expected. The relief that filled her almost made her wobble.

Instead, she smiled at the Molder demon. "Time to leave. And never return."

"You cannot!" the demon said. Then smirked, an insinuating smile that showed its sharp teeth. "You cannot banish me to a realm that isn't mine and hope to keep me there. I will return."

Angie tried to keep her reaction to that comment to herself, tried not to react. But she wasn't entirely sure she was successful.

There were multiple hellscapes, multiple demon realms. Some inaccessible to humans. Some were inaccessible even to other demons. Certain demons could move between those realms, but not all. Most were confined to their own plane.

But Angie rarely paid attention to *which* realm she banished a demon to through her portals. The portal that opened was the one she used. She didn't direct them to specific planes. Didn't think she even could. Until six months ago, the portal that opened depended on the tree she looked through. The portals she'd opened without a tree all seemed to be the same hellscape, the same demon realm with the chittering demons that haunted her nightmares.

The place she'd been trapped twice now.

And she hadn't thought much about that. Because banishing demons to any demon realm was her only objective. Getting them *out* of her realm.

She'd sent the last Molder to the realm it had tried to open using her. She hadn't thought about it getting back from that realm or moving through different realms. She hadn't really cared if she'd banished it to a realm that wasn't its own.

Would that make a difference this time?

She still just wanted the demon gone. But she wanted it gone permanently. If she sent it back to *its* realm, she could make that happen. If she didn't, did she risk this Molder getting back to her world?

Demons lied. It could definitely be lying. In fact, it was more likely lying than not.

Still…

Could she control which hellscape she opened? Could she *pick* the demon realm she sent it to?

The demon surged forward against her circle again, slamming into it so hard, she gasped. The feel of its hit reverberated through her bones. She clenched her jaw to keep from letting out more than the initial gasp, mostly so she didn't scare Sebastian, but that time, the hit hurt.

Yeah, its realm or not, time for the demon to go.

She focused on the space just behind the demon, inside the circle, took hold of that first thread of her demon witch power, focused on that energy coursing through her. Again, the portal didn't open the instant she tapped her demon witch magic.

Instead, she had to give the door a little push.

She smiled as the portal swirled open behind the demon.

The Molder screeched, a noise loud enough to hurt her ears. Carmen slapped her hands over her ears and shouted something Angie didn't hear over the noise.

The Molder scrambled at the edge of the inner containment circle, resisting the pull of the hellscape. Beyond the beast, the black rocky landscape Angie, Sebastian, and Carmen had just escaped spread out. And in the distance, Angie heard the chittering sounds of the terrifying demons she so despised.

But for the first time, that sound didn't set her nerves on edge and send panic rolling through her. She wondered at that, in the back of her mind, that she wasn't panicking or wincing or…reacting at all to the noise that had haunted her nightmares for years.

Strange.

"You cannot banish me!" the Molder shouted. "We were bargaining."

"No. There was never any bargaining. Not on my part. And it's time for you to leave."

The demon resisted, though. Dragging itself away from

the open portal as far as it could get. Angie cursed. She didn't have the will Sebastian had to shove it back through.

But… She had the demon energy. Could she use that?

She gathered some of the new energy that had soaked into her web, the heat, the burn of it sharp. In her mind's eyes, she watched blood drip from her hands again. Dropping through her web.

The power surged with that blood, filled her in a riot of so much strength, she rocked back on her heels. So much.

Too much.

She panicked.

Lifting her hand, she shoved all that power through the barrier of two circles, throwing it at the demon's chest.

The rules of a containment circle, meant that stream of fiery power should have scattered around the edges of the circle. The first circle. Those circles kept demons in, demon magic in, and human magic out. A separation that could be physically breached by a human, but kept the demon contained and the magic separated.

The surge of energy Angie pushed toward the demon should have hit the first circle and stopped. Shouldn't have gotten anywhere near the second circle.

Yet the power cut through the first circle like it was butter.

Carmen hit the ground, her hands covering her head as the magic surged past her.

And cut through Angie's second circle.

That should have released the demon. And later, Angie

would be horrified by what she'd done on accident. But she didn't even have time to recognize the disaster.

Because that surge of power slammed into the Molder demon, hitting it square in the chest, flowing into the beast fast and hard enough to toss it toward the portal entrance.

The Molder screamed. Not in anger this time. A scream of denial. A high-pitched shout of pain.

It flew back through the portal opening…

As its chest exploded. Sending a rain of blood across the black rocks.

CHAPTER THIRTY-TWO

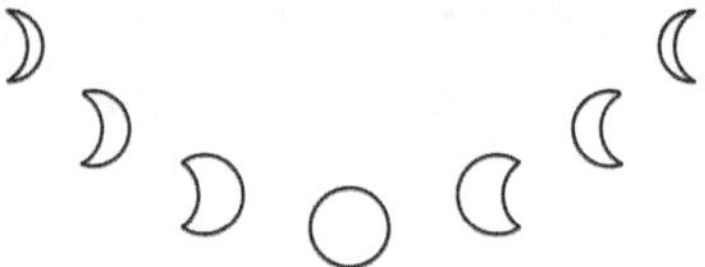

*A*ngie stood with her hands out in front of her, staring into the hellscape on the other side of her portal, as a fine tremor wracked her body.

In the distance, she could hear the chittering demons. A cawing of the winged demons. Under the red sky, volcanos belched sulfur and lava on the horizon, and the stench of the hellscape crept into her world, slithering through the clean desert air.

Demons would scent the Molder's blood soon. They'd come for those remains. She had to close the portal.

Shock left her unable to move.

She felt Sebastian step up behind her, the warmth of him at her back comfortable compared to the heat flowing out of the demon realm. She was vaguely aware of the others. Of Carmen sprawled on the ground a few feet away. Of the still silent Morty and Jacob behind her somewhere. But most of her attention was on the hellscape. And the blood splatter over rock where the Molder had been.

"Close the portal, Ang," Sebastian whispered, close but not touching. "We'll deal with this once the portal is closed."

She nodded, the gesture rapid and jerky. Her trembling so bad now, her teeth were starting to chatter. She focused on closing the realm breach. Just that. That was all she needed to think about in that moment. Just that. Close the breach. Swing the door between realms shut again.

The portal edges whirled, the circular opening shrank. As it closed, Angie watched the chittering demons with their spiked tails and red glowing eyes swarm the Molder's remains. They ignored the closing portal in favor of the blood.

She swallowed hard and tried not to think as the portal winked closed.

Beyond, the desert stretched all around her in quiet, stark beauty. At the edge of her awareness, the sunrise just starting to crest the horizon, a faint lightening of the sky, the red and tans of desert sands and distant rocky hills brightening. The breeze died down, leaving the cool morning air still and eerily quiet. The dry scent of sagebrush slowly overwhelmed the stench of sulfur in her nose.

"I killed a demon," she murmured to Sebastian. The shock making her shake harder. She wrapped her arms around herself, trying to control the shaking. "Not just any demon. Not like… Like there when I was surrounded by all that magic. A Molder demon. A Molder demon."

Sebastian didn't give her any pat reassurances. She

wasn't sure if she wanted any. She'd deny them anyway. It wasn't okay. They might be able to deal with it eventually. But…

It wasn't okay.

"You're trembling," he said instead. "I'd like to hold you. Can you take it?"

She made sure her psychic senses were locked down and then turned into his arms, letting him wrap her up close, letting his warmth and strength seep into her, pulling her away from the edge her shock had sent her toward. She breathed him in, wrapped her arms around his waist, and held tight.

Long moments passed before she was aware of anything or anyone else. Then slowly, she noticed Carmen standing to one side of them, her attention focused over Sebastian's shoulder. She heard the faint shuffling of feat behind Sebastian and realized that must be Morty and Jacob. That meant they were still alive. Right? And not screaming in pain so…not linked to the dead Molder in the hellscape.

A demon she'd killed. The second demon she'd killed tonight.

Humans couldn't kill demons.

That thought sent her careening toward an edge again. She tightened her hold on Sebastian, and he held her closer, keeping her wrapped in the security of his arms.

When she was able, she leaned back. "You're okay? Not hurt after…?"

"I'm fine," he said, running a finger over her cheek. "You're not."

"I'm not. But I'm not hurt. That didn't hurt me."

She would have felt better if it had. She wanted it gone. She wanted whatever had happened tonight to have not happened. She wanted whatever she'd picked up in the hellscape returned to where it belonged. And she wanted to go back to being herself with her own witch magic and no more demons ever ever.

The desire to return to the "before times" and not have to deal with what had just happened overwhelmed everything else for a few minutes. Her brain simply refused to accept that this was a reality that she existed in.

"Got a situation," Carmen murmured as she stepped closer to Sebastian and Angie.

Angie looked over Sebastian's shoulder as he half turned to look at the other two demon hunters.

Morty and Jacob stared at her, their gazes flickering between her and the spot where the portal had been.

Had they seen into the portal? Had they seen what she did?

Morty's expression was impossible to read. Serious. Tight. Controlled. Jacob ran a hand down his face and looked decidedly less controlled. He kept glancing between her, and Morty, and the place where the portal had been. And to Angie's surprise, his hands shook.

They couldn't have seen into the realm. At least, she didn't think so. They shouldn't have been able to. But… either way, they'd obviously seen enough before the Molder fell through the breach.

A little bit of hope she hadn't even known was there died.

Morty and Jacob knew.

"Seems things have progressed farther than I thought," Morty said into the ringing silence.

The sun crested the horizon in that moment, a line of pink separating desert from sky. Casting enough light to see Morty's face clearly. Even with that, Angie couldn't read his expression.

"Are you telling me this is part of that demon witch process you insist I'm on?" If so, if the other witches could kill demons, that was…something she should have known a long time ago.

"Actually," Morty said, "very few reach this level before dying. Very few."

"How few?" Others had done this? Did they also figure out a way to get rid of the power? She thought of what Esmerelda had told her, about being able to cut herself off from her demon witch power. Did that same option exist for…whatever this new energy was that she'd brought out of the demon realm with her?

She hoped so. She really hoped so.

While some, even some demon hunters, might consider the ability to actually *kill* a demon a good thing, Angie was horrified by the prospect. Not that she had much sympathy for the demons. But being able to *kill* them… That put a target on her back. She wouldn't just have trouble from the hunters now. The demons themselves would come looking for her. A human with the ability to kill them couldn't be allowed. *She* wouldn't be allowed. Not without constant fighting.

That wasn't the life she wanted. Even a little bit.

But before the demons, she had to know what the hunters would do.

"As far as we've been able to tell," Morty said, "only two others. Two others, like you. But…that ability took more time. More…things happened before they were at this stage."

"What happened before this? And what happened after?"

"Before…" He shrugged. "The usual demon witch horrors. Things were unleashed. People were killed."

He said that so casually. So much like it was a forgone conclusion Angie wanted to snarl.

"After…"

His expression shifted through emotions she couldn't read, his brow creasing, his eyes narrowing, his mouth pursed. There was a contemplativeness to the look, but more. Suspicion maybe. She wasn't sure. She knew she neither liked nor trusted that expression.

"After," he repeated, "the witch died. The two we know of couldn't survive long, harboring the magic required to kill a demon. That isn't something the human body can take."

Sebastian's arms tightened around her, and beside her, Angie noticed Carmen shift from one foot to the other. But Angie's full focus was on Morty's expression and something…something that didn't sound quite right.

"So, I suppose I don't have to worry about killing you," Morty said. "You've destroyed yourself for me."

"Mm." Yeah, no. She heard the lie there. She wasn't sure *exactly* what he was lying about. But he was lying.

"There has to be a way, though," Jacob said. His voice

sounded hoarse and rough. He rubbed one hand over the back of his neck and glanced between her and Morty, but kept most of his attention on Morty. "There is never a scenario where a hunter can do what she just did. No will, no training would ever enable that. It's impossible. I believe we need to ensure we can fight freed demons, without the help of someone like her. But there are times, moments, when… When destroying the demon completely would be… beneficial."

"Perhaps," Morty said, his gaze still on Angie. "But she can't survive like this."

Still lying. She could hear it in his voice. She wasn't sure how. She just *knew*. And not in her usual psychic way since she wasn't touching him. It was in his body language. He was lying.

And that was very interesting.

"There is no way that you can survive, even if it meant you were a help rather than a threat," Morty said. "I'd say I was sorry about that, but since I've been working to assure we could kill you before you unleashed a plague, I'm certain you'd find my condolences hollow."

"Mm." Angie watched a muscle in his jaw twitch.

Sebastian's arms tightened even more, pulling her close as if he could prevent Morty's words from getting to her by physically blocking them.

"There's a way," Jacob insisted. "There has to be. We can't just…ignore the benefit of this." He finally looked at Angie, though he wouldn't quite meet her gaze. "I realize this is my fault. What's happened to you. Is my fault. And you have no reason to believe me. Or listen to me. But this ability could be a gamechanger for us in the fight against demons. This could change everything."

It had changed everything. Just not in the way Jacob thought.

"She can't help us, Jacob," Morty said, attempting to sound almost sad. "She's dead."

Carmen moved up next to her shoulder. "Don't trust anything either of them is saying," she murmured.

"I don't trust anyone but Sebastian here," Angie said.

"I knew you weren't stupid," Carmen said.

Angie had just told Carmen she didn't trust her. Carmen admitting that was a wise path wasn't lost on Angie.

"We're done here now," Angie said. "I have some training to do. If you come near my family, Morty, I will not release a plague. I will, however, come for you. Consequences be damned."

Morty smiled. "I don't need to go after your family now. I don't need to do anything anymore. This is done now. You'll die well before you can unleash a plague. Soon I'm afraid. You should make the arrangements. Prepare your family." He glanced at Sebastian. "When she dies, I hope you'll realize it couldn't be helped or prevented. There was really no way to avoid her fate, but believe me when I say I never thought it would come to this. You are needed with the hunters, though, Sebastian. The world will not benefit from you rejecting your calling. In fact, the world will suffer. I hope, after you've mourned her, you'll remain with us."

"You're pushing you luck with me right now, mate," Sebastian said. "I would stop talking, if I were you."

Morty lifted his hands in a pacifying gesture. "We're done." He held Angie's gaze. "We're done."

Morty turned around and walked away into the desert in the general direction of the road where Angie and Sebastian had left her rental car. Jacob didn't follow him.

The sky continued to pinken, a sweep of color washing the desert sands. A stillness settled around them as Morty disappeared. A stillness Jacob was the first to break.

"You have no reason to believe me," he said. "But I'm on your side."

"You pushed me into a demon realm to die. Saying I don't believe you is an understatement." Her voice was rough and scratchy. She needed water. And food. And a nap.

She needed whatever had happened to her tonight to not have happened.

Jacob winced but didn't drop his gaze. "I never knew this was possible. I never knew *you* could reach a stage of killing, actually *killing*, demons. That's not in the general lore. Not even hinted at. If I'd known…"

"You wouldn't have tried to kill me?"

"That wasn't… I never planned to… That was a spur of the moment thing that I didn't really think about. The portal needed to be closed and you weren't closing it. I was thinking of the demons getting through. And the fact that I wouldn't have been strong enough to send them back."

"How does my apparent ability to kill them now change anything for you, Jacob? I'll still be a crutch to the hunters."

If she survived the magic coursing through her, invading her web.

Although, when she paused to look, the lines of new magic she'd picked up from the demon realm were still just those two new threads. They weren't blending or mixing with her witch magic, the way her original thread had started to. In fact, her original demon witch thread wasn't blending with her other magics anymore either. Since rearranging her web, rebuilding it, the spread of that purple magic had stopped. All of it stabilized and incorporated.

The addition of the magic from an actual demon realm should have thrown that stability off again. But...it didn't seem to be doing that. The demon magic kept itself isolated. A thing separate and distinct from the rest of her power. She had to think that was good.

At least she hoped it was a good sign.

Because the threads were still very much a part of her web now.

"No," Jacob said. "Not a crutch anymore. Because you're not doing something any of us *should* be able to do. Anything we ever *could* do. We can never strengthen or train our wills enough to kill a demon. Banish a freed one, yes. That's within our prevue, our abilities. It's a thing we *have* to be able to do. Any weakness in that area endangers us all. But what you can do now... Some of those freed demons that shouldn't be here, you could kill them. Destroy them and purify our realm again."

Everything he'd just said sounded wrong to Angie's ears. Especially the last part. The last part sounded like something a zealot would say. Hitting her nerves like a discordant musical note. She was too tired to parse it out, but she knew that last part was wrong. Somehow.

"You're tired," Jacob said suddenly. "You'll need time to consider. To think. But… But even though this wasn't what I'd intended, this could be a great boon to the hunters. Consider it. And to convince you of my sincerity, I'll find a way to keep this from killing you. There has to be a way. Two before you could do this. There has to be something. I'll find the answer."

"Morty seemed to think there was no answer," she said. Morty was lying, of course. But did Jacob know that or was he just desperate?

"I'll make this right," he said, ignoring her comment. "I'll figure this out." To Carmen, he said, "I won't apologize. I didn't mean for things to go the way they did, but… You killed a hunter." He shook his head.

Carmen smiled a falsely sweet smile at him, a smile that showed teeth. "You and I will see each other again. We have some things to discuss."

None of that sounded good. But Angie was too exhausted to intervene just then. She'd worry about *that* problem tomorrow.

Jacob didn't comment. He gave Angie another long look, a look that she could only call…hungry. A disturbing expression given the night that was in it.

Then he turned and walked away, too. Except unlike Morty, who she could still see walking in the distance, Jacob disappeared after only a few feet, using his will to ensure they could no longer see him. She was too tired to fight his effort and try to see where he went.

She had too many other things to worry about.

She turned back into Sebastian's arms and rested her head on his shoulder.

"We're not letting this kill you," he murmured into her hair. "This isn't over."

"I know. Morty was lying anyway. But… But there was some truth there, too. It's not natural for a human to hold this kind of power. That will have consequences."

Sebastian's arms tightened. "We will find the answers we need. But not tonight. Or, well, this morning."

Angie huffed, a sound she wanted to be a laugh but it didn't come out with much humor. The rising sunlight cast lovely pink light across her cheek, sending out long shadows from the few rocks and nearby cacti. The distant rocky mountains to the west caught the first rays, turning the rocks orange. A small breeze picked up again, brushing the fine hairs on her brow.

She glanced at Carmen. "What will you do now?"

"You think I'm going anywhere? When you can kill demons now?"

"I'm not going along with any schemes or plans you have. Anything you think is a good idea will not be. I'm not cooperating."

Carmen smiled. Not a smirk, a pleased smile that lightened some of the harsher angles of her face. She was an attractive woman when she wasn't smirking. But Angie had a hard time not considering that more pleasant look a façade.

"Don't worry," Carmen said. "I don't have an immediate nefarious plan on hand. Never even crossed my mind something like this was possible."

"You didn't know?" Morty had. He said two other demon witches had reached this point. Was that part of the histories Carmen hadn't seen? Or was that the thing Morty was lying about?

Had there ever been other demon witches who could do this?

"Though I hate to admit it, I'm not omniscient. If I was, I would have come up with something already." Carmen stared at her for a long moment. Then her eyes narrowed and that suspiciously calculating expression took over again. "Although…"

"No," Angie said before Carmen could say more. "Whatever it is, no."

"Jacob had a point about some of the freed demons, you know? Few of them…it'd be better if they weren't walking around in this realm."

Carmen had made an enemy of one, according to the mob boss enthralled to that particular freed demon. Angie didn't have to stretch her imagination much to figure Carmen was looking to eliminate that particular enemy.

"The answer is still no," she said. But mostly because she had to figure out what had happened to her and her magic before she decided if she'd use this ability or not.

"I'll be around if you change your mind."

"I won't."

Carmen's smile said otherwise. The expression dropped a

moment later as she gave Angie a considering stare. "Don't believe Morty. When he says you're dying. He was lying about that. At least, that your death is a foregone conclusion."

"You're sure?"

"Good liars always recognize other liars." She shrugged. "And I'm an excellent liar. Morty's not bad, but not good enough to fool me."

"Figured." To Sebastian, she said, "But if he was lying about that, he's still a threat. He was trying to get me to…I don't know. Despair. Let my guard down, maybe."

"Not sure why he'd say that. But he's going to answer for it."

She touched his jaw, the muscle under her fingertips jumped and she could practically feel his teeth clenching. She didn't want to talk too much about this in front of Carmen, but the flare of red in the depths of Sebastian's eyes didn't bode well for Morty.

"Later," she murmured.

Carmen snorted. "You want privacy, you could just say it."

"We want privacy," Angie said, without looking away from Sebastian.

"I'm done here anyway."

Angie reluctantly turned from Sebastian to face Carmen.

"We're not done discussing this demon killing business and how I can use that," Carmen said, raising a hand when Angie opened her mouth to object again. "But I figure I owe you a little time. Since you saved my life tonight." Her mouth flattened and she rolled her eyes. "A few times."

"Is that a thank you?"

"As close to one as you're getting." Carmen turned and headed in the same direction Morty and Jacob had gone.

"You have a car around here somewhere?" Angie called to her.

"I'll be fine. Got some…things to take care of." Carmen turned but kept walking backward as she called. "Stay alive, witch. We have things to do."

"No, we don't," Angie shouted as Carmen turned her back to them again. "Don't step on any snakes. I'm not rescuing you again today."

Carmen held up her middle finger without looking back. And despite herself, Angie laughed.

Damn it, she really hated having any good feelings toward Carmen at all.

She let out a long breath and faced Sebastian again. "Now what?"

"Now, we go make sure your family are all okay. Then we get some rest. We'll deal with everything else tomorrow."

The demon magic had settled. All her powers felt…calm. Nothing hurt. No lightning sizzled on the horizon. But she was exhausted. Her eyes felt heavy. And now that they were alone, without all the enemies and demons surrounding them, Angie felt the last of her strength fading fast.

Sebastian was right. She wasn't going to solve any problems now. She could barely think.

"Okay," she said. "Okay."

Tomorrow.

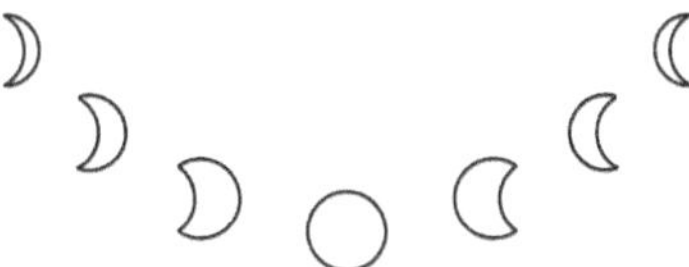

oud music poured out of the house behind Angie, Esmerelda's favorite Mexican rock band adding the soundtrack to the family gathering. Noisy laughter and kids shouting punctuated the rapid guitar beats. The scent of roasting pork wafted through the herby garden, making Angie's stomach growl, despite the abundance of hors d'oeuvres she'd already eaten.

Esmerelda's kids and grandkids had all gathered for the barbecue, along with all of Angie's family, a host of Esmerelda's neighbors and cousins and witch friends. All enjoying the mild, sunny weather and the abundance of food and drink covering the kitchen counters, and a handful of long card tables set out on the patio.

To make her call, Angie had excused herself and wandered deeper into the garden, where she had some privacy. Now, as the call ended, she stood staring at one of Esmerelda's flower boxes, deciding how she felt.

"How'd it go?" Sebastian's voice, quiet, a few feet away.

She faced him. In the bright desert sunshine, he looked cool and handsome in his white cotton t-shirt and light tan dress slacks. He'd shaved for the party, though his goatee still covered his upper lip and chin. And the faint curls of gray in his dark hair caught some of the sunlight, giving him a sparkle that made her smile. She had to look really close to see the faint red in his eyes at the moment.

Without the audience of little kids and neighbors—and her brothers—she closed the space between them, sighing contentedly as he wrapped his arms around her. The way his muscles flexed under her hands sent a little sizzle through her. The scent of him, that faint combination of soap and heat that was so much a part of him, more delicious than the food, headier than the surrounding herbs, teased her and her stomach danced. The fact that she still got giddy around him, after all these years, never cease to amaze her.

They'd spent most of the last week sleeping, training with Esmerelda, and ensuring Angie's family was safe. A phone call to Gabriella the day after the demon fight confirmed Morty had returned to New York. And it looked like his immediate plans to arrange for Angie's death were on hold. There was no word from Jacob, but Gabriella had promised to keep an eye on him.

Angie had, reluctantly and only after a long conversation with Sebastian, confided in Gabriella that things with her magic had…developed. Since Morty knew, and so did Jacob, there was really no point in trying to keep the developments secret. Besides, telling Gabriella gave her a bargaining chip.

Angie had requested access to the demon witch histories. Again.

This time, Gabriella had asked for a week to arrange things.

The text from Gabriella, asking for a phone call, had arrived in the middle of Esmerelda's party.

"She says I've got permission," Angie told Sebastian. "They'll allow me to see the histories specific to the demon witches when we get back to New York." She huffed. "I won't be left alone with the records, of course. Gabriella has assigned herself the task of keeping watch while I read."

"That'll be relaxing," Sebastian said with a straight face.

She chuckled. "Right? But at least I'll have access to all that information finally."

"Does Gabriella think the…demon energy is going to kill you?"

Esmerelda hadn't been able to confirm or deny Morty's assertion. She'd never dealt with the kind of magic that Angie had woven into her web of power. She did say that it looked stable, and was likely permanent. And that, at this stage, cutting off access to the demon witch powers probably wasn't possible.

Knowing she'd missed that window, knowing there was no way to turn back what had happened to her in the demon realm, had hit Angie hard. She still hadn't fully accepted

Esmerelda's opinion on the new threads. Despite knowing she shouldn't, she held out hope that they could find some way to reverse what had happened. And she hoped those answers would be in the histories.

"She says if I'm not dead by now, I'm probably not going to die soon." Angie rolled her eyes. "I asked if that's why she wanted the week. To see if I died."

Sebastian's arms flexed around her. "What did she say to that?"

"She said she wouldn't dignify that question with an answer."

"So she was waiting."

Angie huffed. "Anyway, since I'm not dead and the power isn't overwhelming me, and Esmerelda's training is helping with my control of all the magics, she seems to think I'll survive a little longer. But..."

"But you're hoping we'll find more answers in the records."

"I'm hoping I'll be able to separate out Morty's lies from his truths."

"How did he react to the news?"

"Gabriella says he agreed. Readily. Which is... unsettling."

"Suspicious."

"Mm hmm."

Sebastian sighed. "We're not done with him."

"No. We're not. But now we know *why* he and Jacob have been so...focused on me."

Because of Sebastian. Because Sebastian was so vital to

the hunters, they couldn't afford to lose him. And they were afraid of losing him to her.

The fact that she knew he'd choose her over the other hunters left a conflicting set of complicated emotions in her that she was mostly calling love and leaving it at that.

"When do you need to be back to New York?" he asked.

"I told Gabriella I need another week here." She'd text her bosses about the extended absence later. But she knew they'd agreed to give her the time she needed. They'd said as much before she left. "I want to make sure I can control…all of this before we go back."

He brushed her hair away from her temples, cupping her face between his big palms. "A week will be enough?"

She nodded. "I think so."

"Whatever you need, I'm here for you."

She felt the truth of that statement in the depths of her soul. She sank into a kiss with him, letting the cover of the garden trellises hide them from family and friends, letting her kiss say what she didn't have words for. She wasn't sure there were words for the amount of love and tenderness and gratitude she felt for Sebastian. So she let him feel how deeply grateful she was for him, pouring her emotions into the kiss.

The road ahead was still complicated and rocky. She had no illusions that they were out of the woods. In fact, the future felt darker and more dangerous now. With traps and threats she couldn't even guess at. The demon magic inside her web felt like a ticking timebomb. Her own powers more immense than she'd ever guessed. And the danger posed by Morty and the rest of the hunter council still loomed.

But for this moment, with Sebastian by her side, with her mentor's help with the magic, with her family safe… For this moment, Angie could let herself relax, and love, and know she wouldn't be alone on that terrifying path ahead.

For now, in Sebastian's arms, she was safe.

THANK YOU

Thanks for reading STORM SHADOW WITCH! I hope you enjoyed this latest adventure in the Demon Witch series. Poor Angie. Things are getting really complicated. And that's only going to continue for at least a little longer (insert evil author laugh—mwahaha!). But at least she and Sebastian get to be together in their fight, right?

If you've gotten this far into the series, you already know that Angie started as a secondary character in my Cary Redmond series. There are a few stories in that series that reference Angie's past, so if you want more hints, I hope you'll consider reading Cary Redmond, too. Start with THE TROUBLE WITH BLACK CATS AND DEMONS. Or, if you go to my store, you can get the entire novel series in one bundle of books for one price!

There's also a novella that is outside the main series but directly references Angie's Demon Witch past. And you get to see a…well, not friend LOL, but a character from the Demon Witch series in the future. If you're curious, keep reading for an excerpt from *Cary and the Demon Witch* and consider getting the novella to see what I mean.

And if you've been focused on the main series but are curious about some of the backstories Angie references, don't miss the prequel shorts that go back into Angie and Sebastian's history. *Howling Dreadful* is their "meet cute." Although, meeting during a demon fight isn't a great start. *Moonlit Strange* is the story about their breakup. But if you've read this book and not that story yet, and you're a romantic, you can safely read that knowing they do get back together.

For more on all my books, new releases, excerpts, cover reveals, coupons to my store, and more, please consider joining my newsletter. New subscribers also receive two exclusive, free stories—one in my Tiger Shifters paranormal romance series, and one novella in the Cary Redmond series. If you'd prefer, you can always visit my website or my store for updated information and deals, follow me at BookBub, or follow me at your favorite vendors.

Thanks again for reading!

~Kat

KAT SIMONS
CARY AND THE DEMON WITCH
A CARY REDMOND SHORT STORY

CARY AND THE DEMON WITCH

A CARY REDMOND NOVELLA

EXCERPT

CHAPTER ONE

Cary sat on her back porch, idly tossing a soggy tennis ball to her mundane terrier-collie cross, Fred, with one hand and held her steaming cup of coffee in the other. The scent of fresh roasted hazel nut drifted up and scented the late winter air. Though cold, it was the first dry day they'd had in a week, and she intended to take advantage of it by being outside.

Her basset hound, Pickles, who was actually a foo-lion, rested on the porch next to her, flopped into her basset sprawl, her jowls spread out around her nose. The third dog that made up her little pack, Buck, a golden Lab who was really a demon dog, sniffed the fence border, mostly ignoring Fred as he tore across the lawn.

A bright blue sky overhead and the sharp cold air contrasting with her warm coffee mug made her sigh. This was a rare moment of peace in her ordinarily strange life and she savored it.

The life of a magical Protector was…interesting. But more in the curse meaning of that word. She lived in Interesting Times, and that wasn't necessarily a good thing. Becoming a walking Kevlar vest, whose entire job description was "jump in between good guys and bad guys and keep the good guys safe," using magic she didn't actually control but which flowed through her thanks to her bosses, had been eye opening.

At least it paid well.

After doing this job for a few years, though, she was almost used to the magical world she hadn't known existed before becoming a Protector. Demons, vampires, shapeshifters, witches and wizards… Sometimes she just had to shake her head. What the mundane human world didn't know. It was probably better they didn't know about all the otherworldly stuff going on around them all the time anyway. Humans were a jumpy and reactive species. And not all of those witches and wizards and shapeshifters and such were bad.

Her cellphone rang, breaking into her quiet. She sighed and dug it out of her coat pocket. Probably her mother. Her bosses didn't do anything so ordinary as call her on the phone when they had a job for her. If this was work related, they would have just appeared in her backyard. Or sent her ever-annoying faery mentor, Jaxer, to tell her she had work to do.

She looked at the screen, a little surprised by the name

that flashed up in white block letters. Speaking of one of the good witches…

"Angie, hey, what's up?" she answered, worry creeping into her tone.

Angela Jordan was a powerful witch and one of Cary's best friends. It wasn't unusual for Angie to call at random times during the day. But she had family in town visiting at the moment, so Cary hadn't expected to hear from her for at least another week.

"Can you come over right now?" Angie asked. "Lucy is on her way after her last class and Marianne is due in half an hour, after she closes her shop."

"What's wrong?" Cary stood and hurried inside, motioning the dogs to follow. Because Pickles and Buck came inside immediately, Fred followed without her having to nag him. "Is it your family? Is something wrong?"

"Not exactly." Angie sighed. "Just a sec." Then she called to someone, "I'll be down in a minute. Just making a call. It's work related." She came back to Cary. "Sorry about that."

"Is this work related?"

Angie owned a successful psychic readings business she ran out of her own home. The business thrived because Angie actually was psychic, as well as being a witch. Most of her clients were mundane humans, and according to Angie, were more in need of a therapist than a real psychic, but Angie was good at listening and that was what really made her so successful.

Cary couldn't imagine what issue had come up relating to Angie's business that would require her to call in reinforcements, but Cary had learned over the last few years that life often turned up thing she couldn't imagine.

She locked the back door—even though technically she didn't have to. Between the glamour on her house that kept people away who weren't invited, and the presence of a demon dog and a foo lion, no one could break into her home. But she locked the doors anyway because some habits were impossible to break, and her dad had instilled door-locking into her too thoroughly to be disregarded now.

"Not work…exactly," Angie said. "It's a long story. But I need some help to keep my family occupied while I sort this out, and that help needs to be comfortable with magic and mayhem." She dropped her voice into a near whisper, making her already deep voice even deeper. "And with my family here, I could use a Protector around. Just in case."

"I'll be there in twenty minutes if I don't get stuck in traffic."

"Thanks."

Angie disconnected just as Cary grabbed her keys off the hook near the front door and headed down the side hall that led to her garage. She called a goodbye to the dogs and hurried out, her stomach tight with worry.

If Angie, of all people, needed a Protector, something was very very wrong.

Don't Miss
Cary and the Demon Witch
Out Now

BOOKS BY KAT SIMONS

Demon Witch Series

Howling Dreadful

Moonlit Strange

1-Bone Lantern Witch

2-Spiderweb Witch

3-Storm Shadow Witch

4-Darkling Mist Witch

5-Apocalypse Witch

Urban Fantasy

The Cary Redmond Series

Cary Redmond Short Stories and Collections

Joan of Kerry Series

Friday's Curious Shop Series

Paranormal Romance

Dragon Thief Series

Seven Families: Wolf Series

Tiger Shifters Series

Destiny Cats Series

Romancing the Leopard: A Tiger Shifters-Cary Redmond Crossover Novel

ALSO BY KAT SIMONS

Contemporary Fantasy

Haunts and Howls Collections

**Tombstone Wizard * The Unshattered Sword * Going Out of Business: Everything's for Sale * Anger Management * Demonic Dates * The Museum of Small Art's Everyman * Burning Inside a Stone Circle * Bored Questless * I Just Ate a Bug * Ting Ling * Sophie Saves the World * Black Water Hawthorns * To Dance in Fallow Fields at Midnight * The Troll and the Dressmaker*

Stories from the Café

The Café Collections

Stories from the Café: Volume One

Pick Your Genre Collections

Who Steals a Dragon

Contemporary Romances

Designed for You

Poinsettias and Possibilities

Mystery and Thriller

Ross and O'Neill Adventures

Galileo's Pendulum

ABOUT THE AUTHOR

Kat Simons earned her Ph.D. in animal behavior, working with animals as diverse as dolphins and deer. She brought her experience and knowledge of biology to her paranormal romance and urban fantasy fiction, where she delights in taking nature and turning it on its ear. She writes urban fantasy, contemporary fantasy, and paranormal romance in series which combine action adventure, the otherworldly, and a frequent dose of sexy romance.

The newest book in her bestselling romantic urban fantasy series about Protector Cary Redmond, The Trouble with Shifters and Fae Courts, sees a new direction for the intrepid Protector, her sexy leopard shifter mate, and the entire crew. Kat also launched a new novella length Urban Fantasy Romance series that follows the adventures of a magical thief and the dragon shifter prince she just can't seem to shake—and really doesn't want to. The first season of the Dragon Thief series released throughout 2024. Season Two begins in 2025 with The Crown of Kingship Job.

For something a little different, Kat also publishes fantasy, science fiction, and the occasional hockey romance under the name Isabo Kelly (https://www.isabokelly.com).

After traveling the world, living in places like Hawaii, Germany, and Ireland, Kat now lives in New York City with her family and a library's worth of books.

For more on Kat and her future books

Website: https://www.katsimons.com/
Newsletter: https://bit.ly/KatSimonsNewsletter

KatSimonsBooks

https://www.katsimonsbooks.com
https://www.TheCafeatKatSimonsBooks.com

Social Media

Facebook Page: https://www.facebook.com/
KatSimonsAuthor
BookBub: https://www.bookbub.com/authors/kat-simons
Bluesky: https://bsky.app/profile/katsimons.bsky.social
Instagram: https://www.instagram.com/isabokelly/
Threads: https://www.threads.net/@isabokelly

KATSIMONSBOOKS

Mystery

Urban Fantasy

Romance

And More!

KatSimonsBooks.Com

Join Kat's Newsletter

Stay Up-to-Date

On all Kat's News, Updates, and fun extras

New Subscriber Get Two Exclusive Stories Just for Signing up!

bit.ly/KatSimonsNewsletter